Praise for

A WORLD OF HORROR

"Guignard's editorial prowess is evident throughout; he has selected works that are as shocking as they are thought-provoking. This breath of fresh air for horror readers shows the limitless possibilities of the genre."

—*Publishers Weekly* (starred review)

"A fresh collection of horror authors exploring monsters and myths from their homelands."

—*Library Journal*

"A cultural tour in the sacred art of horror—definitive proof that ghosts, ghouls, goblins, and more are equally terrifying in every corner of the world."

—*Fanbase Press*

"This is the book we need right now! Fresh voices from all over the world, bringing American audiences new ways to feel the fear. Horror is a universal genre and for too long we have only experienced one western version of it. No more. Get ready to experience a whole new world of terror."

—Becky Spratford; librarian, reviewer, *RA for All: Horror*

.

Edited by Eric J. Guignard
Interior layout by Eric J. Guignard
Cover design by Eric J. Guignard
www.ericjguignard.com

Cover art by Albert Bierstadt: *Lake Tahoe, Spearing Fish by Torchlight* (1875)

Interior illustrations by Steve Lines
www.rainfallsite.com

First edition published in September, 2018
Library of Congress Control Number: 2017918605

ISBN-13: 978-1-949491-03-6 (hardback)
ISBN-13: 978-0-9989383-1-8 (paperback)
ISBN-13: 978-0-9989383-2-5 (e-book)

DARK MOON BOOKS
Los Angeles, California
www.DarkMoonBooks.com

Made in the United States of America

(V80118)

This anthology is dedicated as always, and with love,
to my family—Jeannette, Julian, and Devin.

Thank you, also, to all authors who contributed such
dark and marvelous tales. Your imaginations are a wonder
and an inspiration to readers the world over.

TABLE OF CONTENTS

Ultimately, bringing together writers of different backgrounds leads to a richer reading experience . . .

INTRODUCTION: DIVERSITY IN FICTION

by Eric J. Guignard

T HIS, ANTHOLOGY, *A WORLD OF HORROR*, MARKS THE sixth I have edited (fifth published, with another forthcoming). Most of those books involved quite a bit of "slush reading," meaning thousands of submissions coming in from hopeful authors around the world that I would evaluate and discard or accept. Although when I say "around the world," what I mean is that roughly 95% of the submissions came from the same geographic areas of predominantly-speaking English nations (North America, England, and Australia) with a few outliers from elsewhere. It makes sense: I'm posting for stories in English, offering to print in English, and so English-speaking writers respond.

Yet at the same time, I also despair of reading the "stock voice," meaning similar stories of plot structure, similar characters and situations, similar belief systems, similar fears; by no means does that imply what I'm reading is "bad," but just that sameness leads to apathy of literature.

In general, I think there's a lack of cultural diversity in horror fiction, and I also think that's something audiences want to see changed . . . at least I think that based on my own perspective: I love reading stories from authors around the world, because I love *stories*. I love fresh voices, unique ideas, I love discovering lesser-known monsters or fables, I love reading about history and civilizations and other peoples' perceptions and conventions. And, while I think all this, I realize I'm part of the problem. Because of what came in via slush submissions on my prior projects, I didn't look beyond, and I ended up publishing and promoting that very sameness of English-speaking authors who are all generally white, educated, and economically advantaged, and who, really, make up only a small percentage of the global population. Truly, there's no shortage of tales to be shared from the rest of the world, but not everyone has the opportunity.

Which is why I wanted to undertake this venture.

It's important for readers from all walks of life to see characters like themselves, to understand there are others experiencing comparable feelings, leading lives as they do, acting as they do, even in fictional worlds of horror and fantasy. And it's important for readers to see characters *unlike* themselves, to provide exposure to cultures and traditions that are unfamiliar, to increase understanding of priorities, struggles, and perspectives.

Ultimately, bringing together writers of different backgrounds leads to a richer reading experience, one that can stimulate and inspire us with new ideas, can provide normalcy to concepts we might find strange solely due to their unfamiliarity.

Of course there are many other publishers who have put together works of cultural celebration before my attempt, and many others who have done it much better, but the advocacy is still too infrequent (*for some additional reading suggestions, look up: *Nightmare Magazine*'s various issues of "People of___Destroy Horror"; Apex Books' *World of Science Fiction* series; and www.samovar.com, the online side of *Strange Horizons* that publishes translations of spec fiction authors from non-English languages). I think it's necessary to create publications like this, and I think it's beneficial, not just to authors and to readers, but also, selfishly, to me—quite simply, I find it a joy. I find it also stimulating and didactic; it makes me a more astute and assured reader, a more astute and assured *person*.

Anyway, such is my view. And before I sound too proselytizing, I'll take a minute to turn the card and share something different, for those of you interested in such: Here's a bit of statistics and raw data for this project.

For my first time, I engaged in an invitation-only approach to assembling this anthology, meaning there was no open call, but that I reached out directly to writers, writing groups, associations, or referrals for contributors.

I sent out invitations in small "rounds," gauging interest from authors I admired and ensuring that I did not receive too many stories from any one geographic area.

I sent out the first round of invitations in October, 2016 to authors I was already familiar with. Depending on their responses, I then sent out a following round of invitations a few weeks later. I sent out eight rounds of invitations in total, the last occurring in July, 2017 with a November submission deadline. Overall, this anthology took about a year to compile, with much of that time spent engrossed in reading a wide-ranging scope of authors from other nations who wrote dark spec fiction (a worthwhile pleasure in itself!), and who I determined would be a good fit for this book's aims.

In total, I reached out to about sixty writers. Some declined the invitation for different reasons, some accepted and then fell through. Some submitted work I thought was not quite an ideal fit and so passed on. And some, twenty-two in total, I accepted and included within these pages, which includes representation from eighteen nations, and presence from each of the six major (inhabited) continents. As an aside, the nice thing with an invite system is that I can also garner gender equality, and concluded this project with a near even split (about 45% male: 55% female), which makes me happy.

The total cost came in at around US $4,500, much of that financed off my credit card. Anthologies aren't easy to do, nor are they cheap.

But statistics aside, I had a blast. It's every editor's hope to find new and exciting authors willing to work with him or her (or at the least to be made aware of sensational voices, of new trends or progressive or interesting enterprises that others are working on), and, in this, I truly succeeded.

I hope you, dear reader, will agree.

The stories I selected are not horror of a visceral, gory nature—that's never been my interest in books—but rather quiet, thoughtful pieces exploring characters' lives, who generally come in contact with some dark, supernatural element. Ghosts and regrets, death and creeping monsters are often the same in any case: a dread that settles over a character (or yourself!) and must be resolved by confronting or escaping it. But these stories too are mystery, they are thriller, they are weird, funny, bright, telling, and tragic—they are life in all its resplendent diversity . . . which, for all intents, is what this anthology is all about.

Midnight cheers,

—Eric J. Guignard
Chino Hills, California
December 7, 2017

The dried-up pool of water above the sofa was
burgundy and hissing. "*Cheeeedzeeee.*"

MUTSHIDZI

by Mohale Mashigo

I chose this first selection, Mutshidzi, *to open the anthology because it sets a good tone for following stories to come.*

It's everything I was looking for in submissions: heavy in voice, heavy in atmosphere to a geographic area, and it's just good writing. Dark, literary, thoughtful, and horror of both a physical and an emotional kind; for who among us could do better than this young protagonist who must daily endure a number of difficult burdens, and yet no matter how hard she struggles, it seems always only to get worse, sinking, sinking under the hardships life has settled on her?

South African author (and award-winning songwriter!) Mohale Mashigo has had great recent success in her creative endeavors, and it's well deserved. Discover why as you read through a week in the life of Mutshidzi.

"MUTSHIDZI- SEVENTEEN- GOING- ON- EIGHTEEN. Everything is gonna be okay." A Vedic Hymn of sorts, mumbled to myself as I pick up after Boy—sleeping socks in the doorway, pajama pants reaching out to the toilet, and a wet facecloth bunched up next to his toothbrush. "Mutshidzi. Seventeen. Going on eighteen. Every. Thing is going to. Be okay."

Most things were not okay but we had a roof over our heads, food to eat, and Boy was doing well at school. The identity fraud thing... well, that was unfortunate but not a train smash. Somebody pretending to be our dead mother was annoying but so are many other things that I had to focus on, making it through the day without falling apart or feeling sorry for myself.

Mutshidzi-Nineteen-Going-On-Twenty had the day off so I could stay home and be my real age. My seventeen-year-old eyes noticed the water damage above the sofa seemed to be getting darker and larger. The stain was something Mme wanted to fix but her two jobs forced her to fall asleep looking at the offending mark and wake up infuriated by it. "One of these Saturdays I'm going to walk to the hardware store, get what I need, and paint that ceiling myself." She never did. An aneurysm halted her heart's desire. I could have completed most of my mother's unfinished tasks but the biggest one was raising and keeping Boy alive, it took up all my energy and time. Unpainted rooms are in my blood.

MONDAY WAS GOING according to plan—it was laundry day. Not for me but all the other people in the building, and nearby ones, and those surrounding who paid me to do theirs. My hands washing other people's delicates kept my mind off the many things that I had inherited from Mme—rent, grocery shopping, packing school lunch, keeping a few coins from being no coins. Laundry deliveries only happened after Boy came home from school, filled me in on who was very naughty in class, ate a sandwich, and was finally settled. "Boy, latch the door. I will be back in two hours to make supper. Don't open for anyone."

Dimitri called to ask if I could stand in for Neo, though I didn't feel like being behind the bar. Dinner was pap and boiled chicken—Mme's favorite. Boy was in bed by 20:00.

My dreams were filled with blood.

TUESDAY: IN THE MORNING I watched, from the 5th floor balcony, as Boy ran across the street into the schoolyard. Many older people tell me this used to be a good neighborhood—close to the CBD, spacious apartments, schools, and synagogues nearby—but that was in the "good old days" (depending on who you talk to).

Boy watched *Lion King* every morning before school. He knew the exact place he stopped watching the previous morning. "Tshidzi, Mufasa is dead . . . Like Mme."

Outside of Mufasa, he never spoke about our mother. I envied him because it felt like I was constantly talking about her to life insurance people, friends who didn't know she was dead, teachers who weren't familiar with Boy's situation, new adults in our building, relatives who called to check on us, *all the time!* Mme was constantly in my head and on my lips.

Mutshidzi-Seventeen-Going-On-Eighteen, replacement-mother to Boy and an assistant at Luso's Gym in the CBD. Luso was already training, she preferred to train while Johannesburg's inner city was dark and still belonged to shopkeepers who were preparing for the masses, frying doughy amagwinya and getting ready for the first wave of hungry, half-asleep, and angry part-time city occupants.

"You look like hell."

"Thanks, Luso."

"Boy get to school alright? Still having nightmares? Ready to train?" Rapid-fire questions, some of which never needed answers, that was how she spoke.

Luso lived in the flat above ours. After Mme died and family began circling, waiting for whatever little was coming our way, she stepped in quietly and assumed the role of bodyguard, big sister, babysitter, and employer. Nobody wanted to mess with a woman who would easily be heavyweight champion of the world if the world respected and admired the physical strength of women. Even the tough guys she trained knew not to mess with *Malwai Muscles*. Luso's reputation entered a room long before she decided it was a room she would be in.

"You shouldn't work at that place. Alcohol, strippers, and bad men."

"I just work behind the bar twice a week. Nobody bothers me. You told Blaise to make sure nobody bothers me. I'm pretty sure he forces people to tip me."

"Just don't think about doing anything else there. Your left hook is getting better, heh? Ha ha, you're training in secret or what? Ey focus, I almost got you."

After training I busied myself with whatever Luso needed me to do, keeping my hands and mind busy until it was time to go home.

Boy was a little person who sleeps through the constant noise and the gun shot interludes of our neighborhood. At first, I thought it was the pipes that woke me up—Nontobeko always took a shower when she got back from work and the building was very old and nobody was taking care of it. Again, I had fallen asleep on the sofa with letters addressed to Mme, telling her she owed money on accounts she didn't open. There was no time for me to go to the police station or spend on the phone explaining to call center agents. "We need a death certificate, ma'am. You can email or fax it to us. Here's your case number..."

When I opened my eyes, the water damage seemed darker but it also seemed to be moving. The dried-up pool of water above the sofa was burgundy and hissing. "*Cheeeedzeeee.*"

The ceiling was whispering to me. I ran into the bedroom and sat on the floor next to the bed with my hand over my mouth—it tasted like blood.

WEDNESDAY: THE 'LADIES BOXING' GROUP made the gym sound and smell fresh. They giggled when Luso told them to "punch like it's your cheating ex's face."

She didn't really like training people who wanted to lose weight, she was a fighter who trained other fighters. "I'm getting better, right? Did you hear my joke about cheating? Eh, these women are the reason I still have a gym."

Even after a day spent in a loud gym, I could still hear the Burgundy Hissing. Everything else was background noise. After gym, Luso looked after Boy while I went to the club. The night was quiet, I was grateful when Dimitri asked Blaise to take me home early. When I arrived, Luso was reading *Drum* magazine. "I tried to fix the door on that kitchen cabinet but my tools are upstairs."

"It's okay. Mme always meant to fix it. I will do something about it this weekend."

"Night, Tshidz."

"Night, Luso."

The cabinet door hung on one hinge, staring at me accusingly. I gently folded myself onto the sofa and avoided looking at it or the Burgundy Hissing. Our tiny home seemed to be taunting me; above, a sinister hissing and the over-tired cabinet door whistling.

The earphones on the floor rescued me from having to hear this unloved home taunting me.

When we first moved in, none of us could sleep so Mme bought earphones from a young guy at a taxi rank. "At least now you can listen to music you like. It's better than listening to that *goom-goom* noise outside." We never got used to it; instead, we just held a quiet grudge against it. The noise was persistent without being disrespectful. The four young women on the 7th floor had a party at least four times a week, and Akani downstairs was a music producer and DJ, gunshots and sirens were always there. Mme eventually started working two jobs and stopped hearing the noise. Most nights when I saw the kitchen light come on, I would take my earphones off and wait till I heard her snoring on the sofa. I cried for the first time when I tried to fall asleep and couldn't hear my mother snore. The hissing above me and the creaking cabinet hinge in the kitchen carried on singing to me as I slept on the sofa. The whole room smelled like blood.

THURSDAY: "IT WASN'T ME," Boy stood next to the sofa, looking down at me. He was pointing to something in the kitchen.

My eyes were heavy and the back of my throat felt swollen. "What?"

"The cabinets. I didn't do it."

We both walked into the kitchen. My throat made an involuntary squeak. The crime Boy was removing himself from was an echo of a morning routine—a lonely mug in the sink, bread crumbs on the table, and a curious mosaic of handprints all over the off-white cupboards. The mosaic was what Boy was denying, the fact that the handprints were bloody didn't seem to worry him at all. He was already engrossed in a lion's conversation with a meerkat, patiently waiting for his Thursday breakfast of cereal.

FRIDAY: THERE WAS NOTHING special about the night. Simone asked for my shift and offered me a portion of her tips. After supper, I began cleaning the handprints off the cupboards. It occurred to me that I should have told someone about the strange things happening in the house but already so much of my story belonged to other people. People felt entitled to an explanation of our life story in exchange for their unsolicited advice, pity, or misguided prayers.

Boy tried his luck by trying to stay up late, I let him sleep in our room with the door open as a compromise. The TV was off because he would listen and comment on what I was watching. "Who's fighting, Tshidzi? I like that song . . . What does divorce mean?"

The only option was to lie in the body-shaped crater on the sofa until Boy fell asleep. The smell of bleach on my hands and the Burgundy Hissing was nauseating. The Hissing was daring me to look at it. "*Cheeeedzeeee . . .*"

It looked like brown clouds, moving into different shapes: a cow, a two-headed horse . . . A brown chicken with a missing wing had my attention when I heard the labored breathing. My back straightened and I sat up when the breathing got louder.

Blood doesn't scare me. I see so much of it at the gym, coming from me, and on Boy's knees, and on TV. But those tiny droplets falling on the kitchen floor, just a few steps away from me, terrified me. They seemed to hold their shape until they splattered on the floor with a soft cry. The drops marched away from where they began falling and headed toward the sink. When the tap turned and water rushed out of it, I ran to the bedroom, locked the door, and sat on the floor next to the bed where Boy slept peacefully. The kitchen was quiet, followed by a sound I had not heard in months—the heavy footsteps of someone so exhausted, from working two jobs, shuffling around the kitchen and then eventually to the sofa where Mme used to sleep.

SATURDAY: BOY'S ARMS were wrapped around my leg tightly. I said, "Shhh."

"Tshidzi, I want to go to the park," he was crying. The smell of blood filled the room, and my little brother's tears felt slick against his face.

"Shhh." I had finally gotten him to stop screaming. "Boy . . . Where did you put my lighter?" My voice was trembling.

"No. Smoking is bad," he shouted.

With my hand over his mouth, I whispered, "I gave it up . . . would never break a promise. I need it for something else."

"To make her go away?"

I nodded, and he crawled toward the bed.

She was out there. I could hear her humming. The blood from her head was forming a pool that slowly made its way through the door and into the bedroom. Boy pressed a lighter into my hand and stood behind me. The two small backpacks and my bag were all we had time to pack. Boy insisted on taking his school bag and I didn't want to argue with a scared child. The wardrobe was mainly full of Mme's clothes, the rest of our clothes were in the laundry basket. Somewhere in there was her I.D., death certificate, old handbag, and tired old shoes. The ones she died in. The brothers on that TV show always seemed to use fire as a way to get rid of unwanted things. I felt like I had no choice. We had no idea this is how our Saturday would play itself out.

SHE WAS WASHING dishes in the morning. Drops of blood fell from her head but she didn't seem to notice. She wore the blue dress I chose for her to be buried in. The smile on her face made me want to run away. Dead people don't smile. I know because it was my eyes that confirmed her identity at the mortuary. It was my eyes that stared at the strange husk that looked like my mother. She didn't smile, open her eyes, or tell me everything would be fine. For months I struggled to prove to creditors that Mme was dead and somebody was using her identity to buy clothes and not pay back the money. She could have shown up at any time but she didn't. Now there she was wiping her hands on her blood-soaked dress, stretching them out to me. "Happy birthday, Tshidzi."

Our bodies were stuck in that moment until Boy's scream forced us to move. She moved closer to him and he hid behind me.

Boy silently cried into his breakfast of bread and milky tea. There were pools of blood all over the kitchen floor. My eyes followed her around the room as she kept tidying up.

"There's too much to do ... What kind of mother would I be? The mistake on your ID still hasn't been fixed ... Eighteen today, but out of school for two years. Why so many clothes in the basket?"

Her hand kept reaching for her head but never quite touched it. It was like she didn't know there was blood coming out of the cut on her head, but her hand did. "My children living alone ... No. Never. I had plans for us. I need to fix these doors for your birthday, and fix the fraud, and the ceiling and ... Boy, stop crying please. I'm here now. Forever like I planned."

The Burgundy Hissing was much louder than the night before; Boy looked at the ceiling in the next room and bellowed. Mme stopped washing the dishes and turned to him. Blood sideburns and a dress soaked in blood did nothing to appease her son.

"Why are you crying, my Boy? I'm gonna fix that horrible stain and those cupboards and wash these curtains. Everything is going to be okay."

SUNDAY: "MUTSHIDZI—eighteen-year-old   orphan   and permanent mother-sister to Boy. Everything is not fine, but it will be."

This is my mantra.

MOHALE MASHIGO *is a Soweto-born author (including the best-selling and award-winning novel* The Yearning *and the novelization* Beyond the River*), comic book writer, lover of wine, and full time book-nerd. When she has free time, she cooks for friends or writes music. Before she started writing novels, she wrote (racy)* Sweet Valley High *fan fiction.*

Cast on the walls was the exquisite shadow of another puppet . . .

ONE LAST WAYANG

by L Chan

A wayang *is a skillful type of Hindu-influenced theatre art, dating back to the ninth century, in which a story is told through leathery shadow puppets (which are generally always menacing in appearance even when they're not meant to be!). As I've been told, a travelling wayang performance was looked upon by villages with great anticipation as a distraction from life's routine, much as would be a traveling circus or an Autumn harvest festival.*

This art form originated in Indonesia and was popularized throughout Southeast Asia, including author L Chan's homeland of Singapore, from where he relates the following tale of adventure, reminisce, and fright. For even our elders were young once, in another era perhaps, when dragons breathed fire, shadows came to life, and children were taken to One Last Wayang.

the troupes of performers, making the folk of the *kampung* sigh or weep or burst into laughter so raucous we'd rouse the sleeping birds in the trees, that in turn drowned out the song of the crickets with their caws of indignation.

We were in for a treat. A famous *wayang kulit* troupe would be making its way down to our *kampung*. You don't have them here anymore, they've all gone back across the sea to Indonesia. Back then, there were still a few travelling the country. There were many types of *wayang* but the *wayang kulit* was special. There were no actors, only the *dalangs*, perched beneath the stage. Above them, there'd be a screen, big as the wall of our living room now, far bigger than your television. We would watch as the epics unfolded, acted out by shadows on the screen. Such shadows they were! Gods, demons, heroes, and princesses. The *dalangs* would move the puppets with sticks.

(*A lot like that show you watch. The one with the talking frog?*

Sesame Street, *Atuk?*)

It took them a day to set up, arranging a space where the musicians would sit, putting up a screen of fine linen. Behind the screen was a tent, closed off from the eyes of the public, where the *dalangs* worked their mysterious preparations. The *kampung* should have been buzzing with anticipation. The days were hard for our parents, but the nights were long; the *wayang* would normally have been a welcome distraction.

The mood in the *kampung*, however, was somber. The daughter of the headman had taken ill, struck down by a high fever. They'd found her collapsed in one of the nearby plantations, unconscious but shaking like the tall grass in the wind. Some said that we should have sent for a *bomoh*, a spirit doctor. We had not cut down quite so much of the jungle when we lived in the *kampungs*. There were still spirits there, powerful and mischievous. Others said that we should carry her down to town, to the hospital, and get her western medicine. Neither option was cheap and the headman shook his head, refusing to make a decision before daybreak. His wife dabbed at the brow of their daughter with a cloth soaked in water that had boiled the leaves of the hibiscus plant. Through it all, little Aishah shivered and shook under the thin blanket.

(*Atuk, isn't that . . . ?*

Another story, yes. Shut up.)

Night fell and the lamps went up, the chorus of crickets and frogs warming up as the sun dipped behind clouds of rose and ochre. Unbidden, families came out to sit in whispering clumps in front of the screen, waiting for the *wayang* to start.

The band sat by the screen, perched on the dust. Their skins glistened with sweat under the yellow, sputtering light. Percussion instruments and chimes sat ready, flautists puffing up their cheeks in preparation. Then the magic started.

The screen lit up from behind, long shadows springing high. And what shadows they were! Warriors with elaborate headgear and wavy swords. Scowling demons sprang forth brandishing spears to do battle, their tusks almost gleaming with spit and hate. There were kings and princesses, low-scheming merchants and heroes.

The music soared and dove alongside the action and drama. Echoing metallic chimes formed the backbone of the music. Woodwinds darted around the chimes like bright, silvery fish. I saw the crowd nodding and bobbing in time with the music. We were hypnotized.

The audience was rapt. The show was perfect. A little *too* perfect . . .

I stared at the prancing shadows on the screen. The *dalangs* were so skillful that the rods moving the puppets were barely there. After squinting into the bright screen and tracing the smooth movements of the leaping figures I concluded that they were not there at all. Neither was there the slightest motion or stirring in the dark cloth under the screen that hid the *dalangs* from the audience.

There was something strange afoot, something almost magical that the good folk of the *kampung* could not see. But I could see it. And I was curious, itching with that burning curiosity that eats at your belly, stealing hunger and sleep till it is scratched. I would solve this mystery.

THE MUSICIANS and the stage hands joined us for a simple supper. They regaled us with tales of their travels around our island, their homes back in Indonesia. They did not speak of the *dalangs* who worked magic behind the linen screen, neither did the mysterious ones make an appearance for food.

I waited for the tiny space we called home to be filled with the buzzing snores of my family and neighbors before I crept away. There was still light in the tent for the *dalangs*. They must have been making good money to be burning kerosene deep into the night. There was no guard. The other members of the troupe were splayed out on the ground on rough mats, the more senior members putting up with whichever families had room to spare.

My bare feet made no sound as I snuck into the tent. The canvas walls seemed to conceal an expanse that the tent's external footprint did not suggest. It was hard to tell the size of the place. Baskets and boxes piled from ground to ceiling turned the space into a maze, and clothes drying on ropes obscured my line of sight. There were lamps dangling from the ceiling at regular intervals, but the piles and pillars of the place made the entire tent a shifting kaleidoscope of shadows and light.

I found a basket full of the *dalangs'* puppets, carved out of cured leather, held at the joints by pins of brass, supported at the limbs by copper rods. But they weren't the well-loved tools of a master. Rot darkened the leather, the subtle carvings eaten away by mold. The pins and rods were a creeping mass of verdigris. I heard something, a subtle chittering, a sigh. I turned. There was no *one* behind me. But there *was* something new: Cast on the walls of the tent was the exquisite shadow of a puppet—one of the demons—hideously glaring with its deformed face and clawed hands. I looked for a source of light but could not find the puppet that cast said shadow.

The night was warm, humid, but my sweat was cold enough to make me shiver. I hurried onward, only pausing long enough to peer back at the shadow. It seemed like a trick of the light, but the cursed thing seemed to have tilted its head after I passed it, as if to favor me with a quizzical look. I turned a corner and came face to face with another shadow, this one a fearsome warrior, brandishing a pair of curved blades, his armor intricately patterned. Still, there was something wrong with it. I didn't figure it out until I got closer and cast my own shadow over the dark figure. There was nothing between the shadow and I. The light was behind me. Nothing was casting the shadow. Then the lips of the figure turned upward in a leer.

I would love to say that it was courage that brought me forward, but I am old and care little for the admiration of others. I pushed forth because the figure of the demon was still behind me somewhere. The warrior reached for me, a shadow without a body. The questing tip of a sword found my leg, not the flesh and blood leg that shivered as I squeezed by the creature, but its flat black twin on the ground. I felt the cold kiss of steel across my thigh, hissing at the frozen touch. My trousers had been parted cleanly, my fingers found a speck of blood oozing from my leg. Panic drove me deeper into the den.

A step and a turn around a corner brought me to the heart of the structure. Like a spider in a web, the *dalang* sat at the center of his maze. He was a wizened little man, perhaps not much taller than I. The elements had dried him out, his skin so much like the hard leather of the abandoned puppets. And, like the abandoned puppets, he appeared to be rotting. His hair grew in patchy clumps, hanging limply from a scalp spotted with age. Wrinkled lips pulled back to reveal blackened gums and a mismatched collection of brown teeth.

"Finally the burglar shows himself. You were louder than a rutting buffalo."

His hands were still busy with his work. In front of him, barely two paces from me, was a large flat board of wood, so bleached by the sun that it was whiter than bone. On it, pinned down by a collection of sharp wooden dowels, was a squirming black figure in the shape of a man but half the size. I watched as the *dalang* applied a sharp tool to the flat, black thing and teased out a small fleck of darkness. He put the squirming fragment into his mouth and chewed hard, as though munching on dried cuttlefish. The thing quivered, and I imagined a high pitched keening, beyond the range of my hearing. It was another shadow, like the warrior on the wall a moment ago.

"Oh. Now you're quiet, boy. Interrupt my work and just stand there mute as a palm tree. Let me take a look at you."

He set down his tools and groaned as he rose to his feet, only pausing long enough to reach up and pluck a lamp from its perch above. As he

For them. He dies for them.

THINGS I DO FOR LOVE

by Nadia Bulkin

Author Nadia Bulkin describes her fiction writing as "socio-political horror, or, scary stories about the world we live in," and the following is terrifying indeed, in all terms of place, belief, and circumstance.

Asih, Hasyim, Mas Tjapto, Murtawan, and Panggih live in the same Indonesian village, on the muddy banks of a foul, gray river. But as alike as their lives might be imagined, each is an indelible expression of hope, of fear, and of tragedy, driven by how their lives intersect, and how events are set in motion by as diabolical and otherworldly a device as a simple whisper.

Things I Do for Love *was the last story that I acquired for this anthology, and it's one of the best, which goes to prove any number of time-honored adages.*

ASIH HAS BEEN SICK FOR TEN DAYS, OR AT LEAST, that is what they are telling her little sister. Poor sprite is too young, they think, to learn that malice is real; that whatever happens in the dirt of a schoolyard is nothing compared to the things adults will do to hurt each other. But Asih did not raise up her little sister to be an over-sensitive coward, and when the child twists the doorknob and steps into her muggy bedroom, Asih is pleased to welcome her with a mouthful of rotting teeth.

They call it a "curse," and that you "fall" into it helpless and startled, like a house collapsing unexpectedly into a sinkhole, like the knees of a deer buckling as the bullet knits into its hip. This implies your innocence. This implies you were betrayed. This implies that no part of you crawled toward the dark on your hands and knees like a lizard looks for shade, like a termite looks to nest. This implies that *"falling"*—e.g., to *fall in love*— isn't the one thing that everybody wants. As if your bloody, bleeding heart doesn't crave a void.

"Don't be scared," comes tumbling out from between the bleeding gums and blackened enamel, barely discernible through the tongue's dead flesh, "all of this is nothing."

"Rendi says that Mas Tjapto's making you sick," says her little sister, nervously chewing on her finger. "I asked him why. He said he didn't know."

Asih doesn't remember how snarling Mas Tjapto, always sitting on his porch in a ratty sarong with a cigarette that never seems to ease his mood, was drawn into the shadow, the rot. But she knows it doesn't matter. The shadow has taught her that much. Mas Tjapto was always going to be taken apart, whether by an angry mob or lung cancer or brooding Mt. Merapi. "Mas Tjapto" was nothing more than a particular carbon configuration that had mistaken its fleeting sentience for power.

Asih has learned a lot since she slid under the shadow. Including: the look on her aunt and uncle's faces when they peeked into her room, having been compelled by familial obligation and grotesque curiosity to make the drive from Surabaya. Including: the way her friends sound when they are frightened, not just afraid of failing a test or being late for dinner or even of having a rock thrown through their heads when the town is rioting, but truly *frightened* for the purity of their souls, and the way that fear is warped by the closed wooden door that everyone foolishly hopes will keep Asih's "sickness" contained. Including: that there is only the infinite and the irrelevant, and nothing in between. Including: that the origin is the end and the cause is the effect. Including: there is no time, because there is no sequence. Including: that every structure and system and shape we worship is impermanent, mutable, changeable into something better but usually something worse—praise be to God the Unholy. Even cells, even mitochondria, even protein. We hang together only by a thread. That is something her aunt and uncle still need to learn. And learn they will, someday.

"Maybe Mas Tjapto knows how to make you better, too."

The thought is so absurd that Asih begins to laugh—a guttural, primeval predator's laugh that needles under the skin and right into the nerves, blacking out the world—and by the time she is done, her little sister is gone and the only motion in the room is once again the softly-whipping overhead fan, the gently-pulsing walls.

Asih tosses her head in her sweat-soaked bed, panting softly, only faintly aware of the sensation of being vigorously turned inside out. She smells blood dripping from her little sister's finger. She hears a noise from somewhere very far away, coming from just inside her head. Like a whimpering dog, or an airplane in a nosedive. Someone is dying. Just one of one hundred fifty thousand today. Six thousand every hour. One hundred every minute. One of two, this very second.

THE KIAI, HASYIM, has his head in his hands. He can't stop thinking about skin being peeled by fire, about muscle being cut and bones being split, about blood rushing forth to greet the day. He can't stop imagining the pain. There is something to be said for military efficiency, Hasyim is realizing. Surely the poor saps being killed now would rather take a bullet from a soldier's gun than be dismembered alive by a baying mob. That is one thing they have lost since losing the General; one of many small mercies they didn't realize were mercies at the time.

"Things can always get worse," as Mas Tjapto used to say.

Hasyim first heard this earthly truth three years ago, after one of the village's most devout women—Ibu Hartini, a farmer's wife, mother of five—went to the dukun instead of the mosque to fix her ruptured marriage. The thought of a woman who had always had the utmost faith in Allah as the arbiter of the One True Plan turning to magical incantations to curse her husband and his lover had given Hasyim heart palpitations; he saw the whole village tumbling off a cliff into the blazing fire of Jahannam. He tried complaining to the mayor, but Murtawan just sipped his tea and told him they had to "sort this out like grown-ups"; he tried waiting for the dukun to come to town, but of course the dukun wouldn't come near a pesantren, and he ended up marching down to the busted-up little house by the river to see the busted-up little man himself. It was raining, and he had to go wading through the muddy backyard to find him, passing a broken chicken coop and what looked like a broken bird cage. He did not ask why the dukun was throwing tiny bones into the river.

"Waduh," Mas Tjapto said without turning his head. "The honorable kiai, in my simple little home. What have I done to deserve such an honor?"

"Shouldn't you already know?" asked Hasyim. "I thought you were a psychic."

"And I thought kiai could walk through the rain without getting wet."

Hasyim had suddenly become aware of how cold he was. "I cannot stop you from selling people your solutions," he said, teeth chattering, "and I clearly cannot stop people from coming to you for help. But I can make life difficult for you, Mas Tjapto, more difficult than you can imagine."

"You should be thankful that you're sitting so pretty in your little pesantren, my good kiai," said Mas Tjapto, and poked a hole in a small egg with a needle. "Things can always get worse." When he turned his head he was grinning, probably because he knew that sounded like a threat, and not even the most popular dukun could threaten a kiai. At least not back then. There was order back then. "For all of us. We are all just trying to get by."

A small mercy. Hasyim was raised to be kind. In the half-light he could see the lines on Mas Tjapto's face, the lines of years spent in what the old dukun no doubt thought was twisted service to the village. And then Hasyim saw himself withered and wizened, begging a younger guru for a small mercy. The fire in his heart cooled to a simmer. So he said, "I've come to offer you a compromise. Perhaps you could consult me before you prescribe them a solution. Perhaps we could work together. I know we both love this community . . . "

"*Pah*. I don't *love* this community," said Mas Tjapto, and drank the egg. "Full of liars and thieves and idiots. But this community loves me, yes, or thinks it does, anyway. For now."

"Everyone has weaknesses," Hasyim agreed. "Who among us but Allah is perfect."

Mas Tjapto snorted and threw the egg shells into the river. Hasyim hoped he was not implying that he was, indeed, as perfect as Allah, but in the months to come he would learn that Hasyim did not think anyone was perfect—not himself, not Allah, certainly not the General. He was not sure which talk disturbed him more. "Please, Mas, don't speak like that," he would whisper as local cops strolled idly by their favorite warung, but Mas Tjapto would laugh and say they couldn't be held hostage by what he called "the curtain"—the illusion of omnipotence. *Fear will kill you before God or the General can.* He used to say that, too.

And now the General is gone. And God is standing back, somewhere in the sun-kissed clouds, saying, *sort this out yourselves*, and Mas Tjapto is dead—whether burned alive or dismembered or decapitated or simply bludgeoned until broken down into blood and matter, Hasyim does not want to know. The curtain has fallen, and it will take them all with it. *Reformasi*, they call it. *Reformasi total!* But *reformasi* into what . . . ?" No one ever seems to answer that question—no one seems to answer any questions anymore—and now all Hasyim knows is the thought that worms in like a snake and turns to stone in his belly: *You're next.*

The boys of the pesantren lean forward. They have been anxiously awaiting his instructions since Parno ran in with the news that the dukun had been killed by a black-clothed "ninja assassin." In the old days he would have called the police or the mayor, but Murtawan is claiming weakness ("in the face of all the danger") and the police have been bought; so the pesantren must save itself. Some are too young to help—no, they are all too young, and their parents entrusted him with their sons' education—but everything is broken now. *Reformasi total.* Suddenly he understands: no mercies, big or small. Just survival.

"These are frightening times for everyone. I know it feels like everyone has lost their minds. The most important thing… the only thing… we need to do is protect this school," Hasyim says. "Do you boys understand?"

They nod. The younger ones don't understand, not really. But the older ones do.

MAS TJAPTO has met many deadly things in his lifetime. About a hundred ghosts; fifty highly-poisonous scorpions, beetles, and snakes; a green-eyed emissary of the Queen of the South Seas (though not Nyai Roro Kidul herself); three angels; two zabaniyya; and at least five separate species of jinn. The angels are the worst—placid, sanctimonious assholes who use their supposed proximity to God to justify the objectively terrible things they do. Jinn, at least, make no attempt to hide their evil. Jinn don't arrange tinsel military parades for themselves; jinn don't call themselves *The Exultant, The Triumphant, The Providential.* But jinn will make you rip your own face off if they get angry, and a small part inside Mas Tjapto is surprised that after all the many monsters he has known, he will die at the hands of a fifty-year-old carpenter with a hammer.

He likes to think that one of the jinn he has known is behind this—one of the literally bull-headed, quick-to-temper ones that he used to be very good at tricking, when he was a young psychic—that it snuck inside the carpenter's daughter when she wasn't looking and made her flail like a rabid dog; that it planted the seed in her father's mind that poor old Mas Tjapto was to blame; that it was now watching, with sick satisfaction, as her father clubbed poor old Mas Tjapto to death. But this is not real, and every downward swing of the hammer—infused as it is by the stench of the carpenter's homelife, the carpenter's broken heart—reminds him that this is not a scent he recognizes. Whatever is inside that girl, it isn't about him. He's going to die, and it isn't about him.

"I didn't curse your daughter," he gurgles through the warm blood rushing down his throat—*where has it all come from?*—though his ears are ringing so badly that he does not think he will hear his attacker's response. "What has your daughter done to earn a curse from me? Nothing."

But that's bullshit. As if his curses come with any strings like righteousness attached. Well, no, there *is* a string—one single golden string—and that string isn't money, like all the village idiots around here said, but power. Since his grandparents first discovered that his dark little wishes could actually maim livestock and sicken classmates—*try it again just a little, just a touch*—it is the string of power that has jerked him to-and-fro like a wayang puppet. His mother warned him that it would make him nothing more than a loaded gun, a weapon to make the strong even stronger, and she was right, of course, but by the time he grew old enough to understand that, it was too late. Every assassination, every illness, every madness, every thrust of his psychic engine seemed to take him around another corner in a maze so large and so complex that he couldn't possibly remember how to get out.

The fucking price. He's known for years he was speeding toward it, and for the last few months he's been smelling it like the stink of death, lurking around corners. Not even the foulness of the river could mask it.

And because it's bullshit, the carpenter keeps hitting. A little bit harder now. Mas Tjapto has always been lacking in the art of soothing the soul. All the grieving mothers, the worried fathers, the libretto-singing love-struck choir that believes *nothing can eclipse this pain, nothing*—the only thing he ever tells them is: things can always get worse. It's the only solace he believes in. Even now he believes it: *I could always be dead.* Then his vision blurs and a blackness rolls up inside his eyes, and when the world returns the carpenter is saying, "Release her." Something is crawling up the wall behind him—a gecko?—no, bigger. Off to the right, glowing diamond eyes are hovering in the darkness of his kitchen. Fitting that the vultures should gather to watch.

"I didn't curse your daughter," he repeats, more of a whisper now. He tries to swallow; he fails. Ever more viscous blood comes up instead. Either his vision is shaking or the carpenter is, but either way, he decides he owes this desperate man, at least, the truth. "I can't release her. Your daughter isn't cursed. She's... The light from the lamp in the corner splits and the two progeny-lights circle and cross each other's paths like a pair of flying leyak, " . . . inhabited."

The carpenter still hasn't taken off his mask but now it's clear that he's tempted, because why not let the asshole see the wrath in his face if murder's his only option? Well, maybe all that's deserved. Not for that sixteen-year-old demon-possessed know-nothing Asih, whom he never touched psychically or otherwise. But for the others. The journalist, the activist, the doctor, the lawyer, the politician, the student, the teacher, the anonymous endless barrage of bodies that floats slowly down the river outside his house every night.

For them. He dies for them.

THE CARPENTER slowly trudges home, hammer in hand. He has wrapped the tool, now weapon, in the black mask that he tore out of a black scarf, because he couldn't breathe with the mask on. The itchy, choking heat took him back to a childhood nightmare about being buried alive—wrapped in a white sheet and buried alive in a wooden box, the better to rot him with—and the warm blood spatter only made it worse. So now he is walking home without his disguise, confident that nothing matters anyway. Maybe he will be caught. Maybe he will be dragged through the streets by his hair and his heels to the one flickering lamp post and torn apart by a mob of other masked men in torn black scarves, all of whom are trying to unstick curses laid upon their own sick sixteen-year-old daughters.

Or maybe nothing will happen to him. Maybe he will walk home and live the rest of his life in a still, silent peace before succumbing to a heart attack. He is not sure which outcome he prefers. Because either way, there is a little worm chewing through his heart, a blind and deaf little worm that is making him doubt that his daughter has been saved. He has felt it in there since he left the dukun's house—worming around, eating up muscle, making holes. Whispering: *how weak the flesh; how small the spirit*. When he hears this, tears well. The mayor promised him, as much as a politician can promise anything: he promised him, with a squeeze of the hand and a tearful stare into the eye, that this was his last best resort. "The sickness dies with the poisoner," the mayor whispered. "But please, you do not need to do that. Mas Tjapto will listen to reason. I know he will."

Then he thinks he sees a neighbor standing in the middle of a yard, looking over a concrete wall at him. He pauses, takes another look. The sob building in his throat is momentarily hushed in the presence of what he knows in his molecules is not a neighbor. He looks again, but now the "neighbor" is gone.

The gnawing starts up again. It is getting louder, he realizes, the closer he gets to his house. He winces, puts his hand to his heart, and then hears someone behind him whisper his name: *"Panggih!"*

Of course he does not look back. He is not a fool. He remembers telling his own daughters the story of the boy who looked back when he heard his name called on a dark and lonesome road. Asih was ten, starting to grow into the snappy teenager she would become. Indah was four, sitting on his knee. The dying sun drenching their faces crimson, the crickets' chirping almost loud enough to feel. Knowing it would be night soon. *"And do you know what he saw?"*

"No."

"Panggih!" Louder and more urgent now. Like someone tugging on his shirt sleeve. Like Asih or Indah tugging on his shirt sleeve. *Daddy what did he see?* He tightens his grip on the bundled hammer and keeps walking.

"Panggih!" It's almost a yell, and the fear it kick-starts is primordial, animalistic. His house finally comes into view and he breaks into a sprint for the last thirty steps—fumbling with the fence latch, hitting the door shoulder-first, falling into the darkness, slamming the door shut behind him—and only after he has safely shut out the world does the smell hit him. A strange rankness. Like rot wrapped in flowers.

His first thought is of Asih—how he clenched his heart around her name and her last innocent smile as he brought the hammer down on her torturer, *how weak the flesh*—but her door is closed, her room is dark. So he hurries to the other bedroom instead and sees his wife and littlest daughter asleep, limbs wrapped around each other. His pounding heart is searching for relief, but all he sees when he blinks is the dukun's body—head now less of a head than a bowl—splayed where he left it in that house by the river. That sob he's kept swallowed rolls back up his throat as the truth hits him like a sneaker wave that almost knocks him down. *How small the spirit.*

"Daddy."

That scent again. Sickly sweet. Thin arms, cold with fever-sweat, wrap around his neck, pressing gently on his esophagus but not hard enough to choke, even though something about her brittle chicken bones almost feels strong enough to do so. When she was little, she broke her ankle running through the woods from some old long-haired woman that the neighborhood children said lived in the trees, looking for lonely babies to steal.

"He said it would release you. He said the sickness dies with the poisoner."

"What did he see, Daddy? When he looked behind him?"

Pressure of a force he's never felt before tightens his throat. For a second his eyes blur, and when they focus again all he can see is the two bodies on the bed. How peaceful they look. How still.

"Did he see a chasm open up behind him where the world used to be?"

So still.

THE MAYOR, MURTAWAN, misses surfing. He grew up an hour from Plengkung Beach, before the Americans discovered the bay in 1972 and named it G-Land, before the surf camps and the custom beer holders and the speedboats from Bali ferrying in Australians by the dozen—when it was just locals on handmade longboards and the occasional wandering white man with a past and a painted fiberglass board, and when he had a father that used to teach him how to spot good waves rising, how to paddle fast, how to stay balanced. How to look at the wave not as a source of terror but as a vehicle, as a pair of angel wings. Not to look down at the fragility of a liquid floor but forward to the sparkling beach. How to ride danger to Paradise.

He yells for his assistant, voice cracking with sleep. He likes to beat the sun in to work—that hour before dawn when the rest of the village is still floating in a deep lull is the best time to work. Mas Tjapto taught him that. He did learn a few things from the dukun over the past ten years, since he was first elected mayor and introduced, by Ibu Hartini, to their resident "spiritual advisor." Even then, Mas Tjapto looked like he'd been through several knock-out rounds with the Devil, which immediately informed Murtawan that he was a survivor. An aligner. One who knows how to protect himself by jumping quickly from rock to rock. Even if the rock sinks in his wake.

There is one thing that his father did not teach him about surfing, but that he learned on his own in G-Land, getting bumped off waves by older boys, getting thrown off his board even: there is only room for one to ride the crest. Only room for one survivor. And what was the thing Mas Tjapto said to him last month? "Everybody has to pay the price, *Pak*," and from that tone burst forth all the things they'd done together: challengers sickened, bureaucrats blinded, coffers seized. The dukun had become surly in his old age. Started mumbling about God and comeuppance and not Paradise but Hell. Getting ready to jump to another rock.

His assistant—twenty-five years old, looking nervous because the entire country has been thrown into the middle of a fast-breaking wave without a board and everyone is craning their necks backward, just trying to keep their mouths above a thrashing water line, because the world is full of goats in need of a shepherd—hurries in, wiping his eyes. "Yes, Pak Murtawan."

"How is Mas Tjapto?" He picks up a pen and flips open his diary book. "Have you checked?"

"It happened late last night," his assistant says, his mouth hanging open after he stops speaking like a dummy's for just one second too long before he remembers to close it.

"And does the kiai know?"

"One of his boys knows. Parno."

Which means Hasyim knows. Which means Hasyim—so frightened, so unlearned to the ways of the world, and so very arrogant that he had dared tell Murtawan that he had to get this town under control, as if he thought *he* could do a better job—is rallying his boys to protect the pesantren with sticks and knives and fire, if they have to, and boys that age are such easy triggers. This whole village, these days, is such an easy trigger—dragging bus drivers who run over schoolchildren through the street, setting thieves and looters on fire—that his only worry is that he might have overdone it, this time. Chosen too big of a wave—*is that even possible?* No. Stay focused. Stay balanced. Eyes up. Ride the wave. Glide forward. Stand. Lead.

"Send a package to Panggih's family," Murtawan adds, twirling the pen toward his assistant. "Some cakes, some martabak. They've gone through such a terrible time, they'll want to hear from someone they can trust. Check on their girl, see if she's any better."

"I walked past their house this morning..." Again, his assistant pauses. Murtawan glances up—*what is this boy's problem?* "It was very... quiet, Pak. The door was open. I think something's happened."

Now it's Murtawan's turn to pause. He has assumed, until this moment, that there was nothing wrong with the girl—that she was just sick, or hysterical, or mad at her parents. Panggih had just been so upset, banging on his door in the middle of the night, yelling *someone cursed my daughter,* that it had all fallen into place too easily. The perfect swell of hate and rage and fear and love, rising in all its emptiness and will to power, able to drown everything that would ever hope to threaten him. He had seen Mas Tjapto slipping beneath the waves. He had seen the kiai Hasyim swept out to sea. But that was when he assumed there was nothing wrong with the girl.

His assistant's lip is trembling.

"The things I do for love," says Murtawan, and blows on his cup of tea.

NADIA BULKIN *writes scary stories about the scary world we live in, three of which have been nominated for a Shirley Jackson Award. Her stories have been included in volumes of* The Year's Best Horror *(Datlow),* The Year's Best Dark Fantasy and Horror *(Guran), and* The Year's Best Weird Fiction, *and in venues such as* Nightmare, Fantasy, The Dark, *and* ChiZine. *Her debut collection,* She Said Destroy, *was published by Word Horde in August 2017. She spent her childhood in Indonesia with her Javanese father and American mother. She has a B.A. in political science, an M.A. in international affairs, and lives in Washington, D.C.*

"Cheers, young man, to your first time here."

ON A WOODEN PLATE, ON A WINTER'S NIGHT

by David Nickle

There are great existent conversations of the universe, and one of those ongoing is what defines the sub-genre of speculative writing that is known as "Weird Fiction," most often attributed to the writings of H.P. Lovecraft for its modern promulgation, and which otherwise has much overlap to any number of other fiction sub-genres. Jeff VanderMeer, in writing for The Atlantic *(2014), states, "This is the realm of the uncanny, sometimes known as the weird tale, or literature of the strange," and he also sidelines, "The macabre often hinges on the darkly humorous . . . "*

So it goes that the following story most definitely falls into what I would agree with Mr. VanderMeer as defining "Weird."

Canadian journalist and highly-regarded fictionist, David Nickle, shares the anecdote of a simple meal between old friends in a recently renovated restaurant, from the point of view of a certain long-time patron. David confided to me that the incident was inspired by an actual conversation he overheard while dining with his wife in a Hungarian restaurant in Toronto. He did not, however, order what comes On a Wooden Plate, on a Winter's Night.

"A JEWISH GUY," SAID THE AUSTRALIAN. "HE SHOULD be here now."

The waiter didn't know what to say to that, although he guessed who the Australian was talking about. The Jewish guy was in the toilet, up a flight of stairs and just over our heads and maybe back a bit. That guy'd come in ten minutes ago, taken off his coat and gloves and hung them on the rack, then taken a table for two. He was tall, a bit stooped—maybe sixty years old with dark hair combed back over a globe-round skull, and a thin and well-trimmed beard going white. Likely he was the Jewish guy. But the waiter couldn't tell for sure, not the way he could size up this one as Australian the second he opened his mouth.

The waiter shrugged. Could be. And the Australian replied, "Well then," and we were all spared more of this when the door to the men's room slammed open and closed, and the Jewish guy came downstairs.

"Ha!" he said, waving across the room. "Look at us!"

The waiter showed the Australian to that table for two—really a table for four, but it would do—and the two of them sat down.

"Look at you, old man," said the Australian. He wiggled his fingers over his chin, and the Jewish guy shrugged.

"If you could in fact grow one of these," he said, "then you'd have something to say."

The Australian snorted and waved his hand, and the Jewish guy nodded.

According to his driver's license, the Jewish guy's name was David Kruger. He lived on Dufferin Street, pretty far up by the street number, maybe past the highway. In an apartment. He was fifty-eight years old, two years younger than the Australian, whose name was Albert Jackson. Albert Jackson's passport didn't give up an address but, surprisingly, it was instead American.

You never can tell.

The waiter came around with menus. Albert and David didn't bother to open them.

"You still got the wooden plate?" asked David.

"We'll have one of those. We can share it."

"In the old way," said Albert, and the waiter nodded. Would there be anything to drink?

"Some of that Czech beer you got. You do pitchers? Good. One of those. It's good to see you open again. This used to be a hell of a place."

The waiter smiled and said he'd heard stories.

"Is that girl still here?" asked David.

"She's not," said Albert, "how could she be? And how would he know? He just started. Her name was Helen. This one wanted to propose marriage."

Helen. That was a long time ago if it was Helen Katona they were talking about, as it undoubtedly was. Helen Katona had not worked here for twenty years. No . . . twenty-seven years. She was family, but not close family: a pale, freckled beauty, with red hair that kinked and frizzed like a firestorm from the netted bun she had to wear. Helen was not especially friendly, not with anyone . . . but that was probably what had intrigued David in those days, when he was younger and didn't know his way around love, let alone seduction. Even now, the old family gone, new management at work . . . his old infatuation embarrassed him and he tucked his chin low to study the menu he at first hadn't felt need to open.

The waiter went away, slipped back past the stairs to the washroom to the kitchen, and relayed the order—Wooden plate!—and the door to the cellar swung open.

At the table, Albert and David caught up.

Albert had divorced a year ago and there were legal complications, and to a lesser degree, emotional ones too. A much lesser degree by his estimation: Albert had a lawyer but not a psychiatrist.

"Psychiatry is shit," said David. "Complete shit."

"Jill said I should see one," said Albert.

"Is Jill seeing one?"

"Who knows," said Albert.

The waiter returned with the beer and two glasses, and also brought a basket of dinner rolls. Albert poured for them, and they clinked rims.

"God knows," said David, "that's who," and Albert laughed. They finished their glasses of beer and David poured two more.

"This is better," said Albert, and he looked around the dining room, bright with low-rent fluorescents, like it had always been . . . had always been in the lifetime of these two old men, anyway.

stopped him and asked if he would send a pitcher of beer and three glasses over. They were all really too young, and the waiter said so, but Albert said it would be all right. "We have that wooden plate coming, right?" he said, and the waiter nodded yes, that was so. "Then no problem?" said Albert, and the waiter agreed. No problem. He moved behind the bar and poured a pitcher and gathered glasses, and brought it over to the three.

They were not all too young. The boy's name was Jeffrey Albee, and he was nineteen on the nose; his driver's license said his birthday was the day before. The older of the girls, Susan Albee, maybe Jeffrey's sister, was twenty. The third one was not old enough. She was only seventeen, and funnily, her name was Helen. Poulis, not Katona. But there was a resemblance.

These things happen.

"Wow," said the boy, Jeffrey about the beers. The waiter motioned to Albert and David. "Hey thanks!" Jeffrey said, and waved, and Albert waved them over, while David signaled with a different kind of wave, and a shrug: *It's all right if you don't want to.*

None of them really were inclined to. They leaned across the table toward one another and held a short whispering debate to determine that. Jeffrey thought it might be polite to at least stop over and say hello; Susan said fine, as long as Jeffrey took care of it and she and Helen didn't have to; and little Helen Poulis, bless her, didn't want anything to do with them or their beer and thought they should leave, go get some Korean food at one of the places down the road, the one that she and Susan had been to before, that time during the break . . . She didn't care for the smell here. It made her queasy.

That was the flesh.

Sliced, dipped in quail egg, and then battered with the mixture from the sack and the jar and, of course, the tin, it was ready to go. So Pyotr slipped it into the sizzling oil of the fryer—then stood back as it writhed and popped and spattered in four flattened schnitzels. Carl busied himself preparing the sausage, while Mr. Slaut paused slicing the onion and peered out the door to the dining room, curious as he could sometimes be.

"This is a good night," he said, so softly that no one might hear. "Everybody's hungry."

At David's request, Jeffrey sat down in a chair next to Albert and tried to explain with good grace the ladies' reluctance to join them.

"They just want to stay with the coats," was the best that he could come up with.

"Sure," said Albert.

"But here *you* are," said David. "Well. My name is Mr. Kruger, and this is Mr. Jackson. What's your name?"

"Jeff."

"Jeff! Great to meet you, Jeff." Albert patted him on the back. "This is your first time here?"

"It would have to be," said David. "It's only just opened again."

"Sure," said Jeffrey. "First time for Hungarian, too."

"Hungarian?" Albert smiled. "You may have come to the wrong place."

"It's a good place," said David. "Not Hungarian though. There used to be a lot of Hungarian places along here, but this was never one of them."

Jeffrey nodded. "Good to know," he said. "Well, thanks for the beers."

"The cuisine is close though," said Albert, as Jeffrey started to get up. "It's easy to make the mistake. I think Mr. Kruger and I made the same assumption when we first came here. About your age."

"I thought it was new," he said, sinking back into the chair.

"Oh no. It's newly opened."

"*Re*-opened."

"After many years shuttered," said Albert.

"Wow," said Jeffrey.

Susan tried to catch Jeffrey's eye as she sipped at her glass of beer. Helen hadn't even poured one, and had turned her glass upside down, held her hand on top of it. It seemed as though Susan wanted to get Jeffrey to come back to the table, but it was no good. Jeffrey listened raptly, while David told him about how things were here in 1972: the great wagon wheel that hung behind the bar, rusted and with tiny spikes

along its wheel-rim, which came over with the family—"just there!"—
and the four daggers that hung at the compass points around it. "North,
east, south, west," said Albert, and "Midnight, three and six and nine,"
said David.

Helen leaned over and whispered something to Susan . . . softly, too
softly for any but her to hear, at first, until more sensitive ears drew nearer . . .

"—roaches," she said, "beetles, can't you see? All over—"

And like that, with the quickness of a child, she lifted the glass and
clapped it down again. Helen looked away, then squinted her eyes shut.
Susan leaned in close, to peer through the glass at what it had trapped.

Mr. Slaut cursed in the old tongue and withdrew from the kitchen
door as little Helen squealed, and Susan stared. The waiter, who had been
behind the bar, stepped out, hovering uncertainly between the bar, the
front the restaurant, and David, Albert, and young Jeffrey. A moment of
confusion, then he attended the two young women. What might the
trouble be?

"Jeff, get over here!" Helen shouted, and Susan pointed at the glass.
The waiter bent to study it. He nodded in a way that expressed the
mildest of surprise, and apologized. Jeffrey stood and excused himself.
David nodded, but Albert said, "Wait a moment."

Jeffrey stood, confused.

"You know when Mr. Kruger and I first came here . . . well, seeing
you here . . . you and your lovely friends, it reminded us of that," said
Albert as the waiter deftly took a menu and slid it underneath Helen's
glass. He promised to remove it.

"That's not the only one," Helen told him, and pointed—to the
ceiling, to the floor, and finally noticing, to her own shoulder, her arm.
She fell silent, and we felt the gooseflesh rising on her forearm, on her
calves where we tickled and tasted. The waiter lifted the glass, peering
into our eyes as he did, and carried it back through the tables and into the
kitchen.

"It's true," said David. "Mr. Jackson and I were with a girl, so it's not
exactly you."

"But it's a mirror," said Albert. "A symmetry, I mean. This beer's
getting to me."

COUNTRY BOY

by Billie Sue Mosiman

Billie Sue Mosiman has been writing mainstream crime, suspense, and horror fiction from America's southland for over three decades, so having a chance to work with her on this next story was, for all intents and purposes, a genuine honor.

Billie Sue has a distinctly Southern voice in her work, a plain and down-home sweetness that offsets the violence, the bloodshed, the darkness lingering in people's souls. Some of my favorite authors (Joe R. Lansdale, Robert McCammon, Cormac McCarthy, et al.) write in a similar vein, so perhaps it's just a style that appeals to me.

Whatever the reason or preference, it works.

Herein, a young teen is drawn into the mystery of a local serial killer whose victims are found beaten to death. The only monsters in this story come in human form, as discovered by a simple Country Boy.

"Boy, boy, and girl," said David, "and here you are, girl, girl, and boy."

"Lucky boy," said Albert, and laughed a little more loudly than he should have.

The waiter and Mr. Slaut conferred only briefly, and Mr. Slaut told Carl and Pyotr to finish the plate. It was near-to-done in any event, so it was not difficult. Pyotr arranged the turnips around the wings just as he'd been taught, and Carl stacked the last of the cutlets on top of the onion bloom then slid the knives into the compass-point slots of the platter. The waiter slid his fingers beneath the rim and gently lifted it to the old steel tray.

"Go!" said Mr. Slaut.

David and Albert both laughed long enough to embarrass Jeffrey, and he explained that he was here with his sister and her friend, and it wasn't like that.

"Which one's your sister?" asked Albert, and Jeffrey indicated Susan, who was staring at them, her mouth opening and closing, her eyes wide. "Susan," he said. "Helen's her friend."

They stopped laughing, David and Albert, and David smiled behind his whiskers.

"Takes you back, eh?" said Albert, and he raised his glass to clink with David's and then—when Jeffrey thought to lift his—with Jeffrey's. "Cheers, young man, to your first time here."

"The first of many," said David and he looked over his shoulder, as the doors to the kitchen swung open and the waiter emerged, balancing the tray in front of him. David drained his glass of beer and set it on the table, then watched as the waiter slipped past them and to the front. He lowered the tray to the level of the table and slid the wooden plate in front of Helen.

"It's for sharing," he said, when she looked at him with those wide and uncomprehending eyes. David sighed, and Albert shook his head, smiling sadly.

"Looks like your plate's arrived," said Albert.

Jeffrey looked over. "We didn't order."

"Well, it's there," said David. "The wooden plate. It's the house specialty."

"What you want a shovel for?" he asked.

"**G**ARLAND DIDN'T DO SHEILA," DAD SAID WHEN he came in from visiting the store after working the fields.

"He didn't?" I said.

"Couldn't of. Cardinale Bond was found today killed with a shovel. She was down at the creek back of their land, and Garland's been locked up. She had her shoes off and her feet in the water, dead as dead, a shovel by her head. Someone hit her so hard, when she bit down it cracked two of her front teeth."

I couldn't feature it. We called her Card, and she was sixteen with the prettiest teeth of any girl around. That wasn't the point, though. Someone killed her almost the same way as killed Sheila six months ago, and so it sure wasn't Garland.

They never got him to confess, but saw he was too confused in the head to do that anyway, even if he *had* killed her. Garland was put in the asylum over near Andalusia, and he probably wouldn't ever get out. Even Sheriff Bedstone thought it was him did it.

The next day—now that there was a second death with the same method—the sheriff drove to Andalusia and said to Garland in the day room, "You didn't kill nobody, did you?"

This conversation was spread far and wide so everyone knew what was going on.

"I never said I did," Garland answered back.

It was a good day and he was halfway understandable. Some days he just wagged his tongue in the wind until it dried up like a lemon peel and he wouldn't make one lick of sense.

"You never said you didn't either, Garland."

Garland shrugged like he didn't care one way or the other and sat looking out the wired screens on the nearest window.

"God, I don't know who's doing these young ladies if it ain't you." The sheriff took off his hat and pulled his hand through his sparse hair.

Garland had no opinion. "I'm hungry. I'm going to the kitchen to beg for cornbread."

Bedstone let him go. Heaving himself from the chair he looked around the day room with the year-old magazines and the ping pong table with the missing net and figured Garland was just as well off here as anywhere else. Might as well leave that mistaken sentence alone.

I'D KNOWN CARD, who was closer to my age. Sheila had been twenty. Card wasn't like her in having a *reputation*, but that's not to say she didn't take on with two of the Hinch brothers who lived a half mile behind her through the woods. We all rode the same school bus and just about all the boys couldn't help falling for Card's pretty smile. "You're a real card," the country boys would say and grin like goofy monkeys.

Who would do a thing like that to her? Was there someone else in the area as out of his mind as Garland?

I could think of one, but it made me sick to my stomach.

During childbirth, Sheridan Danforth tore his mother asunder sure as a machete. She died before he drew breath. He grew up mean and disrespectful to everyone, even his daddy, who slapped him about with sure resolution. Sheridan still mouthed off to him, given the chance.

I was with Sheridan once in the forest when we come up on a mama raccoon and her babies in a stump. Sheridan went after the bunch like they might be demons and swung the little ones by the tail against the head of the stump and kicked the mama so hard she screamed and died right then.

"What'd you do that for, Sheridan? They done nothing to you."

"You shut up unless you want some." He drew back a fist to make good his threat.

I shut up then and watched Sheridan close anytime I had to be around him. Someone no good like that can't be talked to or coddled or reasoned with. They'd as soon kill you as kill a raccoon with her babies.

Made perfect sense it was Sheridan killing girls. He had one lazy eye and a shock of dirty brown hair that hadn't been barbered, well, ever. He took the scissors to the mop when it got in his eyes. So girls didn't find him fetching. Plus, his temperament was so scary they got afraid to talk to him.

Being rejected, I guess, might cause a boy to go wilder than he might

"Sheriff, I have had an idea about those dead girls," I said from the office door standing open to a breeze.

He looked up from his desk, stood, and turned his back to head out the rear of the building without saying a word.

"Sheriff?"

It was no use. He looked to be a man eat up with guilt and a sense of futility. He was out and shutting the back door with a bang. I could get no audience with the one man needed to hear my theory.

I told my dad instead.

"Have you lost your marbles? You don't know Sheridan stole a shovel—and a rake and a hoe! Why'd he do something like that? Of course the sheriff don't want to hear it."

"But Dad, listen, I know Sheridan, what he's capable of. He's mean. He's . . . bad."

"Bad don't mean killer. And I've known some bad men in my day. You stay out of it before you get yourself in trouble."

Dad hated trouble. Ever since he had a spat with a neighbor over a fence line and was served with a lawsuit that cost him three hundred dollars to settle, he let trouble alone.

I sat on the porch steps and stared into the woods wondering when the next girl would go missing.

FIRST A FEW SHOVELS disappeared from homes. Here, there, all over the county and spread out, so no one took notice for some time. Then shovels went missing everywhere. Every village house, farm, and trailer house, family lost their shovels. At church and the store serving the little area, people began to talk about it. Why would anyone want to steal a shovel, they asked one another, then they'd remember the dead girls and glance away and change the subject. Couldn't be, they might whisper among themselves. That couldn't be why, to be used as bludgeons to murder more girls and women. That'd be crazy.

It certainly *was* crazy, and Sheridan proved he was a game player, a killer racking up a list of victims. The next one was Lana, a young woman who worked as cashier at the store. She wasn't found for a week despite how people rolled out to hunt the woods for her. She was found tucked into a shallow cave in the side of a wall of dirt, her head broken, and the shovel lying nearby.

I felt sick enough to turn away from the sheriff and his two deputies, the lookee-lookers hanging around the bottom of the ravine watching the cave at the top as Lana was brought down. She already smelled, and I gagged before staggering away and home.

Before getting there, Sheridan stepped out of a stand of thick bamboo with a shovel in his hand. My heart stopped and so did my feet and so did my brain. I couldn't think. I could only stare at Sheridan's eyes and then the shovel, the business end of it up in the air.

He smiled, and shivers ran up my back like big black wood ants. I might be dead in a minute and I still couldn't think.

"You figured it out so I made it completely clear for everyone," he said. "I took *all* their shovels. If that's not enough message, they've now found Lana."

I thought, then I was right, it *was* you. Why admit it unless he meant to kill me?

I stuttered, but got it out. "Going to kill me, Sheridan? For figuring you out? Did that make you mad?"

"I don't get mad," he said.

"Why are you doing this?"

"Because I want to."

Then he hit me hard on the side of my head with the shovel and darkness took me down.

"WE HAVE TO LEAVE here by morning," Sheridan told me. "I'm sure you named me to your dad, so he'll bring the sheriff around when you don't come home tonight." He sat across from me, the shovel balanced on his knees.

I sat stiffly tied to a metal kitchen chair. I felt the beginnings of a scab stretching from my forehead to my cheekbone. My eye twitched and, being solidly swollen shut, the movement brought on a near faint. The pain in my temple was like a Chinese gong going off, someone slamming it with a hammer.

"You didn't kill me."

"Not yet," he said, hunching over his knees to peer up into my bloody face. "How'd you know so soon it was me?"

"You're the only one likes killing."

"The only one? Really?"

"Really."

We both heard the crunch of cracking limbs in the yard. Boots walking around the house. I tried to see Sheridan's expression from one good eye, but it was dark in the house.

"Where's your dad?" I asked, realizing we were alone.

"Dead. In the kitchen."

The back door creaked open and Sheridan stood up, hefting the shovel.

I prayed for rescue. Was it my dad, the sheriff, a posse? Someone had to save me because left to the maniac in the room I was chum for the fish in the nearest creek.

"Come on out and talk to us, Sheridan. Put your hands up and come out."

It was Sheriff Bedstone. I sighed with relief until I saw Sheridan's shadow close in on me in the chair and the black rectangle of the shovel head rise up in the darkness.

"Help! He's going to kill me!"

The front door burst open and then the unthinkable happened. Gunfire broke out, fiery blasts coming from two, three, four different weapons. I ducked and screamed.

Sheridan, the shovel poised to strike, fell forward, his head striking my knees before bearing him to the floor.

The men filled the room and turned on the overhead light. Sheridan lay on the floor in a big, widening puddle of blood, his hand still clutching the shovel.

I hung my head, weeping, and I thought, well, I didn't piss myself, that's something.

Back home from the hospital, Dad sat on the side of my bed apologizing for not listening or believing when I'd come to him with my worries. He patted my hand, spoke softly, and in his voice was regret.

He reached over and turned on my bedside lamp. He picked up the latest library copy of a Sherlock Holmes mystery and placed it in my lap.

At the door of my room he turned and said, "He was bad. Just like you said. He was the baddest of the bad. I was the one at the cave this afternoon who told them about how bad he was and said they had to come check him. So you solved the case. My son. My smart son."

He left quietly and I picked up the book. I couldn't see good enough to read, but I ran my hands over the cover and smiled. Reality was worse than fiction, and I hoped to stick to fiction for the rest of my life.

Who wanted to solve crimes like Sherlock?

Certainly not this country boy.

BILLIE SUE MOSIMAN is an author of novels and many published stories. Her latest work was The Grey Matter *from Post Mortem Press. She lives in Texas with her husband, three dogs, and chickens. She travels, quilts, and rewatches* Twilight Zone *episodes.*

Then she said the words he'd been waiting months to hear . . .

THE WIFE WHO DIDN'T EAT

(a reimagining of the Japanese fairy tale "Kuwazu Nyobo")

by Thersa Matsuura

Much of the fun (the gamble!) of editing an anthology is seeing what comes in; different stories may appeal to me for different reasons, although I try to keep in mind this isn't a book of stories set just to my *taste, but they're stories of value (originality or voice or meaning, etc.) that I think the greater general reading audience will enjoy.*

. . . and I think you'll enjoy this next one very much. I sure did.

Writing from the eastern coast of Japan, Clarion West graduate Thersa Matsuura presents her take on an old fairy tale. It's fun, it's smart, it's very, very dark. Be wary the gifts gods grant you, especially when you ask for such as The Wife Who Didn't Eat.

"OH, GOD OF DIRT AND GOD OF ROCKS," SABURO chanted as the blade of his sickle sliced through a bundle of rice stalks he held clenched in his fist.

"Oh, God of Mountains and God of Trees." The sound the sheaths made—crisp and wet—and the feeling of slight resistance and then release always sent a satisfying tingle through his heart. "Listen to my humble prayer, listen to my pleas."

This chant was Saburo's daily incantation; he'd been reciting it for a year. He was still fiddling with the wording, but he believed he'd mastered the emotion behind the prayer. He meant it.

"I'm a humble man. I don't ask for much." Saburo stood and straightened his stiff and sore back.

He gazed over his magnificent fields, square plots of land framed in raised bunds. The straight lines of heavily-tasseled rice plants sparkled his favorite shade of gold under the furious noonday sun. Saburo made a fist and beat at the small of his back. He was too young to be in this much pain.

It wasn't fair.

"I work hard from dawn to dusk and grow very fine rice. The best in town," he continued. "That is, of course, thanks to the blessings of you, the gods."

He glanced around, soggy ground at his feet, neat field after field meeting his house off in the distance, the naked maple that had grown too close, and then the line of Takakusa mountains hazy in the heat beyond. He wondered which gods were listening, which ones he needed to appeal to the most. He wondered if it mattered.

"But there is one thing I'm truly lacking..." Saburo trailed off for effect.

He knew that he only had to get the gods' attention once. And not even all the gods. One or two would do. Maybe three. But once favored, they tended to look kindly on you your whole life. The opposite was also true. But Saburo had faith in the power of his new prayer.

"You see, the one thing I don't have that so many men in the town my age do..." he paused to polish his sickle on his pants in the most modest way he knew. "...is a wife."

Saburo thought about his mud-packed *kura* behind his house and all the rice he had stored there. It was impressive. The backbreaking work deserved a reward. A wife was a good reward.

The most important part of the prayer came next. He was going to try a new approach today.

"A wife. A woman who is beautiful and kind and just as hard working as I am."

He dropped the sickle at his feet, fell to his knees, and prostrated himself. It was an act he'd seen the mountain *yamabushi* doing on the shores of the Abe River. Everyone knew how blessed they were. He pressed his forehead into the damp earth, inhaling the sweet loamy fullness of it. He counted to ten and then pushed himself back up. Mud clung to his clothes and face. He felt embarrassed, but that was the point. He resisted the urge to wipe his cheeks and brow. The gods loved humility.

"What would make her even more perfect, though, is if she didn't eat anything at all." This was his little joke. Didn't the gods have a sense of humor?

"Then I could continue to seed and grow, harvest and store my wonderful rice, and my stockpile would continue to grow, and the town's people would hold me in higher esteem."

Saburo felt the hardening of confidence solidify in his chest. It was a good prayer, he thought. This time it would work. He waited for a breeze to kick up, a flock of ducks to call out as they flew overhead. A sign.

Nothing.

He sighed and scratched the already drying muck from his face. It was a futile prayer. No such woman existed. But couldn't the gods do anything? Somewhere inside he believed. Saburo was nothing if not a believer.

THAT NIGHT under a full moon, Saburo soaked in his wooden barrel-tub. He didn't cool the scorching bath with the usual three buckets of well water though. He wanted to keep it almost too hot. This was one of the punishments for today's overconfidence.

He shifted in the cramped space, resting his chin on one knee and admiring the milky outline of mountains through the steam. He needed to build a bigger tub, one where he didn't have to fold himself up like this. Still, it felt good.

He let the heat untangle the knots of muscle in his back and limbs. Earlier, before climbing in, he'd scrubbed off the sweat, mud, and sins with the prickly *tawashi* brush. More penance. And now as a final atonement, he steeped in the boiling soup of a bath, feeling as if his skin were thinning until it might tear at the slightest touch. It wasn't a bad feeling, kind of like an apology.

Saburo closed his eyes and listened to the crickets chitter and whirr, a chilly bite in the air. He let the disappointment of the day melt away and instead concentrated on the excitement he felt about the coming of winter.

He started calculating how many bushels of rice he'd harvested already and how many he'd have stored before the first frost hit, when a voice startled him.

"*Konbanwa.*" It was a woman's voice, clear as a bell. When he opened his eyes, she was standing beside the tub.

Saburo jumped, splashing the brimming water and extinguishing with a hiss the oil lantern he had set on the ground. It didn't matter. He didn't need the light to see the stranger who had seemingly appeared from nowhere. He could see her perfectly.

The smooth curve of a cheek and a dark, long-lashed eye were illuminated ethereally by her own paper lantern that she held up. She blinked and smiled. This was obviously a woman of some status, for she smiled but did not show her teeth. She was the most beautiful person Saburo had ever seen.

Suddenly, very aware of his nakedness, Saburo made an awkward attempt to hide, thrashing around in the tub as he did. The woman lifted one long sleeve of her kimono in front of her face and giggled. Then she said the words he had been waiting months to hear.

"I'm new to this town and I have no employment and nowhere to stay. If you'll allow me to live here, I will work diligently to keep your house in order. I only require a roof over my head and nothing else. For I do not eat at all."

Saburo pressed his hands in front of his chest and hastily thanked the gods. He didn't know which one or ones to give gratitude to, or what exactly worked with his prayer, but at last he had incurred their favor.

LIFE AFTER THAT took a turn for the better. Not only did Saburo invite the woman into his home, he made her his wife. She was exactly what he'd asked for: beautiful, kind, and worked hard without a single complaint. She mended his clothes, cleaned his house, she even filled his bath and kept the fire stoked just right, so that the water was the perfect temperature when he finished his long day's work.

Every night while he relaxed in the bath, she would drag the heavy bushels of rice he had harvested that day into the storehouse. After stacking them and reporting back how many he currently had, she would use the little bit of rice she'd skimmed off the top to cook his nightly meal.

"*Dana-sama,*" she would call in her lilting voice when dinner was prepared. "It's time to eat."

Saburo would sit cross-legged on the packed earthen floor of his home and dine, while his wife kneeled nearby combing her long hair and quietly humming a song. He didn't have to worry about depleting his stockpile because his lovely, kind, and hard-working wife didn't eat anything at all.

Saburo was happy. The gods had listened to his prayers and they had delivered. He was finally given the reward he deserved.

For six months there was no better wife in all of Japan.

WAITING. HOW MUCH longer? Waiting.

She sits on the mat in the corner of the room and very slowly pulls a comb through her hair, gently teasing out the knots. A lullaby finds her lips. It's calming. It's the one her mother used to sing to her, the one she sang to her own children.

"Sleep, child, sleep
A sleeping child is precious
A child who cries is loathsome

A loathsome child is put on the cutting rack
Chop-chop-chopped like a *daikon* radish
And scraped into the river out back."

Again today she was made to drag five bags of rice from the fields all the way to the storehouse. Her muscles ache. Her head pounds. Her fingers are cut and blistered from mending and chores. There are burns on her arms and face from tending the fires. Worse, hunger consumes her. She wonders how much longer must she wait. How much longer must she endure?

But the daily physical exhaustion of the work is nothing compared to the torment she feels when she remembers her children. Her children.

Another long day. Another long night. How much longer must she wait?

IT TURNED SPRING, and the weather grew humid and warm. It was almost time to start planting again. So one fated day Saburo woke early and trudged out to till the fields and ready them for the seedlings. He was sure that with his wife's help, he would bring in the biggest harvest he'd ever had. He imagined his storehouse full. They might have to build another one before next season.

Saburo grew so excited about the idea of expanding his wealth, that after his hot bath that evening under the stars, even before his wife came out to call him to dinner, he slipped away with his lantern to visit his *kura* and admire all his fortunes for himself. The storehouse must surely be stacked to the ceiling from last year's harvest, he thought.

However, to his shock, when he pulled open the heavy doors, except for a single bushel of rice, the room was entirely empty.

This couldn't be ... Impossible! What had happened to all his precious food? Thinking there had been thieves, Saburo ran immediately to his dutiful wife who was arranging his chopsticks in front of his meal when he burst in.

"My rice," he sputtered, out of breath and heart hammering in his chest, his hair still dripping from the bath. "It's all gone. I think I've been robbed!"

His wife gave no indication of surprise. Instead she took a moment to arrange the pickled radish slices into a fan shape on a tiny saucer before looking up.

"I'm afraid I don't know what you're talking about," she said, and then she ended the conversation. "*Dana-sama,* it's time to eat."

In that moment Saburo was for the first time terrified of this stranger he'd taken in. What did she know? What wasn't she telling him? He was confused and full of questions, but something told him he should not pursue them.

THE NEXT DAY Saburo pretended to go into the fields as usual, but instead, while his wife was out hanging the day's wash, he scaled the maple tree and snuck in through a back window. He then made his way through the high rafters, found the corner where the darkest shadows clung and crouched there, waiting for her return.

Soon the front door flew open and his lovely wife entered with his last heavy bushel of rice. But instead of dragging it, like she'd always done, she was carrying it on one shoulder. In utter horror Saburo silently observed this woman he had called his wife for six months, the one who had made all his dreams come true as she hummed that strange little tune and tenderly washed and prepared the rice.

While she waited for it to cook she sat in the corner of the room and ran a boxwood comb through her hair, rocking back and forth. Saburo waited.

When the rice was ready, she removed a jar of salt from the shelf and began meticulously shaping handfuls of steaming rice into balls and then placing them in a pile at her feet.

Why is she making so many *omusubi*? But Saburo didn't have time to imagine a reason for the odd behavior because suddenly he was very aware of a low growling. It felt like the sound was coming from all around him, the thatched roof, the sticky shadows, even the wooden beams that were sliding splinters into his sweating palms vibrated with the eerie noise.

"Hush, hush," his wife said below him. "Soon."

She finished making the last rice ball and wiped her hands on her apron. Once again she removed the comb from her long sleeve, but this time she carefully parted her hair down the middle before replacing it.

From his position, Saburo watched her grab a handful of hair in each fist and pull. She cried out in pain. All the strength in Saburo's body drained away and it was everything he could do to not topple from his perch above the scene. He watched the part in her hair widen, slowly cracking open to reveal a mouth. A mouth with black-leather lips and too many sharp teeth. A tongue lolled inside and another feral growl reverberated through the house.

"Hush, hush now, *dana-sama*," his wife said, giggling. "It's time to eat." She reached for one of the rice balls and dropped it into the dark maw.

The mouth instantly snapped shut sounding like the crack of a whip. It gnashed and swallowed the morsel, then opened wide again, demanding more. Saburo's wife bent forward and used one hand to support herself. She looked and sounded like she was in agony, but still she fed the ravenous beast living inside her head, tossing his precious rice into the hole until it was gone.

After the monster was sated, his wife collapsed on her side and fell into a deep sleep. Saburo took the opportunity to sneak down from the rafters and staggered his way back into the fields.

"Oh God of Wind, God of Stone," he said. "God of Water, God of Breeze."

Saburo, numb and head reeling, waded out into the tilled flooded fields and absent-mindedly splattered himself with mud. He prayed. "Listen to my pleas."

He went on to explain his unfortunate situation, sure that this time the gods would feel his sincerity at least. He begged for an answer and, almost as if it were delivered from heaven, he came up with a plan.

"*TADAIMA*!" SABURO CALLED OUT as he flung open the front door to find his wife kneeling in front of a mirror, pinning her long tresses back into place.

"*Okaerinasai-mase*," she said and hurried over to help him remove his shoes. "You're home early."

"*So desu ne*," Saburo laughed nervously. The unsettling thought occurred to him that this monster-woman might have known he was in the rafters the whole time. She was obviously some kind of fiendish *oni*, and didn't they have heightened, animal-like senses?

"The strangest thing happened to me while I was tending the crops," he said.

"Strange?"

"Very, very much so." He couldn't find the strength to enter his own home. He stood with his hands fidgeting awkwardly by his sides at the front door. His wife kneeled, placed her hands demurely on her lap, and looked up waiting for him to continue.

"The gods spoke to me today." Would she believe him? Was it obvious he was lying? Did *oni* even believe in gods?

"What did they say?"

"Well, I was tilling the fields, like I was yesterday," Saburo made a motion to indicate his clothes that now suddenly looked too obviously dirtied. "And I was telling them how thankful I was that you had come into my life. They agreed that you were beautiful and kind and hard working." Saburo realized he couldn't look his wife in the eye.

"But then they told me that you are too good a wife for me," the words came out rushed. "They said that I'm a bad husband for leaving you home all day to work and take care of the house. That you deserve better than me and this life I have to offer. That maybe even it's dangerous for you to be left here all alone all day."

His wife raised an eyebrow but didn't speak.

"Then the gods told me that they think you should return to your parents' house where you will be safe and happy. Your parents are getting older and they need you too."

"I see," his wife said. She got to her feet. "The gods said this to you?"

"They did." A stream of sweat trickled down Saburo's back. He tried not to look at her glossy black hair pinned up on top of her head or remember the horrible mouth that was hidden inside.

His wife bowed low and Saburo took a step back.

"I'm so sorry," he said. "I'm really very happy, but I don't think we can go against what the gods say."

"I understand. I will go," she said. She started to turn away but then faced him again. "*Dana-sama*, before I leave, may I ask for two things to take with me. If you don't mind, that is."

"No, yes, of course." Saburo was elated. His plan was working. He would soon be free of the beast.

"I'd like to take with me the wooden bathtub and a long length of rope."

"Yes, yes," Saburo agreed, his heart soaring. He was already planning on making another bathtub and the rope cost hardly anything at all. "I will get those for you now."

His wife followed him outside and waited for him to lug over the heavy tub and hand her a long length of rope.

"*Hai, douzo*," he said, presenting her with the gifts.

"*Arigatou, dana-sama*." She bowed again.

"I think you should leave right away, you know, before it gets dark. It's what the gods suggested."

"Did they now?" She examined the skein of rope. "That's what I intend to do. There is just one thing . . . "

"Yes, anything."

"Before I go, yesterday when I was cleaning the bath, I noticed there was a small leak in one of the slats on the bottom. Could you please check it for me? Maybe you could mend it before I go?"

"*Mochiron*, of course," Saburo said, and without a second thought climbed inside.

In an instant his wife threw the rope around the tub, hefted it onto her back with him inside, and took off running at full speed.

Saburo howled, knowing he'd been tricked. He kicked at the sides and then peeked over the edge only to see that his once beautiful wife had grown three times her size and now had a head of wild matted hair.

She was an ogress, the worst of the *oni*.

He'd have to escape, but she was moving much too fast, and even if he managed to get out of the tub, she'd only stop and snatch him up again. All Saburo could do was hold on and begin praying again to the gods to save him.

He continued his heartfelt pleas until they were deep in the mountains and she started to slow. The gods had heard him. They had listened again. His *oni* wife stopped by a crooked old tree to rest and Saburo got an idea.

While she leaned over catching her breath, he reached up and grabbed a branch and very carefully pulled himself out of the tub and into the tree. There he remained absolutely frozen until she grumbled something unintelligible and, readjusting the rope in her thick hands, started off again.

WAITING. TOO MUCH waiting. There is no time.

Her blood waterfalls in her ears, heartbeat clubbing in her neck and temples. She closes her eyes and collapses against a tree. Through thorny, ill-fitted teeth, she hisses air until her breath returns.

Cannot stop. No time. No time.

Haste. Fear. Elation. Is she already too late? Her children. She heaves herself back up and rewraps the rope around her hands, repositioning her load. She races off again.

Ah. Just a moment's rest and already the burden is lighter. A little farther and my children. Almost there.

The grit of dirt and the slip of grass under her bare feet renew her strength. The animal-scent of night eating away at the day renews her hope. It will be dark soon. This is where she belongs.

My children. My sweet children. Innocent faces last remembered, but how are you now? Cheeks drawn. Eyes hallowed? The snap and yearn and skull rending headaches of the mouths you are obligated to feed. Do you cry? Was that you I heard howling on the wind last night? Was that all of you? Were any missing?

Oh, how you suffered. But I suffered, too. Day in and day out with that man. That fool.

Loathing fed her heart.

Not clever. There was nothing to fear from him, no wit, no bludgeon or blade. Those are the only things that make a man equal to us. Without them he is filth. That man is filth.

She spits.

"Filth and a fool," she says to the man she has trapped on her back. "A friendless fool. I waited, hoping I could ensnare more like you. But to my surprise you have no family or friends." The ogress chuckles at the thought. "No one will even notice that you are missing, I suppose."

"If I had known that you were so despised by the others, I'd have left earlier instead of surviving on that atrocious grainy rice you farmed. Salted, barely edible, a poor substitute for the blood-salt of a man." The ogress feels her stomach churn at the thought of a real meal. Soft, sinewy meat. Her head throbs.

"And then you found me out," she goes on. "I didn't think you were near clever enough. So I had to leave. Only one of you, but you'll do."

Just then the ogress reaches the caves.

"Children! Children!" she calls. Where are they? Hunting? Sleeping? Starving? "Look what I have for you."

There is the sound like a hundred insects hatching, scurrying. They come.

"Bring your knives and your cutting boards. Let's chop him to pieces before the sun sets. We can feast under the full moon."

In the gloaming they swarm, and the ogresses' heart lightens. Thick-limbed, clawed, scarred. Some rub the sleep from their hazel eyes, others growl and scratch. They are beautiful.

"Want to see what mommy has brought for her sweet children?" She swings the heavy wooden tub from her back. The empty, heavy wooden tub.

She screams.

SABURO WAS DEBATING the merits of hiding against how fast he thought he could run, when he heard the scream. His blood iced and his knees buckled. He fell. There was no way he could outrun the monster. It was growing late, the sun had already set, and the moon was rising. He wasn't even sure about the path she'd taken up here. He was so far from home. Would anyone miss him and come looking?

Even if he attempted to flee, he'd probably trip and hurt himself, call out in pain. She'd hear. Or, more likely, he'd get lost until she or her sisters or brothers discovered him. No. He couldn't run away. But where could he hide? Saburo was having trouble finding the strength to stand again.

"Oh, God of Dirt, God of Rocks," he implored. "Oh, God of Flowers, God of Weeds. Listen to my humble prayer. Listen to my pleas."

Saburo began crawling; hand over hand, pulling himself toward a grassy patch of land in the distance.

"I'm a humble man and I don't ask for much. You've already bestowed such great fortune on me and for that I am grateful. But I really need you to protect me. I need you to save me, please, I don't deserve—"

Saburo was interrupted by another howl from the *oni* and what sounded like branches being torn angrily from trees. She was getting closer. When he continued his prayer again, it was in a whisper and with more genuine sincerity than he'd ever mustered before.

"I think I've lived a good, honest life, and my rice is the best in town, everyone says so. Also, I will make amends for any sin I've committed. Forgive me. Please forgive me."

This was it. This was all the strength he had left, all the faith he had left. Saburo looked up and through the pearly moonlight noticed dozens and dozens of irises growing among the snarl of tall grass he was headed. But their sharp leaves were different. They were no longer leaves.

Blades! Katana blades.

The gods were saving him again. With everything he had left, he dragged himself into the bladed fortress, rolled over on his back, and began scraping at the ground, trying to cover himself in dirt and fallen leaves. He needed to become even more invisible. A band of clouds swam to blanket the moon. Everything fell into pitch. Another blessing. A tiny bubble of hope bloomed in his chest.

He heard a slow approaching animal growl and recognized it as the same one from his home, him hanging in the rafters, right before his wife opened up the monster in her head and fed it.

A sharp crack, a foot treading on a fallen branch? She was near, close enough to reach down and grab him. Her breath a deep rattle in the back of her throat, her stench watering his eyes. Saburo bit down on his sleeve to keep quiet. He listened. And he prayed.

The ogress circled his hiding place. Again and again, stalking. But it sounded like she was growing impatient. She couldn't reach him. All he had to do was wait. Soon she'd be gone.

Saburo gave himself permission to begin imagining his home, the home he never thought he'd see again. The maple. He thought about his storehouse and how he'd refill it with rice, how he'd build a second one next year.

Oh, gods, you knew I was worth it. You knew I was worth saving!

Just then the veil of clouds skitted across the sky and the forest was again bathed in the blue underwater light of the moon.

FILTH OF A MAN, there is no time.

She circles the waist-high thicket of weeds. She doesn't understand what he's done, how he did it.

What's this? What trickery?

A hundred *katanas*, hilts sunk into the earth, surrounding him. A trap. A clever trap. She knows he's there. She can hear him, trembling, lips popping in silent prayer. She can smell him, that fetid reek that clung to him every day after he came in from the fields, even after his wretched bath. Even in the complete darkness she can see his outline.

Knives, swords, surrounded by blades.

She blinks again and again, reaches out an arm, draws it back.

Waiting. Too much waiting. My children are starving. I have to feed them.

A chilly breeze wafts through the trees and delivers a different smell. She stops in her tracks and turns. A wild boar in its den, the pups plump and juicy, full with their mother's milk. She can hear them mewl and grunt. She can hear her human husband shift on the ground beside her, an exhalation of breath. She weighs her choices.

The ogress looks up and just then the clouds slip away. The night brightens. She glances back down and laughs. The ground seems to be lit from underneath, an ethereal glow. She can see him perfectly, on his back, both fists clutching a handful of weeds.

"What do we have here?" she asks, noticing the magic that stayed her hand has completely dissolved. "Why these are not swords at all. They're iris leaves."

SHE'S GOT ONE HAND latched to his ankle, the grip so tight he can feel her nails scratch the bone, scrape a nerve. Saburo screams out again. He can't help it. His throat burns.

"*Onegai*, please, no!"

The gods have abandoned him, he thinks. There are no gods.

"Sleep, child, sleep," she's singing. The song has words.

"A sleeping child is precious

A child who cries is loathsome."

Saburo claws at the ground, a passing limb, some underbrush, a stone. Everything is yanked out of his hands. He has the amusing thought that he's being pulled along with so much less effort than she gave his precious bags of rice. He briefly considers his worth against his harvests and then dispels the thought when he hears a sound. Hundreds of clicking noises. They're growing louder.

Saburo garners his strength and readies himself to thrash out again, a well-placed kick. Maybe he can get away this time. He imagines himself bolting into the trees and escaping.

"A loathsome child is put on the cutting rack

Chop-chop-chopped up like a *daikon* radish

And scraped into the river out back."

The *oni* stops and releases her grasp on his leg. Instead of scrambling off, Saburo curls into a fetal position, eye still closed, and whimpers. He can hear them all around him. He doesn't want to see them. There are so many. They scuttle on what sounds like too many legs, curious grunts and wet slurping noises. His stomach heaves as he realizes the clicking sounds are probably teeth, children's heads cracked open to reveal voracious mouths greedy for their meal.

"*Dana sama.*" The sweet cooing voice of his wife whispers warm by his ear. It's calming and for a moment almost makes him want to look, to open his eyes and gaze upon her smooth cheeks, her long-lashed eyes. He resists the urge, screws his eyes closed tighter.

"Hush, hush, *dana-sama,*" she repeats. "It's time to be eaten."

THERSA MATSUURA is an American expat who has lived half her life in a small fishing town in Japan. Her fluency in Japanese allows her to do research into parts of the culture—legends, folktales, and superstitions—that are little known to western audiences. A lot of what she digs up informs her stories, while the rest finds its way onto her blog (thersamatsuura.com) *and into her podcast,* Uncanny Japan (uncannyjapan.com).

She is a graduate of Clarion West (2015), recipient of HWA's Mary Wollstonecraft Shelley Scholarship (2015), and the author of two short story collections: A Robe of Feathers and Other Stories *(Counterpoint LLC, 2009) and* The Carp-Faced Boy and Other Tales *(Independent Legions Press, 2017). She's also had stories published in various magazines and anthologies including:* Black Static, Fortean Times, Madhouse *(anthology), and* The Beauty of Death *(anthology). You can find her on Patreon:* www.patreon.com/thersamatsuura.

FTER SIX MEN, THREE ON EACH END, HAD CARRIED and passed Alyana's corpse through the window facing north, the child's dead body revealed its true form: half a stump of a banana stalk's main trunk.

This proved the prediction by Salvador, the *albularyo*, who wouldn't touch the body even while it still looked like that of Alyana. Salvador was adamant about not touching it when it was first presented to him and was told that it belonged to a seven-year-old who drowned in Kapisan River. He said that touching anything corrupted by the dwellers of Kapisan River would draw their unwanted attention, would mark him somehow.

"How do we get her *real* remains back?" Alyana's mother, distraught but already resigned to her daughter's fate, asked. The trunk's stump faced her. "It would be fitting to at least give her proper burial."

"We can't," Salvador said, making no effort to assuage her grief. "You know how it is. *They* take one life every year, supposedly by drowning. They float something for us to find on the water surface, a likeness of that drowned person, possibly to remind us of our vulnerability. That's the case with the banana stalk. It would look like your child until passage through the north-facing window showed otherwise. This has been going on for a long time, at the same time every year. It was Roberto's child last year. But you already know this, don't you?"

She did not say anything back; there was really nothing to say. If it weren't her child, then it would be someone else's.

Unspoken in the room was the question: *Why did you let your daughter near the river at this time of the year?*

Slumped in one corner of the cramped hut's interior was Alyana's father, a construction worker in Manila. He'd arrived a few hours ago. He did not join the villagers as they went out to bury the stump of banana stalk that once looked like the body of his child. Instead, he absently batted the flapping edge of a calendar showing a scantily clad woman holding a bottle of Tanduay rum. He wore the same expression as his wife: distraught yet resigned. Like the generations before them who insisted on living close to the precarious riverbank.

The two-room hut smelled of dried fish *tamban* and fermented coconut water called tuba. For seven years, it was the smell of home for Alyana, who used to walk three hours every weekday to reach the nearest and only public elementary school, where she was on her second grade and starting to learn about multiplication tables. Alyana's fraying blanket on her cushionless bamboo bed was unfolded. Past treasons stained the folds, presumably leaving only the undersides to be soiled.

The scenic Kapisan River was once again safe until next year.

KRISTINE ONG MUSLIM is the author of nine books of fiction and poetry, including the short story collections Age of Blight *(Unnamed Press, 2016),* Butterfly Dream *(Snuggly Books, 2016), and* The Drone Outside *(Eibonvale Press, 2017), as well as the poetry collections* Lifeboat *(University of Santo Tomas Publishing House, 2015),* Meditations of a Beast *(Cornerstone Press, 2016), and* Black Arcadia *(University of the Philippines Press, 2017). She is co-editor with Nalo Hopkinson of the British Fantasy Award-winning anthology* People of Colo(u)r Destroy Science Fiction *and poetry editor for* LONTAR: The Journal of Southeast Asian Speculative Fiction. *Her stories have recently appeared in* Sunvault: Stories of Solarpunk & Eco-Speculation *(Upper Rubber Boot Books, 2017),* The Cincinnati Review, Weird Fiction Review, *and* World Literature Today. *Widely anthologized and published in magazines, she grew up and continues to live in a rural town in southern Philippines.*

It starts with something as simple as a toothache . . .

THE SECRET LIFE OF THE UNCLAIMED

by Suyi Davies Okungbowa

It makes me very happy to include this next story by Nigerian author Suyi Davies Okungbowa. After enjoying his work in such venues as The Dark *magazine and* Mothership Zeta, *he became one of the first authors I solicited for this anthology, and, in turn, his story ended up becoming one of my favorites: It's smart, suspenseful, and, beside the terrifying circumstances the young protagonist endures, it just feels so* honest . . .

I believe one of the most inherently frightening forms of horror is Body Horror (AKA: Biological Horror), in which the human body itself is used as the primary device by which an audience is confronted with the horrific. Unlike most horrors, there is little escape from things that change within you, and which often spur even greater horror by way of societal revulsion and rejection at your changes. Puberty alone is a horror, but what Aniekan undergoes is perhaps rooted in the deepest of fears, for it is alone that he must endure The Secret Life of the Unclaimed.

T STARTS WITH SOMETHING AS SIMPLE AS A toothache. I'm home on vacation before final session at Ecclesia Boys, so Momsie is the one I run to. She's seated in bed with her glasses on, her hair untamed, the gray streaks standing clear. She has her back on the headboard and her feet buried in documents.

"My teeth, they're painful," I tell her. "I'm dreaming every night that people are chasing me."

She flicks her eyes at me then back to her documents, so I return to my room and curl up like a fetus to absorb the pain. An hour later, she calls me back and says she's scheduled an appointment with Dr. Akpan, whose practice is fifteen minutes away from our estate in the outskirts of town.

I go alone, as always. Momsie says at my age, she was already supporting her parents. *You think sixteen is too young, ba?* To avoid another lecture, I *jejely* take the long trek down Boskel road, to the pockmarked Aba expressway and down to the vine-ridden colossus that is the *Goodbye From Port-Harcourt* toll gate.

Dr. Akpan's practice is two rented shops with a sign that says *TeethWise.* One room is his consulting office where he, a small bald dentist in suspenders, sits me down and asks questions about my teeth. *Where is the pain? When did it start?*

I tell him it's in all my molars, and it started about two weeks ago. He makes chicken scratches on a pad and takes me to the examination room.

He places me in the chair, adjusts it so my blood starts backtracking into my brain, and proceeds to clamp my mouth open. All the while, he talks. My God, he talks.

Your father sat in this chair, you know? I filled six of his teeth, extracted two.

Can you just look at my teeth, sir?

It was the sugar from the beer, you know? Bad for your liver too, I told him.

God. I'm going to die now.

He laughed. Asked me to fix the teeth and let him worry about his liver. Too bad he didn't worry enough. If only he'd—

Then he turns on the light and freezes. The probe in his other hand clatters to the floor.

The light hums, fills the silence. Maybe that's why it seems like ages, the time it takes for him to retrieve the probe. Weirder even, he's stopped talking. He doesn't continue fumbling with my mouth either. He simply places the probe on a side table and walks out of the room on what I think are noodle legs.

A minute later, he returns, slower than before. He has a young lady in tow, an intern from the looks of it. She has her palms linked on her chest and there's a look on her face. The kind you have when someone says, *Come, I want to show you a snake.*

They return to my side and Dr. Akpan smiles, one that doesn't extend to his eyes. The intern tiptoes and peeps into my mouth.

"Jesus!" she says, then zips out of the room. Dr. Akpan flings the probe and follows, calling her name.

It's at this point my suspicions that Dr. Akpan is not right in the head are confirmed. I wriggle out of the chair, unclamp my mouth, and spit in the bowl. There's streaks of blood caked in the phlegm, but no matter. I'm done with this rubbish.

I almost leave the room before I remember.

I retrieve a dental mirror and move to the only double window, where there's proper light. I swing aside the blinds, open my mouth, and tilt the mirror to gain a full view.

This time, it is me who screams.

I KEEP MY LIPS clamped tight together on the way home. The lady in the kiosk at the estate gate, she snarls at me for ignoring her greeting, but it only propels my legs faster. I pass a neighbor. Another neighbor.

Aniekan, how're you? Mummy nko?

Leave me alone! My gums throb to the rhythm of my slippers slapping the dust.

Home is a rented two-bedroom flat squeezed as an afterthought between two towering duplexes in Jumbo Estate, off Kilometer 7. I've never been so glad to see it. I don't expect Momsie to be home. She returns at three to open *Shakara*—her fashion design and tailoring outfit, run out of the garage—after her clerical duties at the State Ministry of Environment. This is enough time to wrap my head around the things in my mouth.

When I burst into the compound, her two helpers are already in, rolling up the garage door: short, buxom Alice and lean, hairy Nsika. They exchange inquiring looks, but before they can ask questions, I slam the entrance door closed.

Once alone in the familiar darkness of my room, I breathe. Then I cry.

AFTER A TUMULTUOUS NIGHT of pain-induced dreams, I'm up and dressed before nine the next morning. Shorts, polo, sneakers. It's a Saturday and I'm on vacation, but Momsie still notices as I pass her, lying on the couch and watching EbonyTV.

She raises her eyebrows.

"We're going to Filmhouse with Kufre's mom," I say without opening my mouth. The words come out in a buzz.

She frowns. "What's wrong with your mouth?"

"Nothing." Buzz.

She waves it off. "I hope you're watching something decent?"

"The Wedding Ringer."

She knows it's a lie, but she's too lazy to argue.

Well, I *am* going to Filmhouse. And Kufre, the only kid in Jumbo I didn't fight with on my numerous forced play dates, *is* going to be there. His mother isn't, though, but I'm safe because I know Momsie will never call to check.

I board an okada, and five minutes of zipping along Aba Expressway lands me at the mall. *Make I buy ticket for you?* Kufre texts as I get in, *No,* I type furiously. *I wan' show you something first.*

We meet under the *Better Together* Coke sign on the ground floor. Kufre is a short, stocky boy with hairy and slightly bowed legs beneath his shorts. Wisps of hair connive between his ear and jaw. An everlasting grin is plastered on his face. Both give him the semblance of a snide older gentleman.

We shake hands and click fingers. He shoves two tickets for *Fifty Shades of Grey* under my nose.

"I chose for you," he says in his nasal voice. "Better hunch your shoulders at the door and behave like eighteen."

"Wait," I say, sluggish. "I need to show you something."

We head for the Men's room. All the while, I'm in conversation with myself, wondering if I should tell him. Kufre is the closest thing I have to anyone—anything—I can trust. He could even have a solution; miracles are possible.

I pull him into the Men's and shove him into a cubicle, bolting it behind me.

"You're my friend, right?"

Kufre frowns. "Why you dey talk like that? Something do your mouth?"

"Answer me. I can trust you with anything, right?"

"I be your guy na," Kufre says. "Wassup?"

"Listen, you can't tell anybody, okay?" I put up my finger. "Nobody."

"Which kain yarn be this? Wetin happen, Aniekan?"

"Promise first," I say. "Promise."

"Film go soon start." He stamps his feet. "Talk fast."

I breathe, then open my mouth. In the mirror behind Kufre, I see it afresh.

Molars, no longer flat and peakless, stick out of my gums with new serrated edges, like mountain ranges. The premolars follow suit, sharper, bulging under the gum with renewed sizes, next to incisors and canines that are slowly morphing into daggers. A tumor growing and destroying from the inside.

Kufre yelps and jerks back. I snap my mouth shut.

"Kufre listen, listen . . . " I'm saying, "I don't know what it is."

But he's hysterical, shaking his head, refusing the memory.

"Kufre—"

He turns to the door and tugs the handle.

"No, no, wait, listen." I'm holding him back, holding down the bolt.

Kufre starts to holler and bang on the door. Two pairs of feet appear under the door, and someone tries the handle from outside. When it doesn't budge, they rap hard.

"Wetin dey happen there?" someone asks.

I look to Kufre, my eyes begging him. *You promised.*

Kufre takes one good look at me, then says, "Na witch, na witch!"

He throws his weight on the bolt and slides it so hard it pulls off, into his hand. The men yank the door open. Kufre steps out, puts some distance between us, then turns right round and swings the bolt at my face.

I feel my left cheekbone explode and particles grind in my mouth as I crumble. I taste blood, and my lips sting.

"See his teeth, see it," Kufre's saying, hysterical.

The men turn to me, a dark cloud descending over their faces, their eyes brimming with menace. They're both towering men, and they lean their sharp-edged faces in close.

"Open your mouth," one orders.

I clamp a palm over my bleeding lips.

"Open am," the second one says, prodding my foot with his toe. "Open it."

I shake my head, slowly.

"Come here," the first one says and reaches for me.

I roll away from his outstretched arm, staining the floor red with my palm, and squeeze past the tiny space between him and the cubicle door. The second one grabs my shirt, but there's too much in my lunge that he's pulled across Kufre and the first man. All three tumble over each other while I jump out of the Men's and scamper down the corridor.

For a moment, I slow down, expecting them not to follow. Then the two burst through the door and come right in tow.

"Witch, witch, witch!" they're saying, echoing along the corridor. A head pops in at the other end, the exit to the mall main.

"Catch am!" one of them screams just as I approach. The man at the end steps in at the last minute to cover the opening. I barge into him and we sprawl into the mall main, to the alarm of bystanders. I roll on my back, and I'm staring into a thousand eyes. A thousand pathways to bewilderment, to denial, to malice.

"See his teeth," someone says. "Blood!"

A leg kicks me. *Witch.*

Another follows, and another. *Witch. Witch.*

Then blows of all kinds rain down on me—my head, my elbows, my buttocks. Round and pointed shoes swing, hit, bite. I catch a glimpse of a child's shoe.

Witch, witch, witch.

Then I am crawling, my joints aching, my flesh stinging. Hands, strong and decisive, pull me back, hold me down, and the blows rain afresh.

Witch, witch, witch.

I'm blind, choking, looking to the light of the exit for respite, to return to belonging, to hope.

Witch, witch, witch.

Then after what is eternity, I suddenly emerge from the crowd, dangling, broken, but sane enough to stand and, with the dregs of strength in my bones, turn my back on the world that will not claim me.

And run.

TWO WEEKS LATER, I'm back at Ecclesia Boys.

I'm glad to be away from Jumbo, to be away from too many reminders. I haven't seen Kufre since that day (God help him if I do; these teeth are going to become useful). Better for him that he attends Federal Government Boys on the opposite end of town.

Still, I know this can't last. I might've left the mall with only bruises and scrapes that would've raised Momsie's eyebrows if they weren't so buried in papers, but now that I'm back at school, I can't remember the last time I opened my mouth. I laugh with my lips pressed together. Every question gets a *hmm?* Every query, a *hmm.* Every threat, a *hmm!* If I had any friends, I would've been found out long ago, but for once, I'm grateful I don't.

I could manage through the rest of the session if it was my teeth alone, you know? But now I wear thick, black woven gloves everywhere—to bed, to prep, to class.

Because my nails won't stop growing.

Then, Ibanga says, "Hold him!"

Seven hundred hands reach out for me at once. Seven hundred pathways to bewilderment, to denial, to malice.

"Catch am," they're saying, their words overlapping hisses. "Witch! Catch am!"

I've learned enough to know I must move quickly.

I wriggle out of the first arms that grab me and dive under a desk. I move—left, right, between rows—just enough to get out of each new grab. Hands recoil when I pass them by.

Don't touch me, animal—

The door is there, wide, freedom. I sprint out, down the concrete steps, into the blazing heat. If they're following, I don't know, don't care. I kick off my school loafers, hop, take off my socks. Pull them over my hands.

The school gate comes into view ahead. I speed past school security before they have time to react. Outside the gate is a motor garage, blessed with a beehive of rusty blue-and-white commercial buses, street hawkers, and hiding places. After running circles around plantain chips sellers and parked okadas for a minute, the security men who'd followed me to the park give up. I slip into one of the buses with the conductor singing a string of bus-stops and squeeze myself between a mechanic and an old woman carrying a chicken on her lap.

After an eternity of a thundering heart, dripping sweat, and questioning looks from strangers, the bus gets filled with passengers and moves. I realize I've been holding my breath.

I don't let it out. Not yet.

FIVE HOURS LATER, I'm sitting in the dark, in a corner of our sitting room at Jumbo, my knees to my chest and my arms around my legs. My cheeks are wet, but I don't remember crying. The only things I feel are those moving in my body: contorting, changing, transforming, parts of me I will not look at, that I will not accept.

I focus on breathing, on controlling my body. If I sit still, maybe? If I don't move, neither will they, right?

The gears keep on rearranging.

All I want is for Momsie to return from the Ministry, and I hope the school hasn't already poisoned her mind against me? *Madam, we need you to know: Aniekan is not Aniekan anymore. Be careful when approaching.*

There are footsteps outside. I wait to see if it could be Alice or Nsika. But then the door opens, and light streams in, before it's shut and darkness returns. Momsie is feeling for the switch when I rise.

The light comes on.

"Jesus!" Her handbag thuds on the floor. Her hands fly to her mouth.

I no longer wear socks over my hands or a shirt over my torso. The hairs on my chest, arms, and legs have tripled in density. The hair on my head is wild, bedraggled, and stretched enough to plait into cornrows. The shorter end of it creeps into my face, covers my cheeks. My jaw feels too long and heavy. Under the hair on my arms, my skin is scaly like armor, like if I rubbed it the wrong way, it would peel and bleed.

The two of us stare at each other.

"They just grew there," I say. My cheeks are wet again.

She gapes past me with dead eyes.

"Mummy," I say, "help me."

She starts to cry. She comes over, so slowly, lifts my hands, caresses the hard core of my claws, encloses them in her small hands, cries into them.

"I'm sorry," I say, "I'm sorry."

She holds me for a while. I think I feel the gears breathe, become tranquil.

"It's okay," she says, more to herself than me. "It's okay. It's okay."

She lets go of my hands and backs away, as slowly as she'd approached. She picks up her bag and opens the door with her back to it. Before she shuts it, she reaches a hand in to turn the lights off.

The lock clicks from the outside.

THE NEXT TIME there are steps outside, it's a multitude. The door unlocks and flings wide open before I can react, and men pour into the room.

Someone must've told them about all the good points of escape, because they enter in a formation that allows them to immediately block all exits. I squint and slowly begin to recognize them. Pastor Richard—tall, yellow, skinny—at the front door. Brother Jerome with the stick—a thick rubber pipe. Brother Hilary with a similar pipe, at the door to the kitchen exit. Brother Marvinus to my left, Brother Akin to the right, both holding small steel chains used for leashing mongrels.

Outside the door, Momsie, her face in her palms, sobbing. Nsika, Alice. Neighbors.

"Mummy?"

"Catch am, catch am!" someone says, and they all move at once.

Like that, there are hands on me again. Pulling, dragging, unrelenting, deaf to my screams. They pull me out of the darkness and into the light. Past Momsie who will not look at me nor acknowledge my cries. Past the neighbors, out to the courtyard, where they dump me on the ground.

Someone pins my arm to the concrete with his knee and wraps the chains along my wrist. Someone else sprinkles something wet and salty on my face.

"In the name of the Most High Lord," Pastor Richard yells, "let loose His servant!"

They chorus *Amen.*

I kick out at the person trying to bind me—Brother Marvinus. My knee catches him in the face.

Someone whacks my thigh with a pipe. "The Lord shall prevail!" He whacks me again. "The Lord shall prevail!"

Another pipe joins in whacking me into submission—on my thighs, my legs, my biceps. I cover my head in my hands and press my knees to my chest. The crowd about me begins to pray loud, fervent, sibilant prayers.

"The Kingdom of God does not beg," Pastor Richard bellows. "It taketh by force!"

"Mummy!" I'm wailing. "*Muhmee!*"

My mother does not claim me.

They hit and hit until there's no physical sensation, no hurt, until I am only half-aware of the pain. I'm rolling over and over, aligning new parts of my body to take in the fresh blows. Each new hit reminds me that every surface has been touched.

I let out a long, hard growl I do not recognize as my voice.

"Jesus!" someone says. "It's manifesting!"

The crowd jumps and half of it scatters. Those that remain circle around me, a murder of crows, eyes peeled and foreheads gleaming. The concrete on which I'm sprawled digs into my elbows, urges me on.

Go now, run!

I want to, I swear. But my legs are sick of running, my lips sick of pleading. My body, tired, is no longer mine.

So I scream again. Long, hard.

The scream rouses something in me, a dormant ferocity snapped awake, a fountain of indefinable rage suddenly flowing. I open my mouth and drain my lungs of all power. Each scream gives me fire, unleashes the fountain.

My body is awake, and it is no longer mine.

They must recognize the bestial fury in my eyes, because the rest of the crowd peels away. Only my mother and the men who brought me out are left.

Pastor Richard dinks salty holy water on my head. Without thinking, I shoot out a hand and grab him by the neck, pull him down. He gurgles, but I can't hear it, will not recognize it. My claws cut deep into his skinny neck, drawing bright red blood.

"Aniekan," Momsie is saying, "stop!"

The rest of my assailants are stilled by shock. Then they backtrack, scuttle, fall over themselves, then finally turn and fade into the sweltering afternoon.

I squeeze harder, watch the veins appear on his neck, on his forehead.

"Pluhz," he gags. "*Pluhz.*"

I hurl him a good couple of yards, my anger pulsing hard. He lands and rolls on the concrete, raising dust. He's skinned in several places, drawing blood and staining the concrete. He doesn't move when he stops rolling.

My mother is the only one left. She shuffles toward me, her elbows pressed together at her navel, her hands folded under her chin.

"Aniekan?"

I rise, gingerly, each movement recognizing new tissue, new muscles. I flex them, accept them, claim them. When I get to my feet, a hand so tiny, so human, rests on my bicep.

"Aniekan," Momsie says, "please."

"No," I say, my voice gravelly, unrecognizable. "No."

I turn my back on her and walk. Out of our compound, past the kiosk at Jumbo's gate, down Boskel, down Kilometer 7, past the toll gate, and out of a world that will not claim me.

SUYI DAVIES OKUNGBOWA writes speculative fiction and associated matters from Lagos, Nigeria. His fiction and essays have been published in Lightspeed, Mothership Zeta, The Dark, Omenana, *and the anthology,* Lights Out: Resurrection, *amidst other places. He is a charter member of the African Speculative Fiction Society. When not writing, Suyi works in visual communications. In-between, he plays piano, guitar, FIFA, and searches for spaces to fit new bookshelves. He lives on the web at* suyidavies.com *and tweets at* @IAmSuyiDavies.

In the midst of the hall, they see the troll king on his throne . . .

HOW ALFRED NOBEL GOT HIS MOJO

by Johannes Pinter

Title alone, when this next submission came across my desk, I was very eager to read it, and it did not let me down. For a horror story, it's fun. It's also heart-breaking. It's also about the life of famed Swedish chemist and philanthropist Alfred Nobel, though where certain elements may have been "inflated," I will leave to you, dear reader, to decide.

Coming from Stockholm, successful writer and movie director Johannes Pinter has access, I believe, to certain anecdotes of Nobel's life that are not attainable by the rest of the world. Following is one, How Alfred Nobel Got His Mojo.

1896. December. Afternoon.

PALE WINTER LIGHT GLINTS THROUGH THE FINE lace of long curtains, illuminating specks of dust floating in the dense atmosphere of the chamber as if underwater. A clock passes the seconds one tick at a time, the building creaks as if moving and settling in its sleep, and for a moment an exhale of light voices pierces the wall of wood and silence.

The sun highlights the wool structure in the worn red Bokhara carpet, carves creases and patterns on the duvet on the bed above, on which an old man's hand rests with a porcelain cup clasped in its fingers. The skin of the emaciated hand is aged and spotty, stretched over bones like a worn old glove, but so perfectly steady that it does not spill a single drop.

Alfred Nobel rests propped up against pillows at the head of the bed, watching the slow swirls of steam rising from his cup.

"Like ghosts," he mumbles so quietly that only the sharpest consonants are audible.

In the shadows next to the illuminated glass rectangle of the window, a figure moves, causing the worn leather armchair to complain with a dry creak: It is Robert, Alfred's older brother.

"Did you say something, brother?" Robert asks and coughs.

Alfred's bleak eyes shift, because beyond his brother's words he catches a sound just outside the room. Then the door slowly opens, and a groaning bleat is heard, and it is impossible to say if the sound comes from rusty old hinges or from the throat of whatever is intruding. Alfred's free hand immediately reaches under the pillow, and the next second a black revolver points at the open doorway.

Now the hand trembles.

Not even three feet high, a blond tousle of hair appears from behind the door accompanied by light, uneven steps upon the floorboards. It is young Saga who boldly stumbles into the chamber in a red dress, one foot bare and the other sporting a large boot. The six-year-old stirs up the room's dust, making it twirl in a dance, before she notices the tension and slows to a halt. But she has not seen the revolver that Alfred swiftly tucks away back under the covers.

"Will you not come down for supper?" Saga asks and tweaks a loose front tooth with her thumbnail. "There is pea soup and pork."

Alfred puts away his porcelain cup, and Robert nudges a sheet of paper on the tablecloth in front of him with his elbow. "We still have some doings to take care of," Robert says and puts his hand over his mouth to suppress a cough. "Tell mother we should like to have our soup in the chamber in half an hour."

Young Saga wrinkles her nose thoughtfully. Then she stops poking her tooth, walks to the bed, and clutches the sleeve of Alfred's nightshirt, the one that hides the revolver. A short tug-of-war commences between Saga, who wants to take his hand, and Alfred, who wants to keep hiding the unsecured gun, until the girl eventually gives up and crosses her arms over her chest.

"Uncle Alfred, while grandfather writes, can you not get dressed and join us for supper?" she asks and adds again, "It's got pork!"

Alfred shakes his head wearily. Explains that he has to take part in this work, as it is he who decides what to write. He and grandfather will be pleased to eat later.

Saga considers this. "Mother will want to open the windows when she brings the soup later, it smells stuffy in here."

With great effort, Robert gets up from the armchair and closes the door when his granddaughter leaves. He crosses over to the bed and with one harsh tug pulls the blanket off, uncovering Alfred's skinny legs under the nightshirt, and next to them the black gun.

"What in heaven's name, Alfred?!" Robert keeps his tone down, not wanting anyone outside to hear, but his voice quakes with fury. He grabs the gun, which Alfred does not want to let go, and a short, weak tussle takes place, a tussle Alfred loses as he is the smaller and in poor health besides.

Robert carefully puts the gun on the table next to the paraffin lamp, muzzle toward the wall and asks, not without accusation, as he taps his temple, "Still alive in there?"

Alfred's only response is to pull the duvet tighter around himself.

"You aimed at Saga," Robert says. "Admit it: *It* is still in your

Alfred holds out the box, watching her reaction surreptitiously. "Open it and find out."

Bertha sits in the middle of the bed, adjusting comfortably before placing the box in her lap. Carefully, she opens the lid, allowing the light to illuminate its content.

On light pink, sand-washed satin lays countless shimmering pearls in rows that twist and turn around each other, and in the middle, the tiny silver clasp of the necklace.

Bertha sighs deeply, at a loss for words.

"Here," Alfred says. The string of pearls clatters against each other as he lifts the necklace and gently places it around her neck. The pearls move smoothly around her, and with steady fingers he hooks the clasps into its tiny drop-shaped silver loop.

With one palm resting over the necklace, as if she wants to hide it and relive the moment of surprise, Bertha stands on the red and not-so-worn Bokhara carpet in front of the room's patinated mirror. She lifts her hand, once again astonished by the luster of the jewelry. Her ivory skin enhances its shimmering beauty even more.

"This is your love," Bertha says breathlessly.

"Yes. My love on a silk thread around your neck."

"But, Alfred, you are crazy!"

Alfred, still on his knees, can do nothing but stare. "Yes . . . crazy for you."

Bertha leaps onto the bed, embracing his face and gives him a gentle kiss, and then another.

Alfred's expression changes and he is suddenly very tired, as if Bertha's positive reaction took his energy and replaced it with fatigue. He falls back onto the bed, stretches, and pulls the blanket over his legs.

"But Alfred," Bertha exclaims with fingers that won't stop fingering the necklace, "how do you think I will be able to sleep now?"

"It is late and cruel of me to tire," Alfred says, "but tomorrow is an important day for testing the explosive, nitroglycerin."

"Tomorrow is tomorrow, and tonight is tonight. Let us go for a walk. Look at that moon!"

The big full moon shines through the thin lace curtains framing the window. The courtyard and stables are lit up as if it was daytime, and beyond them shine the forest and the mountain Båsberget, although the light is cold as ice, and where the light does not reach, the shadows are impenetrable.

He can barely contain a yawn when he says that no, going out for a nightly walk he cannot, for he has to be well rested and alert tomorrow. They still have not come as far as they wish to find more practical use for the nitroglycerin. These are important things for his career, for science, even more important than watching the moon.

"Very well. I shall go by myself then," says Bertha, and she gets out of bed and laces up her corset.

Temper and independence are two of the things that Alfred values the most in Bertha. But at this moment, both that and her retort pass far above his head, as he already snores like a boar, deep among the pillows.

Bertha smiles at his wheezing. She leans in to give him a light kiss on the nose, then swiftly pads over the floorboards and out through the chamber door.

CAREFULLY BERTHA closes the main door and pushes the padlock, slowly to not make it creak. Then she walks out onto the yard. It is late spring, and wild roses already bloom along the porch railing, yet her breath mists in front of her face. Happy that she brought the wool scarf, she drapes it around her shoulders and walks over the hard-trampled courtyard that leads around the stables.

By the pasture she pauses, scarf covering her hair and one elbow resting on the fence. In the middle of the field the two geldings, Tor and Skogsstjärna, stand head-to-tail, sleeping with hanging heads. It's really fantastic how bright the moon is tonight. Bemused, Bertha watches the pale sphere in the sky, letting the shiny pearls around her neck wander one at a time between her fingers as she contemplates what just occurred . . .

Alfred gave her a necklace. A gift of love.

Perhaps the most beautiful gift she has ever received. And the gravity of it all dawns on her: he wants to marry her, a thought that has passed through her mind lately, and for every instance she's got used to it a little more.

The night suddenly turns sober as a grave.

Bertha shivers, is about to turn back to the house, when something snaps behind her. She turns—and sees giant shadows charging at her, blocking out the light of the moon. She manages a scream, then a giant hand covers her face and the sound is cut off.

WITH A JOLT, Alfred wakes in the darkness of the bedroom. It's dead quiet, but within him something ominous still echoes, as if there's just been a terrible occurrence. It takes a few seconds for him to adjust his mind to the waking world. Then he leaps out of the bed, exits the chamber, and hurries down the stairs. With his feet crammed halfway into his boots, he stumbles through the front door into the yard. To the right of the stables, he notices the outline of people by the pasture. He has to rub the grit from his eyes to recognize his three brothers.

"The scream woke us all," says the youngest brother, Emil, as Alfred approaches.

"Do you know who it could be?" Ludvig asks. "We're not missing anybody."

Alfred looks around. At the far end of the field, Tor and Skogsstjärna huddle near the fence. *What could have spooked the two horses?*

"Look!" Robert, the oldest of the brothers, cries out and picks something off the ground. He holds up his find for everyone to examine: a shimmering pearl that reflects the moonlight.

"What is this?" he asks.

"And what is *this*?" Ludvig lifts his feet high, as if he was standing on a heated flat rock that burned his soles.

The four brothers look at the ground. Footprints are evident in the grass, not from one but from several visitors, and they are abnormally big. *Could they have been made by animals?* The prints look humanoid, yet each has only three toes instead of five.

"What is this that could have scared the horses?" Robert wonders aloud.

"And who screamed?" Emil asks again.

Bertha, is Alfred's only thought as he looks around. Farther away something glistens in the grass: another pearl. His gaze sharpens, exploring every unevenness in the grass that might be yet another footprint, and he spots another pearly glimmer. Together, the pearls form a trail, and he looks in the direction that they lead. There in the distance, beyond the forest, the forbidding silhouette of Båsberget sits under the moon.

After a brief counsel, the brothers agree: There is no time to wait for dawn, they must follow Bertha and her kidnappers immediately while the tracks are fresh and the pearls not yet collected by thieving magpies.

They bring winter coats and caps to combat the cold, bottled water for the thirst, and two lanterns to light the way through the dark forest. And last but not least, two revolvers and a carbine rifle. But when they bring the watchdog Garm to the trail, they meet resistance: facing the giant footsteps, the dog whimpers and crawls away in fear. When they force him toward the forest, Garm tears himself loose and flees in the opposite direction, not to be found again.

The brothers must brave the forest on their own.

The walk through the woods is lengthy and exhausting; they drudge through the rough undergrowth, over logs and rocks and all the obstacles that such a primeval forest might summon with brushwood, windthrows, and crevices hidden by thick moss. When they think they have lost the path, the clouds disperse, and when the moonlight gets brighter they spot another pearl. For every step and every pearl, Alfred's love for Bertha increases. For despite how overwhelming her anguish must be, being abducted by monsters through the dark Värmland forests, she is yet able to summon the courage to occasionally drop another pearl from the necklace, like Hansel and Gretel's breadcrumbs.

After two hours and halfway up Båsberget, the moon has passed the mountain top and begun to sink toward the saw-toothed forest silhouette, and they finally hear something: dull pounding.

The farther up they come, the stronger the sound, and ultimately it is clear that it originates from inside the mountain. One pearl clearly shows the way to another, and finally they stand in front of the colossal mouth of a cave. Its edges are lined with cracks like wrinkles around a hag's toothless mouth, and from the throat of the cave a frenzied drumbeat echoes.

The brothers gather a few feet away from the opening to discuss how to proceed. It is decided that Alfred and Robert, the strongest of them, will go in, each carrying a revolver, while Emil and Ludvig wait outside with the loaded carbine.

It's the hour of the wolf when the two brothers enter the cave. Something crunches under their feet, and when Robert holds up the lamp they see what is covering the floor: piles, drifts, hundreds and hundreds of bones, remains of animals big and small lining the entrance. Whatever inhabits the mountain, they eat these creatures and then leave each carcass where it falls. Doubt overcomes them both, but when Alfred sees another pearl shimmering among the bones, he is once again filled with courage. He leads the way into the dark with Robert trailing behind.

Finding the way is easy, for there is no other path than the tunnel. But the walk is horrifying: the restlessly moving shadows beyond the lantern's flickering light, the hollow scraping when they brush against dry bones and skulls, and the muffled throbs of the drum—the very heartbeat of the mountain—that come closer the deeper they go. If not for Bertha, Alfred would have taken Robert's arm and rushed back up and out and home to Björkborn.

They start to think that the mountain is infinite, an endless maze, when they round a corner and see a warm light beyond the next turn, and suddenly the music is no longer subdued but clear and sharp and louder than ever. Alfred puts out the lantern, and they grip their guns tighter as they sneak up and peek around the corner of the rough, arched stone wall.

The unexpected and terrifying sight almost knocks them off their feet...

Trolls.

In front of them are tens, no, hundreds of ugly, hairy trolls dressed as trolls do, in patchwork shirts of animal hides, loin clothes of fur, sheets stolen off washer women's' lines. The beasts are either gargantuan or just plain big, have sweeping tails and ragged hair, they growl and cheer and move clumsily in a synchronous dance to the rhythm from an orchestra of troll drummers in a far corner. The cave is like a throne hall, lit by rows of torches along the walls. In the midst of the sweeping movement is an elevated stage with two impressive thrones cut from the rock. On one of the thrones sits an enormous troll, with bigger hair and thicker nose and longer tail than any other troll, and on its head sits a mighty crown that shines of purest gold.

It takes Alfred a moment to sort through all the impressions and realize what it is he is looking at, but when he does the shock almost brings him to his knees—on the other throne sits his beloved Bertha! She wears the same pretty, light dress as when he saw her last, her hands are neatly folded in her lap, and her wide eyes sweep over the celebrating masses.

Then Alfred notices the necklace. She still wears it around her neck, but the silk thread hangs limp and empty—except for one remaining pearl.

They have seen enough! Alfred and Robert back away and run as fast as they can through the winding tunnel until they reach the outside where the waiting brothers greet them.

The moon has left the sky, and a thin shard of sunlight gleams over the tree tops as the four companions hurry back through the woods. As they walk, they decide on a course of action. Quite simply, Bertha must be saved, and they decide they must blow up the cave with their stock of nitroglycerin and bar the opening so that these monstrous trolls can never get out again.

But back at Björkborn, reality slams the door on Bertha's rescue, for Alfred is faced with the very problem he's been testing so long to solve: How can they bring the nitroglycerin through the woods without setting off the oil-like and shock-sensitive liquid?

While Emil and Ludvig rest, Alfred locks himself inside of Björkborn's laboratory with Robert in search of a solution. The nitroglycerin must be mixed with another substance that makes it more shock-resistant and easier to transport. They experiment with charcoal, sawdust, and cement, but the substances prove too crumbly.

Frustrated, Alfred leaves the building for a solitary walk along Timsälven, a nearby river. He needs to sleep, but has no peace of mind. How could he sleep with Bertha confined in a cave, surrounded by an army of trolls? This predicament, finding a better-suited packing for the unstable nitroglycerin, is something that has confounded him for a long time. The key to the solution is near, he can feel it, but it just has to reveal itself to him.

He walks along the river, speculation and exhaustion making him careless, and suddenly he trips and falls flat on his face, one shoe stuck in the sticky brown of the river bank's mud.

First he swears, his face spattered with brown filth. But then he composes himself and scoops up a fistful of the sticky substance. His brain begins to calculate, putting two and two together as he examines and feels the mud, and after a minute he arrives at a conclusion.

The rest of the day is dedicated to productivity. With extreme caution, and greatest respect for the balance, Alfred and Robert, and later, Emil and Ludvig, mix the nitroglycerin with dried diatomaceous earth, the special algae-rich mud from the bank of Timsälven that Albert had stepped in. They roll sticks, attach a detonator in one end, then wrap it in paper and stack them in a robust wooden box.

When all the sticks are finally packed, and the sun has started to set, they strap the box to Tor's back, bring a heavy roll of fuse, and put a sheaf of phosphorus matches in the bag with the revolvers.

This time they move slower as primeval forests are not a horse's natural environment. But they still have the trail of pearls to follow, and the thoughts of saving Bertha as a driving force, and finally they stand outside the cave again. It is very quiet now: no drums are heard, no sound of birds, not even a breeze through the trees. In some ways the silence is far more frightening than any other sounds in the world.

As quietly as possible, the brothers prime the sticks of baked nitroglycerin in the crevices around the cave and attach the fuse to them.

"Dynamite," Alfred exclaims suddenly.

"What?" Robert asks.

"A lot of power is needed to close this cave," explains Alfred. "These sticks come with that power—*dynamis* in Greek."

The brothers agree that *dynamite* is a very suitable name.

After a brief discussion, they decide that, in addition to Alfred, Emil should come this time. Emil is the youngest and fastest, which is needed if there is a chase. They must do this swiftly for everyone knows that trolls sleep during the day and wake at sundown, and the dusk deepens with every passing minute. Robert and Ludvig will stand ready with the matches and the fuse.

Fleet-footed, the two brothers move through the tunnels. For each turn they make, and the deeper they go, the more the pressure increases. Like deep-diving in a lake, even breathing becomes harder, a combination of the mountain's atmosphere as well as the rising anxiety for what they are about to face.

Finally they stand at the entrance to the throne room.

And there are the trolls.

But this time they lay still, sprawled haphazardly across the ground: the stone floor is covered by large, deformed, ugly, sleeping bodies. In the midst of the hall, they see the troll king on his throne, snoring loudly. On the throne next to him rests Bertha, a sleeping beauty with her eyes closed, in every aspect the polar opposite to the rest of the creatures in the room. Probably asleep from exhaustion, Alfred assumes, as the situation must be inhumanly trying for her, surrounded by hordes of tailed beasts.

Alfred gestures to Emil to stay by the entrance, then carefully makes his way through the room and the heaps of snoozing trolls. There are tails here and outstretched limbs there, restlessly moving legs here and dirty mops of hair there. Alfred moves as fast as he dares; he must not step on anyone, but he cannot be too slow and let the sun set and the night—trolls' daytime—begin.

The hall is hot as a blacksmith's forge and Alfred is sweating so much that his shirt sticks to his back, but he finally reaches the podium. He glances at the sleeping troll king, who is hideous like no man he has ever seen, with spongy, dimpled skin, nose like a loaf of bread, and a filthy shrub for hair. Then he looks at Bertha, and she is indeed the king's opposite with her smooth skin, full red lips, and hair as soft as a lamb's coat. He puts his hand over her mouth and shakes her gently. When the first attempt fails he tries again, but still she does not wake. In addition to fatigue, her body must be suffering from shock.

Alfred considers the alternatives, then lifts and puts her over his shoulder like a sack of turnips. With this extra weight, he begins his walk back through the heaps of bodies. He follows the same path, where he knows he can place his feet.

Three-quarters back he sees Emil waving from the entrance. Later, as he contemplates the outcome of the adventure, he will think that it was a spectacularly stupid thing to do. But there in the room, with a rising sense of triumph in his chest, he instinctively waves back. This brief misstep is enough. One of the trolls moves slightly, and it flicks its tail, which unfortunately ends up right under Alfred's descending foot.

With a guttural cry, the beast sits up and groggily looks around, whimpering in pain. At first, it does not notice anything. Then it spots Alfred's back, and the woman hanging limply over his shoulder, and it understands what is happening. With a deafening howl, it alerts the rest of the room.

A few steps more, and Alfred can join Emil at the cave entrance. Seeing Emil's terrified gaze, he turns his head and, in the corner of his eye, beholds how the floor comes to life. It is like a seething melting pot, with bodies rising and dashing about, colliding and barking and fussing without really knowing what is going on.

"Run for god's sake!" Alfred wails. And O yes, they run! With all the strength they can muster, they run through the winding mountain tunnels, and far behind they hear the beasts come to their senses and begin pursuit.

"Run ahead!" Alfred gasps, Bertha's body getting heavier with every step. "Warn them! When they see me . . . they light the fuse!"

Emil, younger and with no burden, bolts and is gone.

What moves through Alfred Nobel's head as he stumbles and fumbles through the underground darkness, chased by a howling and raging horde that appears closer for every turn and unevenness, is not easy to know. But one might assume that two things drive him: the fear of what is behind him, and the love for who he carries.

There are things you just have to manage, although the task seems inhuman, and your body and mind should have shut down long ago. The struggle Alfred now faces is exactly that, because of what is at stake.

When he thinks he will never reach the end of the tunnel, and his heart feels as if it is about to explode, and the trolls are literally around the corner—he finally sees the mouth of the cave and the pine forest outside and Emil waving him on. He forces his legs to carry him the last few steps, then Emil is there to support him and Bertha. Together they stumble out of the cave, and Robert and Ludvig light the fuses.

They have only moments . . .

Bertha, with a spasm and a moan, comes to life besides him in the grass.

"Hurry, we must get away!" he warns and takes her cold hand.

He gets her on her feet and starts to run—and feels her hand slip from his grip. He fumbles, and his fingers catch something thin that tears when he pulls at it. He turns—and witnesses Bertha running in the opposite direction, slowly though like she is moving under water, back into the darkness of the cave. *But why?* In the corner of his eye, he sees Robert and Ludvig dodge in the shadows behind a windthrow.

Emil is nearest and darts to her, intercepting Bertha and grabbing her arm.

Bertha halts.

"Emil, get out before it blows!" Robert screams at the younger brother.

But everything happens so terribly slowly.

There, Bertha turns and her eyes look straight into Alfred's, and it is as if they are completely empty, or even dead, but in the next moment something ignites in them like she suddenly remembers him and everything they have shared . . .

There, the roars grow louder from inside the cave when the first trolls emerge into the moonlight, and when they see the men outside the cave they howl in triumph . . .

There, Emil releases Bertha's arm as he sees the beasts, and he turns to flee . . .

There, the fire devours the fuse, runs toward the dynamite sticks that are wedged in the crevices around the cave, and the fire is quicker than any living being, it speeds to meet the detonators . . .

There, Alfred looks down at his hand, uncomprehending—what did he catch?—and in his palm lies a torn silk thread and the last pearl from her necklace . . .

And then the dynamite explodes, and the world becomes a roaring vibrating white hell . . .

1896. December. Dusk.

OF COURSE he misses her. Like he has missed her every day and every minute since that cursed day.

Alfred leans against the pillows, looking at the sun caught in the window drapery's crocheted lace web. It is setting now, the sun, maybe for the last time.

He is reminded of Robert's recent words: Balance had always been essential in his life . . .

He needed the balance of *her*. Life had been filled with success and honors, he was given the opportunity to do what he was meant for, he has 355 patents with dynamite being the jewel in the crown. How many people are blessed with a life like that? But here he is now at his end, wifeless and childless, with the love of his surviving brothers, though which, however, cannot be compared to the love of a woman.

In his time and by his doing, the balance has been made uneven: Great destruction against a lack of love. He sees it now, viewing his life as it turned out. He is a powerless old man on his deathbed, and it pains him so much that his eyes and chest burn, because it is too late to do anything about it.

But wait . . . *Is that really so?*

Is it truly too late?

Alfred Nobel contemplates for some time while the sky slowly darkens outside the window. Then he clears his throat and addresses Robert who slumbers in his armchair.

"Brother," Alfred says, "I want you to tear up the testament that you have in front of you."

"What are you saying?" Robert asks. "Should we throw away a full afternoon's work?" Then he brightens. "Do you feel better, Alfred? Is it not time yet?"

"Unfortunately, in that, the situation remains unchanged," Alfred replies, wheezing. "But there is something I want to add to the will, something that must be a priority."

"Alright," Robert says, ripping the sheet in two and letting it drop to the floor, because he knows when there is no point in arguing. He uncaps the fountain pen and asks wearily, "So what should it say?"

"You know about my wealth?" Alfred asks.

"Yes, I know about that," Robert smirks and strokes his moustache. "That is what we have been discussing all afternoon."

"I wish it to be used for the benefit of humanity." Alfred smiles for the first time throughout the day. "There is going to be a prize."

"What?" Robert leans forward, making the leather armchair creak, unsure if he's heard right.

But Alfred does not repeat himself, because there is no time. He just asks Robert to take his pen and write down his words.

When Alfred Nobel gets an idea, it's no use to argue, so Robert does not, but takes his pen and writes as his brother speaks:

"I, the undersigned, Alfred Bernhard Nobel, do hereby, after mature deliberation, declare the following to be my last Will and Testament . . . "

JOHANNES PINTER, born 1965, is a Swedish writer and movie director. He has three novels published in Sweden: Beautiful Churches of Sweden, *about a hunter of Scandinavian folklore beings; the vampire drama* 1007; *and the co-written supernatural crime novel,* Stained by Darkness, *the first part in a trilogy. He's also published several short stories in both American and Swedish anthologies.*

*As movie director, he's directed two feature films; of those, Hollywood producer Mark Johnson (*Breaking Bad, Chronicles of Narnia*) has recently bought the remake rights of the thriller,* Sleepwalker. *He's written movie scripts including the adaptation of the Swedish crime novel,* The Beast, *from Roslund & Hellström (*Three Seconds*) and two uncredited drafts of the US fantasy action hit,* Pathfinder, *from director Marcus Nispel.*

Johannes lives in Stockholm, Sweden, with his wife and two teenage children.

The ghost exists because the bottle does.

SICK CATS IN SMALL SPACES

by Kaaron Warren

To work with Australian author Kaaron Warren is a joy. She brings decades of talent, experience, and sheer enthusiasm to all she does, including this next story, in which I had fascinating conversations with her discussing the nuances of language, those subtle context quirks between how words are understood, or distinctions to what they allude, when the same language is spoken in different parts of the world.

It's since been a further joy to also work on a new book project with Kaaron, examining her writing in depth, analyzing her heart-rending tales of horror and fantasy, and I would be remiss if I did not suggest that if you enjoy the following selection, to immediately pick up a copy of Exploring Dark Short Fiction #2: A Primer to Kaaron Warren *(2018) from Dark Moon Books.*

But first, come along with Tara and Dale as they take a road trip through the scorched, sparsely-populated outback of southeastern Australia, a bonding trip with their son, and a chance to photograph the condition of ailing towns. What they discover are that some towns are meant to be isolated, while the family bond is not.

So go ghosts in the sand, as do crawl Sick Cats in Small Places.

FTER SIXTEEN HOURS ON THE ROAD, THE DISTANT sight of the old pub was a relief. The flatness of the road meant they still had half an hour to drive but there it was ahead of them, promising cold beer, food, maybe air conditioning.

Tara knew this last would be a vain hope; rather there'd be a sluggish ceiling fan, the doors—with their ineffectual fly strips flapping—left open so the men didn't stifle inside and the dogs could go in and out at will.

Every outback pub was the same.

It was warm inside the station wagon, even with the aircon blasting. The thermometer said outside was 45 degrees Celsius, and Tara could feel it when she put her palm on the windscreen.

They planned to spend the night at the pub, although Tara hadn't been able to book. Hopefully there'd be rooms so they could have a night off from sleeping in the hitched caravan. They'd share a room if they had to.

"Look, Jonas!" Tara said. Her son raised his eyebrows. He was in the back seat, having driven the last stint, five hour's worth, and was tired now and more than usually unresponsive. "I wonder if they'll have internet. You can get in touch with your friends," she said, a statement she instantly regretted. Dale took his hand off the wheel and patted her own, their married couple secret language for, *Fucked that up, move on.*

Twenty minutes later Dale pulled up in front of the pub, where half a dozen vehicles sat parked on the red dirt. Three utes, a battered Holden, a long-haul truck, and something that looked like it was made out of corrugated iron. There was plenty of room for the caravan they towed behind; they could have pulled straight in but Dale did his usual ten-minute-back-the-caravan-into-position thing. By the time he was done, the verandah was crowded with men and dogs, come out to watch. They broke into applause as the O'Briens got out of their car, and Jonas went bright red.

"Nice job, mate," one of the men said, and Tara could only be grateful she hadn't been driving. Dale took a small bow but the men had already turned to go back inside so the joke was lost. Tara smiled, making sure he saw it.

Dale hadn't worked since his job disappeared in a company reshuffle six months earlier, but he'd tried hard to stay positive, making little jokes, keeping things light. This holiday was almost a reward for that. A break in the routine, a change; they all needed it. He'd received an excellent severance package.

Outside the car was like a furnace; she'd stood next to bonfires with less heat to them. Tara stretched carefully but still her knees buckled when she tried to walk. When they travelled so much each day, she felt much older than forty-seven.

"Do I have to go in?" Jonas asked.

Tara had a quick look around. "There's no shade anywhere so yeah, you have to come in."

"The Three Musketeers!" Dale said. He was always trying to get them to call themselves that; Tara and Jonas never did.

INSIDE THE PUB, they stood for a moment, getting their bearings. "Welcome to the Digger's Arms," the barman called out. "What'll it be?" He was tall and broad, with a bright red face and a shock of red hair to match. He gestured for them to come to the bar and they did, Jonas tripping over the paws of a large dog on the way. An old man sitting by himself at the counter gave them a quick glance, then went back to his beer. Nearby, a middle-aged man with a priestly collar sat with three younger men, all of them in blue sleeveless t-shirts, the table filled with empty beer glasses. Other tables were filled, too; it was Saturday evening, the big night. No other women though, Tara noted.

"G'day," Dale said.

"What'll it be?" the barman said again.

"What would you like to drink, Jonas?" Dale said.

"Jonas is the name, is it? They call me Bluey. Obvious reasons," the barman said, running his fingers through his red hair.

"I'll have a gin and lemon," Tara told Dale. "And get Jonas a beer. Choose him something."

She knew if they were in Victoria he'd order VB, Queensland it'd be XXXX, but they were in New South Wales so he asked for a Toohey's for them both. He was always eager to please and didn't understand that it held him back.

"And some beer nuts, too, on me." It was the man with the priestly collar, standing at the bar now. He shook hands with Dale and Jonas, and bowed to Tara. "I'm Father John," he said, "and the burning question is, what brings you here?"

The whole pub wanted to know, it seemed, because the room fell silent.

"So it turned out my job doesn't exist anymore, so here I am out of work and at a loose end, so we decided to take a road trip," Dale said. "We're following in the footsteps of my wife's family. Her great-grandad travelled around taking photos of country towns in boom years, then her grandad did it of them when they were going into decline. By the time her dad did the trip, some of the towns were waking up again. So we're doing the next look. Taking photos, you know. And seeing where her roots are."

"I wouldn't mind seeing her roots," a man from the other side of the room called. Someone had called that out every single time Dale had used the line. Father John sent a stern look in that direction.

"Good on you. Most people see more of overseas than they do their own country."

"I don't get a chance to travel much in my job. I'm a school photographer. So I see the inside of gyms, kids lined up, you know, *Say Cheese*." Tara mimicked holding a camera to her eye and Bluey grinned broadly.

"And what do they call you, love?"

"I'm Tara."

"Like the house in *Gone with the Wind*?" Bluey said. The men in the bar jeered at him. "Movie buff!" they called out, and "Smart Arse!"

"It is, actually. Not many people know that." She felt such a powerful attraction to Bluey she felt flushed, so to cover it she said, "This is my husband Dale."

"Call me Dazza," Dale said. He looked pale, almost see-through, compared to the sun-burnt men sitting around the room.

"So we thought we'd visit some of the places my family went. Take more photos of how the towns are now," Tara said.

"Photos of shit heaps? Can't see much point in that," one of the men said.

"Surprisingly," Dale said, and Tara did the hand pat thing, but it was too late, he'd said the word so he already sounded like a wanker, so rambled quickly on, "Surprisingly, many of the towns that were ghost towns in her grandfather's day have come good. Full of people and life. We're finding that a lot of the towns have reinvented themselves. There might be ghosts, but there are people, too."

"Not all the towns," Tara said. She'd already developed some of her photos along the way and thought her grandfather's 'bust' pictures were more desolate than the ones she was taking of towns entirely deserted. His were full of people who knew it was all over. Going through the motions. It was almost like they were already ghosts.

They'd visited many towns, each of them resonating with Tara in one way or another. She'd known them for most of her life, from the framed photographs in the hallway of her childhood home. She knew every building, the way the road lay, where the lone tree stood.

She loved the way her family photographs showed that everything is cyclical. From dust to boom to bust and ghost town, dust again, then recovery and renewal. Some towns feel thick with memory. Some are wiped clean. Some towns carried a great sense of emptiness, even when there were signs of past occupation. They carried a sense of absolute vacancy. Other towns seemed to writhe with unseen life.

Father John nodded at them and went back to his table with the workmen. They laughed amongst themselves and Jonas smiled with them. Tara knew he was bored on this family trip, that he missed the company of people his own age, and she imagined he wished he could be a part of that group of young men.

Bluey said quietly, "Flash lot, aren't they?"

The workmen really were showy, standing out amongst the other men in the room, but there was something underlying, something about the way they followed the priest's every word, that interested Tara.

"Aren't you all?"

"Us?" Bluey threw his head back and laughed. "Yeah, nah. Most of us are just country boys in one way or another. Trying to make a living on a shit heap. Those boys have figured it out."

The lone old man at the bar whom she'd noticed on the way in nodded, turning to face them. "Eighty years my family have been on the land." He had the skinny legs of a long-term alcoholic, sitting high on a bar stool, his heels resting on the brass rung that ran close to the floor. "Shearing, slaughtering, whatever it takes. That lot," here he pointed at a row of bottles along the bar, each containing layers of colorful sand. "That's what the priest and his boys come in with. Bottles of sand. Take a look. See the little tracks in the sand? The tunnels? Imps, I reckon. Trapped for all eternity by *them*." He tilted his head at the priest and the young men.

"What'dya mean, imps?" Jonas said. "Sounds like bullshit."

"Imps. Like little demons," the old man said.

"And they're trapped?"

"It's bullshit, Jonas," Dale said. "The old fella's having a go." Dale struggled lately with Jonas having his own opinions. He wasn't ready for him to become an individual. An independent man.

"Anyway, if so, you should lettem out," Jonas said. "Nothing should be trapped like that." He gave a shudder.

"Tell me about it," Tara said, and she laughed, giving Dale a gentle punch on the arm. "Tell me about being trapped."

Bluey poured her another drink. "Ya can't let the little mongrels out," he said. "Otherwise they'll jump onto your shoulder and suck the life out of you." He whispered this last, so quietly Tara had to lean close to hear.

The priest and his men all laughed. Tara didn't mind; the sound of it filled her with a sort of gentle joy.

"Lucky charms, they reckon," the old man went on. "People pay a bloody fortune for them."

"People call 'em *bottle imps*," Bluey said. "They reckon they ward off bad luck. You ever read that story? Robert Louis Stevenson? Bloody terrifying. But what they are is ghosts, crawled into those bottles, like scorpions or spiders. Just wanting to rest for a bit."

"Ghosts in bottles?" Jonas said.

"It's bullshit," Dale said again, although Tara knew from past experience he was a great believer in ghosts.

"Not just any bottle, though," Bluey added. "There's a heap of bottles, somewhere. No one knows but the priest and his mates over there."

"You can't find it on the map. People have gone missing trying to find the heap," the old man cut in. "Missing till their bones are found."

"Precious jewels, all of them," Father John called out from across the pub. "Diamonds in the rough."

Jonas stared at the bottles, then at the young men. Father John waved a hand at him. "Come over, Jonas. Sit with us for a bit."

"Go on, then," Tara said. "They might let you use their phones or something." Dale tried to follow, but Tara put her hand on his arm. "Leave him."

Jonas left his beer on the bar. He wasn't like the men in her family; her grandfather had been a legendary drunk, and her father was famous for his lively drunkenness as well.

She watched Jonas amongst the men. He still looked younger than his eighteen years, with baby fat around his cheeks and a haircut that was years out of date. They tried to get him to eat well but all he liked were potato chips and orange American cheese he made her buy at Costco. Dale was handsome, though, in a fresh-faced cheerful way, and she had good cheekbones, great eyes, so she knew Jonas would come good.

She felt a deep weariness, watching him. She constantly worried about him and what he would be. *Who* he would be. Since Jonas had finished high school he'd been adrift. He didn't know what to do next, and day by day it ate away at his parents, far more than it did him.

The idea was that this was their last family holiday before he was off. Started university or full time work or travel the world or . . . something. Truthfully, Tara knew none of that was likely. She was just happy to get away from her work, all the fake smiles, the "say cheese," the poor kids who forgot it was photo day. A large part of her was happy Jonas stayed with them. There were stories . . . a friend of his from school had died overseas in a boating accident, his body never found, and Tara didn't think she could bear that. Dale said he was in no hurry for the boy to go, joking that she'd leave him once they had an empty nest.

Here, she was desperate to talk to others after days on the road. Dale got all blokey in the company of men, a trait she found both annoying and endearing.

He ordered more drinks for them, and asked Bluey, "We're thinking of staying for the night. I don't suppose you've got any rooms?"

Bluey shook his head. "Me wife's done a runner so I've got room for one of you at mine," he said. "It'd have to be the lady, though. Blokes'll call me a poofter otherwise."

"Is there anywhere we can park the caravan, in that case?" Dale asked. The bar laughed, and he added, "I mean shady. Near water, maybe."

"Shady Tree Hill, 'bout fifty K up the road. There's a billabong there should be wet. I haven't had a look for a while, but."

TARA WENT INTO the bathroom. She looked flushed, and her hair was lank from the humidity, but she thought she looked all right. She'd always liked attention; she admitted that.

When she went back out, Bluey said, "Another gin and lemon?" Dale sat at the bar playing happily with the dogs. The young men and the priest left in a noisy jumble, clapping people on the back, and all of them saying, "see ya later" to Jonas. The place felt empty after they were gone, as if they took the soul of the pub with them. There was a great rattle from outside as they loaded up the empties.

"God's gift, they are," the old man said. "Taking away the rubbish."

"They don't do it for free, mate," Bluey said. "But yeah."

Jonas made his way slowly to the bar where his parents were. He stopped at each table along the way, collecting bottletops.

"You after a job, mate? Chuck us your resume and I'll think about it," Bluey said.

"He's always been a collector," Tara said. It was true, although in recent years this had stopped. Someone had told them the stoppage was a sign of depression so she was happy to see him stash the bottletops in his backpack.

Jonas' eyes glittered. His lips were pressed tightly closed as if he was trying to keep a burp in. He picked up his mother's backpack and handed it to her, indicating the door with a tilt of his head.

"I guess we're leaving," she said. She was too tipsy to drive so she planned to sleep while Dale took the wheel.

In the car, Jonas burst out, "I know where the bottle heap is! They told me!" He was sitting forward in his seat without his seatbelt on so Tara wished Dale would stop suddenly, throw the kid forward, teach him a lesson. She felt light-headed, slightly queasy, from all the lemon squash she'd drunk. How many was it? Eight? Nine? She'd lost count.

"No one knows but me! We have to go!"

"We'll stop for the night soon," Dale said. "Sort out our itinerary tomorrow, ay?"

They all knew they'd be going to see this bottle heap.

Tara slept well that night, topped up with the scotch Dale laid out for her. She slept without her inner voice, her worrywart inner voice *at her, at her, at her . . .*

THEY WERE WOKEN by a loud, then louder, rattling, the clink of thousands of empty bottles. It was the young men, the bottle collectors, in their ute, which was filled with bottles, collected from every pub they'd earlier stopped at.

They pulled up beside the caravan and Tara wished she'd changed into pajamas rather than stand here in the clothes they'd seen her in yesterday.

"Follow us if you like," Father John said. "We're heading for the heap." He named the ghost town in the surrounding area; Tara recognized it as one her family had photographed.

Without speaking, Jonas climbed into the driver's seat, and revved the car.

They only had the toilet to empty, then they took off, following a couple of hundred meters behind the ute to avoid being smothered by dust from the road.

The ute left a long shimmering tail.

"It's the ghosts they've collected," Jonas said, and he looked at her, back and forth from the road, until she agreed.

AS THE TOWN loomed in the distance Tara felt the air in the car thicken, feeling it like a pain in her chest.

They were found far apart and that made Tara the saddest, to think of them dying alone.

She read about a father and son, drowned in a water tank fifty years earlier. The father saving the son, she was sure, something that happened often.

"They all die different," Father John said. He was even redder than before and his shirt completely soaked. "It wasn't always this way. Do you know the town used to be full of children? There was a school and all. Couldn't keep them in when it rained."

He poured a glass of water for himself and one for her and said, "Come on, love. Come have a look at what you came to have a look at. Your two fellas have stepped in to help. Good men, both of them."

THE HEAT COMING OFF the heap of glass bottles was intense and the noise of it, too, a constant clinking as the bottles shifted in the red dirt or were collected by the men. Jonas was out there and Dale, too. Jonas held bottles up to the light and sorted them; Dale just gathered armsful.

"That's a good boy you've got there. Very sensitive," Father John said.

"That's a nice way to say it," Tara said.

"What he's looking for are the ghost bottles. Some have ghosts, some have insects, some have both. That young man, he can tell the difference."

"He's always said he can see ghosts. I used to, a long time ago."

"I can pick a believer at fifty paces. Everybody can see them. Most people though don't believe their own eyes."

They watched Jonas collect another bottle and hold it to the light.

"I've had to train the rest of them," Father John said, "but he's a natural. I'd like to keep him forever."

"I think his girlfriend might have something to say about that," Tara said, not sure why she lied about it. She walked to the edge of the heap. "It's astonishing how many bottles there are. That's a lot of alcohol."

"Lots of men in lots of places over lots of years," one of the workmen said, or the priest. She wasn't sure; all the voices of men started to sound the same out here.

"There are a lot of stories on that heap, so many we'll never get them all. Thirty thousand alone died in one town. Typhoid took a lot of them.

And the meatworks; you'd be surprised how many of them died from eating meat thieved from there. Men were hungry back then. They'd eat anything. They'd eat the tongue out of a bullock if they had the knife to cut it."

Tara walked to where they were sorting the bottles into size, color, contents. "The ones with the insects are worth the most," Father John said. "All the clear ones go into that pile for sale. The green and the brown are for the church. We'll show you the church later."

It was so hot the ground shimmered as far as she could see. She saw images, squeezed her eyes to clear them, still saw them. *People,* she thought, *shoulders slumped, going about their business in a town close to death.*

She recognized the slump of the shoulders from her grandfather's photos.

"The old bloke at the pub told me the bottles had imps in them."

"What the fuck's an imp?" the priest said. He shook his head. "All our customers take the bottles all right, take the luck, but not one of them gives a shit about the work that goes into it. Us out here in the heat, collecting these poor lost souls up."

"So it's ghosts, not imps?" she said, as if that made sense.

"We don't know why they come here, but they do. From all over. Mostly country people, but we've got some from the city too. Maybe they've got family in the bush, who knows." Father John wiped his brow. "I'd been travelling a long time, visited many towns, before I saw my first ghost."

As they watched, a silvery shape hovered over the bottles. Tara could see a face, she thought, and perhaps limbs, but the thing was like thick, oily smoke. The ghost sank down, disappearing into the bottle. The young men raced over to the place, searching each bottle, holding it up to the light, till they found what they were looking for.

"What happens to them? Once they're in the bottle?"

"Don't know. But we do know they're at peace at least."

"Can we release them? I mean, if a family member wanted to. Could they smash the bottle and let them out?"

"Been tried. But there's nothing inside. Nothing at all. When you smash the bottle, it's empty. The ghost exists because the bottle does. That's about all we know. God works in mysterious ways, all right. You can keep your loved ones the way they are. Perfect preservation. Nothing changes. It's a way to keep a loved one close by. You'll never lose them this way."

TARA HELPED sort for an hour, then Father John asked her to help him take a load to the church. "Your station wagon is perfect," he said. "A good afternoon's work, then we'll eat a feast, ay? Leon caught us a 'roo and he'll fry the steaks in their own fat. Bit of desert fig, some finger lime, your bush tomato, and we're eating like kings."

They loaded up the station wagon. She adjusted the driver's seat and started the car, saying, "Where to? Have we got far to go?"

Father John sat beside her and one of the young men sat behind. In the closed environment of the car the priest's scent was strong. She wasn't sure what it was. Not body odor, exactly. More like a chemical being exuded.

"You haven't noticed?" Father John pointed at a derelict, large gray building. "Over there, behind the meatworks."

The old meat processing plant hadn't been in operation for decades. As she drove closer she saw enormous pieces of corroded machinery, tipped over, useless. They had the windows down and she was sure she could smell the place; it was the smell of boiled, bad meat.

"Pull in around the back," Father John said. As she drove behind the meatworks, she saw the church and gasped.

It was maybe waist-high and stretched ten meters along. Built entirely of green and brown bottles, it seemed to shimmer as the rest of the place did, but with a more fluorescent hum.

"It is a miracle, isn't it?" Father John said. She parked the car. The buzz increased, a thumping in her ear that could have been her blood beating. The wind was high out here, high and hot and irritating.

"How long have you been building the church?"

"A dozen years or more. It's a lifetime job. I can't seem to leave." He said it quiet so the ghosts couldn't hear. "I'm doing it to give the souls rest. Most of these poor souls, we don't know who they are. They follow the bottles or they're already here, they've already crawled inside.

Sometimes, though, lucky times, a person will die nearby and we'll know who they are. We can provide a certificate of authentication and reunite the person with their family."

"Really?" she said, thinking he was joking, but later he showed it to her:

This is to certify that _____ died in unsuspicious circumstances and crawled into this bottle.

"Imagine a long rope, I tell them. Each member of the family holds onto it. Each person holds a knot in the rope. If you've lost track of a family member, they have no knot and their part of the rope is frayed, or broken. We can weave it back together."

"I guess they know about ropes, out here in mining country. My grandad always said, don't go anywhere without one."

"I guess he was right."

The wind rose, whistling in the bottles, stinging her face with sand. "I can't bear this wind," she said.

"I love it. But then I was born in a cyclone," he said.

They unloaded the bottles as Dale arrived in another full car. It was hot work in the wind, and no one seemed to have water or beer to drink.

"Why didn't you build the church near the bottle pile?" Dale said, sounding as cross as he'd ever been.

"No shade, mate. And the water is over this way. Hard work now but worth it."

It was burning hot in the walls of the church. Light came through bottles making scorpions and other insects seem alive. There was movement. Noise. Whispering.

She sat, mesmerized by this activity in the bottles. If she squinted, looked closely, she could see faces, imagine fingers beckoning her.

"It's beautiful at dawn," the priest said.

AFTER DINNER, over a third and then a fourth bottle of wine, Father John asked them for a donation. He said they only survived on the kindness of supporters and the money they received from bottle collecting and sales.

"One of the boys can run you into the Big Smoke if you like. You don't need much for yourselves, not out here."

"We won't be staying out here longer than a couple of days, though," Dale said. "We're planning to travel. So I really can't." He pulled out his wallet anyway, offered a twenty.

"Nah, mate, thanks, that won't really do it," the priest said, and he turned away. "Let's get some sleep, ay? You two can have the Bank. Good walls in there. Jonas can bunk in with us if he wants."

Strangely enough they made love that night, realizing how long it had been since they had a night on their own. "You see?" Tara said. "We'll survive without him," but Dale didn't respond.

At dawn, Tara found herself walking the main street. She walked near the building her son was in and closed her eyes and focused until she thought she heard him breathing.

ALTHOUGH THEY'D all had too much to drink the night before, the young men seemed lively and bright. In the morning light, though, Tara thought she could see signs of damage on all of them, tears in the skin she hadn't noticed before.

For breakfast there was coffee and eggs cooked over the coals, still hot from the night before. They'd covered the old oil drum, surrounded it with rocks, and it was good to go.

After breakfast they all went to work on the heap. Jonas greeted them first thing, bouncing on his toes, begging to stay. "They said I could help them again with the ghosts today." Tara had never seen him so alive. "The *actual* ghosts. Father John reckons I'm a natural at finding them."

"That would explain you staring off in the distance half the time," Tara said, and there was a hand pat from Dale. So many hand pats these days.

"This place has a habit of making people forget. Doesn't it, boys?" Father John said to the workmen. "Every last one of them has a family who has let them go. Forgotten them. This is family now, for some of us at least."

"We could spend another day or two," Tara said. She felt rested, as if the deserted town somehow settled her. "What do you think, Dale?"

"Two days at most, then we need to head off," Dale said firmly. "I'm sorry none of them have families anymore," he said to Tara quietly. "But that's not up to us. We've got family. The Three Musketeers."

She smiled at him, but was sure the pity she felt for him must seep through. He was trying to hold onto something only he couldn't see was slipping away.

THEY SPENT the second night away from Jonas and they barely saw him all day. She couldn't remember what he looked like. It wasn't just the booze, but that helped; it helped forget and to keep things quiet.

"It feels a bit odd, only Two Musketeers," Dale said as they settled into their beds.

"How about you be a Musketeer and I'll be the Lone Ranger," she said.

He turned away from her, curling himself into a defensive ball that made her think of Jonas when he was a child.

ON THE THIRD DAY, Jonas stared off into the distance, his face moving as if having conversations. He and Dale had angry words, though neither would tell Tara what they'd spoken about. He loaded up the car with clear bottles. Tara thought he seemed tanned already and that he walked tall. She'd spent the morning filling bottles with sand and her hands were numb, freezing to the touch, no matter what she did.

She was entranced by the ghosts now. She watched them for hours as she sat and worked, watching them crawl into the bottles, like beaten dogs into a corner or sick cats into small spaces.

"Don't you love it here?" Jonas asked.

"No," Dale said. He'd hardly spoken since his argument with Jonas, and he wouldn't answer her when she asked him about it. The men barely acknowledged his existence and he seemed to fade in Tara's eyes, minute by minute. "We should head off today."

"I want to stay," Jonas said.

Dale and Tara exchanged glances. Dale didn't want to stay a minute longer; he'd leave the caravan behind to get away. A lethargy had come over both of them which he didn't like, an inability to make decisions for themselves. They'd fallen into the strange routine of days by the bottle heap, and they both knew it was time to move on. They'd talked about it during the night, in whispers, and Dale had snuck out to try to hook the caravan up, but he couldn't do it alone. It was facing the wrong way. Not backed in.

"Jonas, you can't stay here. This is not your life."

"This *is* his life," Father John said, joining them at the station wagon with another box of bottles. "You need to find the serenity to accept what you can't change."

"There's a life for all three of us back home," Dale said. "Together."

Tara was torn. She could see how happy Jonas was here and knew he wanted to stay. He was a grown man, or close enough, and they couldn't force him to leave. But she'd worry about him. How would he get away if he needed to? What if something happened? And truly, she imagined the hours on the road alone with Dale, and such a deep sense of boredom came across her she felt ashamed.

They were quiet then, and Dale spent the rest of the day preparing for an early morning departure.

That night they drank more heavily than ever, and before ten Tara was finding it hard to walk, hard to keep her eyes open. She felt herself weeping openly and Jonas patting her kindly, not saying anything, just giving her moments of his time.

SHE VAGUELY REALIZED she was asleep in the caravan and wondered who had carried her there. She'd done this in the past, slept while someone was driving the car ahead, and found it very comforting.

Dale was driving, she discovered. When he stopped, hours later, she sat up, her head pounding, as he opened the caravan's door.

"Where are we?"

"On our way."

"I didn't get to say goodbye," she said. "Why'd you drive off like that?"

"It's okay," he said. '"He's with us in spirit."

She joined him in the car. She offered to drive but she knew she shouldn't, she couldn't, so they drove in silence for another hour or so. They were smack in the middle of nowhere, *atom bomb testing country*, Dale called it.

She reached for water and saw a note on the floor, from Father John, thanking Dale for a donation.

"Oh, you gave them money." She looked at the note. "Shitloads of money. I guess they'll look after Jonas, then."

There were scratches on his face. His arms. Blood in his hair. She thought she'd dreamt it, that they'd fought, her husband and son, she'd heard it but not seen it, yet here he was, damaged.

"Are you all right? You're beat up! Is Jonas all right? We should go back and see. I'll call him."

Dale put his hand over hers. "This is my gift to you. To us," he said. "This is the rope that binds."

He reached into his side pocket. She saw that his ear was bloodied and he hadn't cleaned his neck, or changed his shirt, but it wasn't until he placed the bottle between them, sand-filled, already run through with tiny tunnels, that she understood what he had done.

KAARON WARREN *is an Australian author of horror, science fiction, and fantasy short stories and novels. She is the author of the short story collections,* Through Splintered Walls, The Grinding House, *and* Dead Sea Fruit. *Her short stories have won Australian Shadows Awards, Ditmar Awards, and Aurealis Awards. She's also a Bram Stoker Award Nominee, twice-World Fantasy Award Nominee, and Shirley Jackson Award winner. Her novels, published by Angry Robot Books, include* Slights, Walking the Tree, *and* Mistification. *Her latest novel is* The Grief Hole *(IFWG Publishing Australia).*

Kaaron Warren has lived in Melbourne, Sydney, Canberra and Fiji. You can find her at http://kaaronwarren.wordpress.com *and she tweets* @KaaronWarren.

"You are like me," it said.

OBIBI

by Dilman Dila

I'd previously read several of Dilman Dila's submissions over the past years for various other enterprises, and although they weren't quite fitting for the projects then at hand, I always thought in the back of my mind that Dilman had unusual and compelling stories that were well written, and that I wanted to find an opportunity to someday work with him.

That day came with this anthology.

Remember, writers, even when an editor must pass on your submission, if they say they enjoy your work, they most often mean it, and they do remember you. Especially when you're someone with talent such as Dilman who's involved with so many creative endeavors (novelist, screen writer, film maker, world-travelling social activist, etc.), it's a wonder he can keep up with it all.

He explained that this following story is based on old superstition, in which children born with disability would often be abandoned to die in the country, for it was believed their bodies had been corrupted by demon infestation. So it is for Agira, a crippled hunter who must save the village who shuns him from the Obibi, a shapeshifting monster . . . or is it the monster in him that shapes the world around?

A GIRA COULD NOT RUN ANYMORE.

The thorn, buried deep in his sole, sent rivers of pain up his leg, like the bite of a great-toothed beast. He crumbled into the undergrowth. The ground was damp, the forest muggy, insects whirred about, stinging him, but his attention was on the thorn. He had never hurt his foot before. He'd learned long ago to limp without stepping on thorns or sharp rocks. Sometimes a snake slithered ahead to clear his path. Other times his crutch rattled if he was about to step on something.

But this time, a monster—an *obibi*—was hunting him.

He ran in panic. He had no snake to guide him. The crutch alerted him, but he was too slow to respond, and the terrible thorn ripped through his sandal. Blood spilled onto the thick mat of dead twigs and rotting leaves, rendering his spoor-mask spell useless. The obibi would now easily sniff him out.

Or am I the monster?

Agira undid the straps of the sandal, clenched his teeth, shut his eyes tight, and yanked out the thorn. It came off with bits of flesh. The pain was unbearable, and he screamed. He heard a nearing rustle, the thump of elephantine feet, a gigantic body crashing through the undergrowth, knocking weak trees out of its way. The obibi was coming.

He would see it. Finally. After five days of hunting, when fate had turned and he was now the prey, he would see it.

When you see it, you'll think you've looked into a mirror.

Ignoring the pain, he struggled to his feet, leaning on the crutch, a *shongo* in one hand. Though charmed to hurt any demon, the knife did not reassure him. He had to let go of the crutch to throw it far and hard, and thus he lost balance and fell every time he tried. He preferred arrows. He'd fashioned his crutch into a bow and he could shoot without losing balance. But he had no arrows... A warrior had taken them all. He should have resisted, he should have held on to his best weapon. He let the warrior take them for he'd imagined he would have time to make more arrows. He did not think all six warriors would die so easily. They were the bravest, the most fierce, each with dozens of powerful defense charms, yet the obibi killed them as though they were ants.

He should have stayed home. He was no warrior. His crippled leg meant he would never be one, nor part of any society. He came because Mama insisted that the warriors needed him to hunt down the monster. He had the ability to see birds fly far above clouds, he could hear ants crawl on the other side of the mountain. Without him, they had no chance of tracking down the obibi.

But when the warriors saw him, which was the first time in his memory that anyone else had seen him, they saw his twisted leg, and they spat, all six of them. They spat. They believed a demon had possessed him, so they spat to discourage it from jumping out of his body and possessing them too, and crippling them. They ran from him, chanting prayers of protection, spitting.

Mama always cautioned him to stay hidden because of this superstition. He lived with her in the wilderness, and a huge swamp separated their home from the nearest village. The villagers never dared cross the swamp for they feared her. When they needed medicine, or charms, or prophecy, or to conduct funeral rituals, or birth rituals, they lit a fire on a tall rock to summon her. He, on the other hand, never had any reason to cross the swamp to their side. Everything he wanted was in the wilderness, his snakes, his monkeys, his cattle, they were his best friends. He spoke to them, he played with them, and they gave him love and company. Why would he ever want to cross the swamp? He stayed isolated until he had to help them hunt a monster . . .

And now the obibi got closer. Its odor grew so strong that Agira struggled to breathe. It stunk like a mix of smoked fish and rotten beans. It was no ordinary smell. Only those the ancestors had blessed with special gifts could detect it, which is how he had tracked it from the site of its last kill, a maize garden that its victims, a pregnant woman and her little daughter, had been weeding. It ate them, even the fetus, just as over a period of twenty days, it had eaten its previous twelve victims, who were all from the same family.

"They need our help to catch it," Mama had told him.

And yet, the warriors spat on seeing him. It hurt.

He'd lived with rejection all his life, beginning with the fact that his father ordered for his death because of a twisted leg. He'd imagined that if strangers spat on seeing him, he would simply shrug it off, but it hurt so bad that tears ran down his face like boiling water. If his oldest friend, the yellow spotted cobra, was nearby, he would have sent her after them, but he was on the wrong side of the swamp. He could not have immediate revenge.

When you see it you'll think you've looked into a mirror, Mama had said, and as he'd thought of sending the cobra against the warriors, he wondered: *Did I ask the monster to attack the village? Why were all victims from the same family? Are they my family?*

"I'm going back home," he'd told Mama. "Let obibi eat them!"

Mama had followed in silence as he limped back to the canoe. She waited until he'd climbed in, and then she spoke in a tone he'd never heard before.

"You'll soon need a wife," she said. "This is a good opportunity to show them how useful you can be."

Her words stirred pain deep inside. Playing with snakes was fun, and romping with monkeys and rolling in the grass with hyenas was a joy. But when he heard boys of his own age in the swamp, swimming, laughing, fighting, he would hide in the papyrus and watch them and wonder whether he would ever laugh like that. Sometimes he lay awake at night and tried to think what his real mother looked like, what it felt like to snuggle against her bosom. Sometimes he cried when Mama was away for days looking for herbs and he had no one to talk to. Conversing with wild animals was not like conversing with Mama. He talked, and they understood what he said, and obeyed his commands, but they could not talk back.

He'd sat in the canoe, tears blurring his sight. Mama, a small, wiry old woman, made her way back to the warriors, who stood a good distance away. She talked to them for a long time. They looked youthful, while still twice his age, and probably all were married with children and in big, happy families. He wondered if any of them were related to his biological family.

He was not born with a twisted leg. Mama said he fell sick shortly after he'd learned to walk, and he became crippled. He should have been dumped in the Bush of Ghosts and left to die, like all other crippled children. Some were given poison to quicken their departure, others were strangled, most were tethered to a tree and condemned to a slow death because their parents thought it was better than outright murder. To them the child was no longer human but a possessed creature that could infect other children with demons. He would have ended up in the Bush of Ghosts, but his father, being very wealthy and with no heir, at first refused to sentence his only son to death. He instead asked the *ajwaka* to drive out the demon. Many seasons passed. His father eventually bore other sons, and then he asked the ajwaka to kill Agira. However the boy now called her Mama, and she'd become fond of him, and so she decided to reject the villages' practice of throwing away maimed children.

She told his father the deed was done, while instead presenting Agira to the ancestors, crying out to them to stand with children like him, and they agreed to make Agira her apprentice. They blessed him with special gifts, and she trained him to one day become a medium.

Then the monster attacked, and Mama finally spoke the truth to the village, explaining she had not killed the child because the ancestors had accepted him.

The village kings and elders thought she was telling lies, for they believed all cripples were possessed by demons, and so could never harbor ancestral spirits. They threatened to drown her in the swamp for they thought she must have lost touch with the ancestors to say such things.

"He's still young," Mama had replied. "But he's been given special gifts and can use them to help the warriors track down the obibi."

The kings and the elders were in such a state of fear that they grudgingly accepted to give him a chance. If he did help destroy the obibi, it would prove her true, for evil cannot destroy evil. Only good can destroy evil.

She reminded the warriors of this, and they reluctantly agreed to take him with them, but they treated him worse than they treated their dogs.

Now, as he stood in the middle of the forest, his foot bleeding, the obibi getting closer, he wondered if it was worth it. He would die because his people—his own father, his own mother, his blood family—did not love him enough to bear the burden of looking after him. Any crippled child, even those who lost a finger in some accident, were condemned to die in the Bush of Ghosts.

"The ancestors saved you for a reason," Mama said. "You'll stop them from throwing away their children."

But Mama was wrong. The obibi would kill him. His life would be for nothing. He should not have come. He should have stayed on the other side of the swamp. He should have stuck to his original plan of migrating to a faraway place, where Mama said people did not treat cripples like this. Or to that magical place his monkey friends thought was somewhere in the middle of the jungle. Somewhere he could live a happy life.

When you see it you'll think you've looked into a mirror.

He heard it grunt like a pig as it sniffed at his blood. Any moment now, he would see it. The mirror . . . Survivors of its attacks never agreed on what it looked like. Some said it was apelike, with four horns and tall as a tree, others said it was a monstrous bull with a long machete for a tail, while others thought it was a fire-breathing cock. It had no definite shape. It took the form of their worst nightmares. Is that why Mama said that when he saw it he would think he was looking into a mirror?

"I know what this monster is," Mama had added. "But I haven't told the village for it would undo everything I've done to make them accept you and to stop them from throwing away their children. Remember that."

What did she mean? Am I the monster? Did I send the monster? Mama never told him exactly which family he came from, or even in which village his family lived, but from the moment she told him about looking into a mirror, he feared that he had unconsciously sent the monster after his family in vengeance. *Why else are all the victims from the same family?*

A bush trembled as the monster brushed past, creeping toward him, its grunts seeming to shake the ground. Any moment now he would see it . . . He did not want to look into that mirror!

Fire, he thought. No demon can survive fire!

He chanted a spell, and at once flames burst out of the bushes, forming a ring around him. The fire grew strong, the heat pressed against him, and his hope flared for he could feel the obibi retreat. He said another prayer and the flames chased the obibi, to devour it. Just as he started to relax, a strong wind blew, putting out the fire as though it were a candle. When the smoke wafted away, it revealed a large area that was scorched and bare. He was in a green patch in the middle of the burned area.

Exposed.

Panic returned. His heart beat fast. The shongo felt heavy, greasy in his palms. Sweat drenched his loin cloth. In a heartbeat it would be upon him, and then he would look into that mirror. He could not run. He could not fight. If only he could hide ... But where? He'd burned down everything around him. Now there was only scorched tree trunks and black soil. If only he could crawl into a trunk ... If only he could turn into a tree, the obibi would not find him.

At that thought, something strange happened to his body. It splintered into a thousand pieces. His bones, his flesh, his blood, all tumbled about in the air like leaves in a whirlwind. Had the obibi got him? Was he dying ... ? No, not dying. Transforming. Evolving. It took less than ten heartbeats for his body to morph into—he frowned at his torso—*a tree?*

He looked down at his feet and saw the shongo and the crutch in the foliage beside a pool of his blood, a tree trunk going into the ground where his feet had been. The remains of his loin cloth, torn into several pieces, were scattered about, as were the beads that once graced his wrist and neck. He had seven arms and a hundred thousand leafy fingers, fluttering about in the wind.

Had he turned into a tree? Just by thinking it? Mama had told him of shape-shifting ajwaka, who could morph into animals, or birds, but never into a tree. Only spirits could turn into plants and rocks. So how had he changed into a tree? Was he indeed demon-possessed, or did the ancestors favor him so much that they blessed him with abilities no other ajwaka had ever acquired?

Or had the obibi turned him?

A bush to his left trembled as the monster stepped closer. Another step, and it would walk into the burned area. Agira closed his eyes. He did not want to look into the mirror. Maybe the obibi would not notice he was a tree and would walk past and go away. But when he heard feet on the ashen ground, he looked, against his will, as something forced his eyes open. He saw a boy walking out of the bush. Not walking, but limping, for he was hunchbacked and had twisted legs, and he used two crutches.

Is this what Mama meant by a mirror?

The boy cast a shadow, even though there was hardly any sunlight this deep in the jungle. The shadow fell on the foliage, as though the light came up from the ground, in the shape of a monster from Agira's nightmares, something like a cross between a leopard and a cock, with a spiked tail wriggling like an earthworm. The boy's eyes held a bright shade of brown, almost like a sweet potato, with lips twisted in what could have been a snarl.

"You are like me," it said, in an adolescent's voice.

Now Agira wondered if he understood Mama's mirror. Had she thought that he, like this hunchbacked boy, would let rage overwhelm him, and that he would also misuse his gifts and go to the darkness? He wanted to protest that he was no monster, but his mouth hung open and no word came out. Instead, a dry wind blew into his throat.

"Strange," it said, stepping closer, staring hard at Agira. "You turned yourself into a tree . . . We are not supposed to do that." Agira could no longer smell the bad odor. "But I can see you, just as you can see me even though I wear a monster's body."

Agira wanted to ask a thousand questions, but his mouth just hung open and the wind continued to blow into his throat, making him long to drink from Mama's pot.

"Where do you come from?" the obibi asked. "Why are you helping them?"

Its shadow changed from a leopard-cock monster to a monkey, and Agira thought this meant his fear of the obibi had ebbed away. But why was he not afraid anymore? Just because he had seen that it was only a crippled boy?

You are like me.

No! No! No! Agira fought the accusation. He was no monster. He did not kill and eat pregnant women and their fetuses!

"We live in our own village in this forest," the boy was saying. "The cripples they throw away, we save those we can. But you, you are not with us, and it doesn't make sense that you are with *them*. Where do you come from? Why are you helping them?"

Agira finally found his voice, a husky sound deep from within the tree. "Mama asked me."

"Mama?" The anger in the obibi's voice was like hailstone. "You have a Mama?"

Agira got tired of the wind blowing into his mouth. He wished he was not a tree anymore. At once, his body disintegrated into a thousand pieces again, and he crumbled to the ground. His foot throbbed in pain, blood oozing from the thorn's wound. He felt he was no longer in immediate danger, and he plucked leaves from the foliage and wove a bandage, which he stuck onto the wound and then chanted a spell to stop the bleeding.

When he looked up again, he did not see the hunchbacked boy or the leopard-cock monster or the monkey. In their place stood a man, tall and mighty like a warrior. Agira frowned, and the man smiled quickly.

"It's still me," the obibi said. "I take many forms. I turn into a man and live in their midst and they never know it's the child they discarded. My people say I must stick to our village and forget that my own mother threw me into the bush. But I can't forget. Not something like that. I can't ever."

In the man's eyes, Agira saw anger that had simmered for ages, the same anger Agira felt, and a grim thought cropped up: Did this man kill and eat his own blood kin? Was the pregnant woman his mother?

It's not a mirror! he screamed to himself. He was not a demon. The ancestors blessed him with gifts to be a helper. Eventually he would succeed Mama as the ajwaka. He would make medicines and charms and see prophecies and perform rituals. He would not kill and eat people.

A lump formed in Agira's throat. If the villagers knew a child they threw away had returned as an obibi, it would prove their idea that all crippled children really *were* demon-possessed. All the work Mama had put into changing their attitude would evaporate, and Agira would never swim and laugh with other boys in the swamp.

"Come live with us," the man said. "You'll find it better than staying with *them*."

The invitation blazed through Agira's head. If he followed the man to the village of cripples, would he find a new home, people to talk to and play with? Would he find a girl to love and marry? Or were the others monsters as well?

He struggled to his feet, leaning on his crutch. The man took that to be an acceptance of the invitation, and so begun to walk away.

"Change into a strong man," the obibi said. "Our village is very far. I could have turned into a bird to fly, but the ancestors didn't bless me with that shape."

Agira's hand trembled as he clasped the shongo. Pain throbbed in his foot. He hesitated for a moment, only for one moment, and then, before his conscience could stop him, he let go of the crutch and threw the knife, using all his energy. He lost balance and fell. The shongo whistled through the air. The man noticed it a heartbeat before it struck, and tried to dodge it, but too late. It changed direction to keep track of the target, and then it cracked open his skull. He fell, blood and brains oozing out, and his body transformed into that of the hunchbacked boy.

Agira struggled to his feet, leaning heavily on the crutch, and hobbled to the corpse. He looked at the body for a long time, thinking about asking monkeys he had seen nearby to help dig a grave. After that, he would have to find a carcass, maybe that of a hippopotamus, and transform it into a monstrous ogre, which he would present as the obibi. Maybe that would be the first step toward making them accept him. Later, he would have to find the village of cripples and he would have to think of building bridges to ensure this carnage never happened again.

He was only a little boy, but he could feel a huge burden on his shoulders.

DILMAN DILA *is the author of a critically acclaimed collection of short stories,* A Killing in the Sun. *He has been listed in several prestigious prizes, including the BBC International Radio Playwriting Competition (2014), the Commonwealth Short Story Prize (2013), and the Short Story Day Africa prize (2013, 2014). His short fiction has been featured in several magazines and anthologies. His films include the masterpiece,* What Happened in Room 13 *(2007), which has attracted over six million views on YouTube, and* The Felistas Fable *(2013), which was nominated for Best First Feature at Africa Movie Academy Awards (2014), and which won four major awards at Uganda Film Festival (2014). More of his life and works are online at* www.dilmandila.com *and you can watch his films on YouTube channel* www.youtube.com/dilstories.

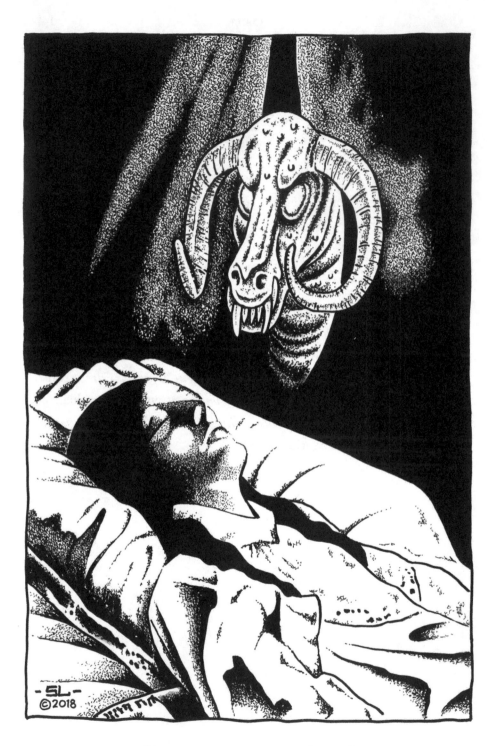

"I assure you, it was no dream."

THE NIGHTMARE

by Rhea Daniel

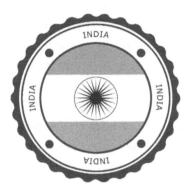

I read this next story during open call for a different anthology project that I edited. Although it didn't quite fit for that book, I fell in love with the characters' voices, the circumstances of the afflicted, and the Doctor's greater predicament, not to mention the Freudian discernment that so eschews this period setting of an Edwardian, Colonial-era world.

Simply put, I had to have it.

Artist Rhea Daniel writes from Mumbai, India, and this is just her second fiction publication credit. If she continues penning such eloquent and astute work as The Nightmare, *I hope for many, many more to come.*

I WAS FIRST INTRODUCED TO MISS LILY M. THROUGH her uncle when I was holidaying at a summer resort.

During that brief introduction, I found she was an intelligent young woman who possessed a vibrant character—that is, until the rest of her family arrived on the scene, after which it were as if a cloak of gloom had been cast over her.

Her female relatives complained that she tended to cut herself off from society by turning inward. They thought it was a self-indulgent pastime and was the very reason behind the fits of anxiety and restlessness that she complained of. During such daydreaming sessions, she had to have her name called several times before she woke from her "happy place."

Her case was referred to me with the warning that her conservative, church-going mother and two sisters had a strong dislike for the newfangled ideas of psychoanalysis.

With the help of her uncle, an authority in many of the family's decisions, Miss Lily managed to convince her mother that the treatment would not involve the devil's work. Moreover, it would be conducted with utter secrecy within the privacy of their own home.

Having dealt with many cases of such hysteria amongst young women of a similar age, I was tempted to waive my fee, for I had already identified the cause of poor Lily's psychoses in that brief introduction and expected to successfully cure her problems in little time.

I saw that the family was not short of funds, however, when my carriage entered the vast estate and quickly changed my thoughts of working *pro gratis*. The gardens were simple but meticulously manicured and the family mansion, though old, was not badly maintained. Her sisters greeted me at the door with the politeness of the upper class, managing to convey their distaste for my kind without words.

I was led to a vast parlor which held the scent of a bygone era, where past owners had entertained ladies dressed to the teeth, many of whom had posed prettily for the paintings that adorned the walls. As for the most recent paintings, the resemblance to the originals was uncanny, the painter a genius. The elder sisters sat beside their mother, prim and buttoned up to the neck with nary a hint of smile, the eyes similar to the cold, fish-eyed gray of their progenitor. I couldn't imagine what it was like growing up under those watchful eyes.

Lily's portrait stood last and low enough so I could examine the bluish tint beneath her eyes, her mouth pressed into the shape of a crushed rose-petal that could burst into anything between a laugh or a cry. How long had she wanted to run into the middle of a field and scream her lungs out?

Our first in-house meeting was overseen by the mater, her eyes observing me occasionally as she pretended to work on her needlepoint, her ears, I assume, sharply tuned to hear every word.

Lily, though open and relaxed at our introductory meeting at the summer resort, was incapable now of more than a few pleasantries. I politely asked Mrs. M. to leave so that I could conduct the treatment in privacy. She wasn't pleased at all but, having stipulated this as a condition of my treatment once before, left with a swish of her skirts.

Once she was gone, it seemed as if the bars of a cage were raised. Lily stuttered her thanks and wept copious tears, while trying vainly to compose herself. I gave her some time, assuring her that her tears did not offend me and that I was here to help. She stammered out something about there being "a devil on her back," to which I assured her that her situation might not be entirely unique and incurable.

"But, sir, I'm deeply afraid!" she cried out.

I instructed her to breathe evenly until her anxiety had passed, then explained how hypnosis could help in her recovery.

"I see," she said, pressing her lips into the same crushed rose-petal shape. "I will have to relive my nightmares."

"It will be different this time, you will be a spectator to them and confront them. I know it sounds contrary to my intention, so I will explain this simply: If a thought or experience you can't fully comprehend is tucked away, and buried within layers upon layers, be it by time, or by your own denial, it can fight back and surface in the oddest ways. Do you understand?"

"And this thing can be the source of my vexations?"

I nodded. "We have to turn back time and get to the source."

"But what if it takes a turn for the worse?"

"The difference this time is that I will be here to guide you if you falter."

She nodded and lowered her eyes. "I have the barest inkling of when it first occurred. At first it was just small things, flitting past the corners of my vision, distracting me from my godly duties."

She swallowed nervously and laid a shaky hand to her breast. "I . . . I was so afraid, thinking I'm going mad. And then I saw it, as real as life!"

"What did you see?"

"Perhaps I can show you?"

From a pocket in her skirts she removed a folded piece of paper that she carefully opened. Its image revealed a woman's body stretched across her bed in a most vulnerable pose, with a glaring imp planted on her abdomen. I recognized this copy of a famous painting immediately: Fuseli's *The Nightmare*.

"He's the one," she said, her tone accusing. She was pointing to the imp. "Or something like him."

"And there's no one else in the background around you, like this black horse?"

I pointed to the head of a black horse peering out from behind the curtains in the painting, its eyes glazed with a watchful, eager deadness, reminding me of the cold gaze of Lily's own mother.

"No, none that I remember," she replied.

"Was this all your dream?"

"I assure you, it was no dream."

I nodded, it was important for me to gain her trust. I handed back the piece of paper.

"Keep it," she said. "Mother already admonished me once when she found it. She said it was vulgar and made me throw it in the fire."

"Well, the original painting did cause a sensation in its day. How did you find it in the first place?"

"A pamphlet left in a book. Luckily there were two of them. I was so struck at how closely it resembled my experience . . . "

She trailed away as if going into some daydream.

"Lily," I called and when she did not respond, called her name in a sharper tone.

"Oh, did you say something, Doctor?" she asked with a smile.

"With your permission, I would like to place you under hypnosis."

"Will it hurt?"

"No," I replied reassuringly. "I would not bring a patient to harm."

"Will it make it worse? After all, my daydreaming is, as my dear uncle puts it, almost pathological."

"Miss M., I can assure you, you are an intelligent woman in control of her faculties. I have seen symptoms in some people that have manifested into physical disabilities, and your case is not even close to such a condition."

"Then, I suppose, I must give my permission."

However, when Lily lay down on a chaise longue, her expression betrayed her apprehension.

"Breathe deeply, relax," I said, and continued speaking to her in soothing tones, asking her to concentrate on my finger before her.

She turned out to be an excellent subject for hypnotism. She followed my instructions without missing a heartbeat before slipping into a peaceful trance, her body relaxing and the look of apprehension etched on her face slipping away.

"Now, Lily, I want you to go back to the day you might have first seen something that upset you."

"I am there."

"How old are you?"

"Fourteen."

"Are you at home?"

"Yes, in the parlor with my mother and my aunt. My cousin Mika is there too. He sits down next to me and asks what I am reading. We are talking."

"What happens next?"

"Mother sends me to my room. She is displeased."

"Do you know why?"

"No, she doesn't say. But I have never felt so bad before. I feel as if I did something wrong."

"By speaking to your cousin Mika?"

"Yes. Mother makes me read a passage from the Bible: *If your hand causes you to sin, cut it off. It is better for you to enter life crippled than with two hands to go to hell, to the unquenchable fire . . . "*

Her forehead grew tense and a tear rolled down her cheek.

"My wrists grow cold," she continued. "I feel as if I've done something unforgivable."

I argued with myself for a moment and then decided to wake her. "The scene fades. Come away now, Lily."

But she seemed to resist my instructions.

"I see a garden," she said, a faint smile on her lips.

"Do you want to linger?"

"Yes, yes," she replied, "I am at a garden party."

"Is Mika there?"

"Yes. He smiles at me but I am afraid to smile back. My sisters are watching."

"What do you do next?"

"I make an excuse and go inside."

"What do you feel in that moment?"

"I feel terribly glad that Mika noticed me. My heart flutters like a bird within a cage, and I am flushed. But I feel that it is wrong, because my sisters are still watching."

"Go on. What happens after you go inside?"

"It is afternoon and the clock in the parlor strikes two. The curtains are drawn and the shadows are sharp."

"What happens next?"

"I am alone at the piano, but something is distracting me."

"What do you think it is?"

"It dashes away the moment I set eyes on it. It is too quick for me to focus on."

"Is there anything at all that you can tell me about it?"

"No, no, it's gone, it's in my bed now. I see hair and fur, a cloven hoof. It is dark."

She whimpered and her chest began to move quickly, her voice rising in a panic.

"Oh God! He's on my chest, he bears down on me! I can't breathe! I can't breathe! Mother! Mother, tell him to stop!"

She waved her hands in the air as if trying to ward off something. I stood beside her reclining form to prevent her from rolling off the chaise longue and falling to the floor.

"The scene fades, breathe deeply, you are safe." I repeated these words until she woke from her trance.

"Oh," she said. "Was I asleep?"

"You were under hypnosis. Do you remember anything we spoke about?"

"No," she said, wiping away her tears and sitting up. "Should I?"

"Not necessarily. I will need you to tell me how you feel in the next few days till our next meeting, so keep a record of it in your mind."

"Doctor," she asked, placing a hand on my wrist, "did I say something that I might be ashamed of?"

"Nothing at all. In fact, you are a very good patient and I believe we will progress admirably within the next few sessions."

She looked pleased as I took my leave. I met the two sisters at the door of the parlor and gave them a few instructions on how to care for Miss Lily in the next few days. Mrs. M. appeared by their side, and I repeated my reassurances and instructions for her daughter's care.

"How long will this take?"

"A minimum of four to five sessions. I believe I've identified the source of Miss Lily's problems."

I fixed my eye on Mrs. M.'s cold gray ones and added, "I would advise you to allow her a little more freedom of movement. All young women of this age clamor for activity of some sort. Besides needlepoint, that is. It will do her a world of good."

"You needn't advise me on my duties as a mother, Doctor," Mrs. M. responded curtly.

I felt relief at leaving the oppressive atmosphere of the ancestral home. It was obvious that Lily's psychosexual development had been hindered by her mother and sisters, to what end, I didn't know. She was of marriageable age now, and ought to be meeting many young men, but for some reason the matriarch insisted on keeping her cloistered. I would not know the reason why unless I treated Mrs. M. herself, but an abreaction with someone who frightened her own child with grisly passages from the Bible would be like opening up a basket of snakes. I could only appeal to her as a doctor, by bringing Lily's poor health into the picture.

By next week, Lily's pallor had shown no sign of improvement.

"I remember everything, Doctor," she confessed as soon as her mother left the room. "I remember what happened after... after the nightmare, for it couldn't be anything more than one."

"I see," I said. "And did the memories return in a rush, or little by little?"

"Slowly, I pieced them together. After the Devil crushed me under his foot, I began screaming for help, calling for my mother. She came and she slapped me awake and began to speak words from the Bible, telling the demon to leave my soul alone. I heard a voice in the darkness, pulling me in, drawing me down a dark path. When I couldn't open my eyes, she slapped my face several times again. And then my sisters called for me and did the same."

"They slapped you in the face?"

She nodded.

"When I woke finally, they were staring at me. They told me that Satan had almost taken my soul."

My face must have held a look of incredulity, for she smiled in sympathy at me.

"Oh Doctor, don't be upset."

"You remember all this?"

"I do now. Our last meeting might have something to do with it."

"And are you not shaken by such a severe chastisement on behalf of your mother and sisters?" I asked, unable to help myself.

"I believe I needed it," she replied softly.

"Oh dear God..."

I removed my glasses and rubbed my eyes, then placed them back on my nose.

"Miss M., you are, in my opinion, a kind and sensitive soul. You may also have several talents that have not been allowed to bloom. In three years you will be a legal adult. I cannot recommend enough that you find someone suitable to marry and leave this house as soon as you are able. I would suggest getting a job, but I know your family would consider that unsuitable for someone of your class."

She stared at me as I spoke. "But . . . but why should I leave?"

I sighed.

"It is unhealthy to be cooped up like a hen within a cage. I am a product of a regimental upbringing myself, and I cannot recommend enough that you absolutely must get away, as soon as you are able. It might be the only the key to your happiness."

The look on her face turned thoughtful.

"The Devil, he left a mark on my body. Would you like to see it?"

"I'm sorry?"

She began, to my utter horror, to open up the neck of her bodice.

"Miss M., stop that at once! You needn't prove anything to me!"

She didn't listen and, releasing two more buttons, revealed a bruise just below her collarbone. If anyone walked in at that moment, I would be in danger of losing my license.

I leapt up and striding up to her, caught hold of her hands.

"You don't believe me, do you, Doctor?" she said, tears filling her eyes. "It was a nightmare but it was real, real to *me*!"

"I believe every word you say, I'm just helping you make sense of it," I said to her, adopting a soothing tone. "Do you remember me telling you about how certain mental ailments can manifest themselves physically? This too might be manifestation. It was real to you, I understand!"

She looked at me, a tear balanced at the corner of her eye, and squeezed my hands.

"Your hands are so soft," she said.

"Miss M.," I said, my voice carrying the faintest warning.

My hands trembled as I drew away and took my seat opposite her. There was a moment of silence as we both composed ourselves.

I realized that Lily had interpreted my advice as a dismissal of her hallucinations. As a doctor, I had allowed my past to interfere with my patient's treatment.

Hopefully, I had not failed her completely.

"Miss M.," I said, "I must apologize. When I said you need to find a partner and marry, I did not mean it as a dismissal of your experience. In fact, we needn't discuss the subject at all. We will concentrate on betterment of your health, until I feel you have my trust again."

"You do have my trust Doctor," she said. "In fact I think you understand me *too* well."

"Then are you ready for another session of hypnosis?"

She took a deep breath and answered, "Yes."

Again, she slipped into a trance easily. We returned to her past, to the time she experienced anything that might have left a psychological imprint and filled in the gaps in her story. She spoke of Mika again, whom she hadn't visited with in several years since, as her mother had seen to that. She spoke at length about her schoolgirl friends. She spoke about how she hated sleeping alone. Then she began to hum a tune that I hadn't heard before, a small smile playing on her lips. Then, she began to whisper words that I could barely hear. I leaned down and put my ear near her lips.

" ... There you are, you little bastard ... you're smaller than the old hag ... do you want to fuck her? Turn her around ... give her a good spanking ... no, no, she's mine ... I know what you're thinking ... "

I could feel my hackles rise as she let out a low chuckle, much too unfeminine to be hers.

" ... whip her, whip her good, hear her scream ... she likes it, the little bitch ... pinch her, slap her ... "

I said immediately, "The scene fades, breathe deeply, you are safe."

Lily woke with no memory of the words she had spoken. I announced that the session was over and expertly avoided the other women of the house. It was dark and rainy when I stepped outside, my mind reeling with questions.

Lily's case, apparently, was not as simple as I'd thought.

I needed a different view. Without disclosing my patient's details, I called a long-trusted colleague whom I hadn't spoken to in years. We met the next evening in my room over a glass of port.

"I remember you didn't take too well to the pipe the first time," he said. "But now this room positively reeks of it."

"That's not entirely my fault," I protested. "Many other boarders have passed through here."

"I wonder why you stay here," he remarked, casting a glance around my poorly lit room. "I thought you were doing well for yourself."

"I am. I just like to live beneath my means."

He snorted at my answer and took a sip from his glass.

"So, what is you wanted to ask me?"

I let out a contemplative breath, caressing my pipe. "I have a new patient, one that might have cracked my walls."

"Oh my," he said with a grin.

"Her symptoms include chest pains, anxiety neurosis, hallucinations, insomnia, and night terrors. She has a tendency to go into auto-hypnotic absences. I have witnessed her slip into one during our first session."

My friend grew serious, listening intently to every word.

"She comes from a well-off family. The mater's quite the harridan, a real Bible thumper. I strongly feel that her psychosexual development has been interrupted from birth."

"Anything else?"

"Yes," I said, finishing my glass and setting it down. "I have twice so far engaged the patient in hypnosis. The first time, she recalled a traumatic nightmare from which her mother and sisters woke her, slapping her awake like it was some sort of exorcism. For the second session, she said some things that . . . that I can't imagine a woman of her station would say aloud, let alone think."

"What things?"

I chewed on the stem of my pipe, wondering how to convey Lily's words.

"Like someone had bent her into a state of complete submission."

"So she's a masochist."

I sighed, stroking my mustache.

"And yet, it wasn't her, it was a part of her that had taken a monstrous aspect."

"A dissociative identity?"

"Maybe. But think of what could happen to a child's psyche when they are treated harshly. The self-abuse . . . a bruise below her collarbone that she claims a demon from her dreams caused. Or it could have been done by her mother or sisters. Either way she feels she needed the chastisement."

I frowned and leaned forward, rubbing my forehead. I admitted, "She reminds me so much of myself at that age."

He narrowed his eyes at me, recognizing my gestures of worry, and seemed to reach a conclusion. "You can't stand the rest of her family because they remind you of your own."

"Anyone would dislike them."

"You're hoping she's *not* a masochist because you want to rescue her."

"Because victims of abuse secretly want what they're getting?" I demanded, resenting his presence.

He returned my gaze steadily.

"You've contaminated the treatment with memories from your *own* complicated past. Perhaps it is you who needs treatment. Have you been feeling vulnerable lately?"

"I just . . . I know what she's going through, that's all."

I argued silently with myself as he stared at me over the rim of his glass.

"Back out," he said quietly. "Let someone else take over the case."

"I can't, I've only just gained her trust."

"Back away, my good man. You need to remain aloof to treat a patient with any success."

"It's not that easy."

"It is. Think of everything you've worked for."

I met his eyes and saw the sense in his words.

"Pass her case on to another doctor, so that you don't leave the poor girl hanging," he said, downing the contents of his glass and rising from his chair. "Now if you'll excuse me, I have to meet a patient with a piece of metal embedded in the right side of his brain, who makes the most delicate sculptures of American Indians, only he has no education and has never set foot on American soil."

"Fascinating," I remarked, with a hint of sarcasm.

"Do it," he warned me, before leaving.

It took me two more weeks to arrange an appointment with my patient, during which time I was able to think about my personal involvement with her case. I had to conclude that my friend was right, and steeled myself to end our doctor-patient relationship.

Lily greeted me in the parlor with a smile, and I could see that something had changed. Her mother, I noted, didn't like the way she smiled at me and hovered, glancing shiftily at both of us.

To my utter surprise, Lily said, "Mother, my meetings with the kind doctor are meant to be private. Could you please take your leave so we may continue?"

Mrs. M. glared at Lily so hard I thought she might bore a hole through her smiling face. Rather than cause a scene, she mentioned something about a guest she had to attend to and left as if it were her idea in the first place.

"Well, Miss M.," I said as I sat down, "you seem . . . happier."

"And I owe it to our meetings, Doctor," she said, clasping her hands together. "I have found the strength to shake off my nightmares, both in the living world and the dreaming."

"Can you . . . explain what happened?"

"You see, when the Devil beckons, it is the sinner's temptations that draw him down. I listened to your words and realized that I had not sinned, not the way our Lord and all the saints in the Bible had described it. The Devil had put those very thoughts inside me. Moreover, I had been running from him all these years, by hiding in a room inside my mind."

"I see," I said unsurely.

"I am pure, I told him, and I cast him off with all the strength in my soul. Look . . . "

She opened her bodice and I did not stop her this time. The bruise below her collarbone had faded to almost nothing.

"No nightmares," she said, buttoning up. "And if he knocks at my door again I have the strength to cast him off. I drew on it from within, with your help and our Lord Savior's."

Well, I thought, I certainly can't prevent my patient from making parallels with her faith, however simplistic they were, as long as her symptoms had improved.

"Miss M., do you mind if we have one last session of hypnosis?"

She agreed readily and, slipping into her trance, coasted down the stream of memories without showing any signs of anxiety. Even her past interactions with her mother were, to my surprise, recalled with acceptance, as if she were very much a mature observer rooted in the present. The session lasted over an hour.

I considered her recovery nothing short of miraculous, and possibly owed it to her character, which I had initially expressed to be intelligent and vibrant. She had confronted her monstrous aspect once it surfaced. She had overcome the strictures of this corset of guilt and orthodoxy that her female relatives had imposed on her, and done so in the most graceful manner. This had been evident from the moment I'd entered the parlor today, when she asked her mother to leave us to conduct our treatment alone.

Mrs. M. accosted me at the door and without mincing her words, told me never to return.

"I have lost my daughter to the world, Doctor," she declared. "And I can only blame you for it."

"On the contrary, Madam, she has been nudged out of the nest and is now mentally free to pursue her desires."

She shook her head, narrowing her fish-eyes at me with barely controlled anger.

"You are wrong. My daughter was under her mother's guidance so far, and was restrained from indulging in the caprices that come with our nature."

"Whose nature?" I inquired.

"*Us*, women," she replied without jest.

I was tempted to give her a much needed lecture on the history of the struggle endured by the fairer sex, but doubted it would have gone down well.

I left in a self-congratulatory mood, for I had saved my patient. I received my fee in full the next day, with a letter of thanks from her uncle.

Contemplating my success, I decided to consult my friend for a treatment that was long overdue.

It gave me great relief to let down my walls and make myself vulnerable to my own demons, for I had struggled long and hard over the years, guarding my emotions behind a wall that I had built while I walked the thorny road to success.

Three weeks later I received an invitation to a wedding. Lily was to be married to her cousin, the very Mika whom she had been expressly told to avoid by her mother. I had no idea of the details, but assumed they had somehow managed to find each other again.

The wedding was a discreet affair held in the garden of her uncle's home. I arrived late and hung back, a glass of champagne in my hand, watching the couple exchange vows under a beautiful sunlit arbor. Lily's mother and sisters were not present.

I've always been wan to the outdoors, and the bright sunlight seemed to quickly bring on the onset of a headache. Sharp shadows played at the corners of my eyes. Something flitted here and there, like the black tail of a cat, an annoying creature capable of tripping up a careless guest. I did away with the glass of champagne, in case it added to my headache.

I removed my glasses and, reaching for my kerchief, found a piece of folded paper in my coat pocket instead. It was the image of *The Nightmare* that Lily had given me during our first session.

"Doctor."

I glanced up. Lily looked radiant, her wedding dress an elegant cream-colored satin and a spray of flowers pinned to her corsage.

"You came," she said simply.

"I wouldn't miss it."

"You must excuse Mika, he's busy greeting the other guests, but you mustn't leave before meeting him. We owe you everything, especially this."

"I'm truly glad for you. But what about your family?"

"They will understand."

I nodded.

"You mustn't judge them, Doctor. They were only trying to help me."

"Of course," I said, feeling an inexplicable irritation at her saintly acceptance of her female relatives' behavior. I kept a polite smile to prevent her from guessing my thoughts.

"I might seek out some form of employment. I feel as if I could get bored with marriage alone," she said.

"Of course," I agreed.

"As my mother would say, 'an idle mind is the devil's workshop.' I haven't spoken to Mika about it, but I hope he agrees."

She met my eye and added meaningfully, "You know what it's like, to be a woman in a man's world."

I stared at her.

"Splendid," I coughed.

She took my hands suddenly and brought them to her lips. I froze at the physical contact, a whirlwind of thoughts rushing through my head.

"Thank you," she whispered, her eyes brimming with tears, then quickly left to be with her husband.

I made my way through the garden and out the front door, feeling utterly exposed, the ache in my head now a thunderous, pounding symphony.

Returning to the safety of my room, I called on the landlady to prepare me a hot bath and bring me a cup of chamomile. Against my own common sense, I downed a glass of port while I waited for the hot water to be prepared.

I went to the almirah where I stored my suits and, opening the trunk on the bottom shelf, reached for a piece of clothing I hadn't touched in fifteen years.

"Your hot water's ready," came a voice at the door.

My landlady was a belligerent woman who collected her rent with the attitude of a taxman. After I sent her off, I put away the rest of my disguise and sank gratefully into the tub, making a supreme effort to relax my body and my mind while sipping my tea.

Tears filled my eyes and my throat constricted with the onset of a sob. I wept, allowing the tears to find their way out. I had not cried, and had no reason to, for years. I allowed the memories of my childhood to surface, the memories of my first years at the university and my decision to suppress every aspect of my feminine self to earn a place in a man's profession.

Thankfully, I was alone and no one there to witness my turmoil.

Drowsy with the effects of the hot water combined with the port, I rose and dried off, then slipped under the sheets, and fell asleep almost immediately.

I woke to the sound of a voice that was a murmur in the darkness, as if someone were cursing in a low tone. I reached for my bedside lamp but felt nothing but air. I got up and felt hard cold stone beneath my feet instead of the wooden floor of my room. The air was cold and held a light breeze, covering me with gooseflesh.

It was a dream, quite obviously, and a very vivid one.

There was, in the very dim blue light, the curve of a long road before me. I heard a rapid clip-clop noise as if a horse were thundering down the road in the distance. Panic seized me and I began to run on bare feet. I felt a wind course up behind me as if something were rushing upon me, and then felt the blow of a whip on my back that knocked the air from my lungs and sent me sprawling on my hands and knees.

"There, you are, you little bastard."

I turned around, trembling, to see the inky outline of a tall shape and a face, half human, half animal. It drew back its lips to reveal a set of shining teeth. Steam rose from its feet and up its flanks.

I stood and stared at the tall creature before me, trying to make sense of it through the fading sting of its blow on my back.

I matched the creature's manner to the tone of voice that had come from Miss Lily's lips during our hypnotic session, her monstrous aspect. I told myself that somehow this nightmare was the result of empathic distress on my part, manifesting itself into a vision similar to hers within my exhausted psyche.

"That's right, lad, I'm there, in your head. You lost me a good one, a real virginal soul. I'd been trying to get her for years." It grinned. "You'll have to do instead."

The creature raised its whip and struck me again. I stared disbelievingly as the whip twisted like a snake and tore through the cloth of my nightshirt, leaving a trail of burning skin in its wake. I let out a shriek of surprise and sank to my knees with the pain.

"Feel real?"

It struck me again with an expert flick of its whip, this time ripping off my nightshirt completely. I fell backward with a gasp, unable to remember the last time I'd experienced such pain.

The creature took a step closer and, to my shame, I began inching away, whispering and begging for it to stop. It peered at me, blocking the sky with its fearsome visage, two curving pointed horns outlined against the dark purple sky.

"Tits? Who'd've thought."

I cried out once more as I felt the weight of one hoof on my upper chest, pressing down and crushing me with a terrible weight. I gasped for air when all at once its hoof grew orange hot and seared my skin just below the collarbone. Unable to scream for I could barely breathe, I twisted under it, the smell of my own burning flesh stinging my nostrils.

The creature released me. I found my voice and began to scream incoherently for my friend, for the landlady, for my mother, for anyone to come to my aid, to slap me awake.

"Scream all you want, no one can hear you."

It leaned in close to me and whispered with a sulfurous exhalation, "You're mine now."

It laughed and kicked my sides and commanded me to rise, the hoofs sharp and cold against my flesh. I summoned all my strength and rose to my feet, knowing that if I didn't I'd be struck again.

I began to tumble forward, nearly fainting from my injuries. The road grew soft and my feet sank into crevices. I tripped and fell, hitting the ground. I felt the flesh of arms hooking around my neck, pulling me down.

"Help! Help me!" cried a face that could have been my own mirrored in front of me, mouth open and gasping, eyes ridden with despair.

"Keep going!" the creature barked.

I pulled away and tumbled down the river of flailing arms, legs, faces, and torsos, a mindless fear driving me forward.

"Walk," it said. "We've got a long road ahead of us."

And behind me, the creature began to hum a tune that I had heard once before.

RHEA DANIEL *is an artist and aspiring writer living in Mumbai, India. She loves making jewelry, bookbinding, hand lettering, journaling, dancing, and has her fingers in way too many pies. To keep up with what she's currently up to you can follow her blog @* rheadaniel.tumblr.com.

"Look!" Jonas said. Outside the town was the bottle heap.

At least two meters high and stretching, Tara thought, a hundred meters or more. There had to be many, many thousands of glass bottles there, brown, green, and clear. Decades of men with nothing else to do but drink, and no one wanting to pay the money to move the bottles, and to where? Now the bottle collectors brought more in, adding to the heap.

Jonas parked the station wagon and caravan head first, sitting it next to the ute. Dale sighed.

"I'm not backing it in, Dad," Jonas said, but he smiled at his father.

The priest, his sleeves rolled up, his face a sheen of sweat in the heat, said, "Welcome to Bottletown. We're just brewing a cuppa so your timing is perfect."

Tara thrust a hat on to keep the worst of the rays off and they followed the priest up the main street. They'd seen two dozen or so derelict worker's houses on the way in; here was where they'd spent their time when not working or at home. Five pubs (with a sixth burnt to the ground), a general store, a police station, a bank, and a post office, all built of galvanized iron, their red roofs dull now.

The sky was wide open all around them. The three trees she could see were spindly, long past rescuing, although by the rocks placed in a circle around each one, somebody had cared once.

The Post Office often represented the center of community in these towns and here was no different. The front yard was like an art exhibition of things left behind: children's bikes, long bones, petrified pieces of wood, and concrete garden gnomes. Tara wondered why they were still there, why the yard hadn't been stripped.

Inside, the tea was laid out. It was much cooler in there, almost bearable, and after the tea and dry biscuits Tara lingered, curious about what else was left behind.

Very little, she found, just the odd stamp or two and an old milk can.

The community noticeboard held Christmas cards from decades earlier, notices of land sales, an invitation to a wedding, death notices, obituaries, and news stories. She read about an elderly German couple whose car broke down in the outback and who were found weeks later. "They panicked and left their vehicle," a policeman was quoted as saying.

He hums as he plays, stacking blocks in tall wooden steeples . . .

CHEMIROCHA

by Charlie Human

Readers' Advisory: Although this anthology has been classified as "horror" (albeit broadly-themed and quiet), the following selection has no horror in it.

Really, it hasn't a dark aspect at all, but rather it's a beautiful little anecdote about the personification of a pop song in South Africa.

Such is the fun and license of editing an anthology, that the editor can include rich voices such as author Charlie Human's that help expand the boundaries of this book's vision. For at the least, this is still speculative fiction and that embodies any number of aspects to progress the unique, the expressive, and the literary imagination: And herein lies all that in the mystical legend of the Chemirocha.

A POP SONG GETS CAUGHT IN BARBED WIRE. Entangled, the sweet and repetitive murmur starts to rip, tearing at the corners and dancing hopelessly in Cape Town's southeast wind. There it stays through hot, dry days and cold, wet nights.

Passersby don't notice it whipping like a flag in the breeze. But as they pass, its murmur, its whisper, its sad, lonely lullaby grasps at their minds and makes them whistle or hum or dig their hands deeper into their pockets.

The song is locked in a deadly struggle for survival. It could give up, let its harmony unwind, its structure unravel and slide limp and lifeless through the chain-link fence. But it doesn't. It may be a pop song, designed only as ephemera, destined to be discarded. It could die like a one-hit wonder is supposed to.

But it doesn't.

Something... It could be part of the dark river, some fluid, some ooze that splashes across it. In the moment of that splash the song is galvanized, it yearns: the stolid men and women who slump by on their way to work. The stubbornness, the resilience, the sheer, harsh *fuck-you!* that seems to resound in the human heart like a constant ringing bell. That is what the pop song wants.

It draws bits from the humans that walk by. It goes for the shiny parts like a magpie. It goes for the hidden parts like a hunter. It weaves itself together until it has arms and legs.

It weaves itself together until someone sees it.

"My god, boy!" a man says, and he cuts away the barbed wire with shears. "How did you get up there?"

The man puts the boy—the song—gently on the ground and wraps a coat around his tiny bloodied flesh. "We need to get you to a hospital."

A murmur in reply, the pop refrain is ragged and torn. But still there. Still playing. Still alive.

Then come bright lights.

"What's your name?" a voice attached to a face with glasses asks.

He doesn't know. A song is a song. It doesn't need to know what to call itself. But now he's no longer just a song, so he must try.

"Tok," he says, the sound of his voice, the word, tinkling in his own ears; it resonates, this opening note.

Tok, he repeats to himself. A name he knows from somewhere. One of the passersby perhaps? Or a nametag on a nurse's uniform?

"Tok," the doctor says with a short nod and a flourish of his pen. "Good."

Tok, tok, tok. The sound of bird at the window. *Tok, tok, tok. Screeee, screee.*

The song is a boy, and the boy is alive.

Then come more doctors who watch him play through the glass.

"We can't find his parents," the doctor with the glasses says. "We can't find anything. It's like he doesn't exist."

But he does exist, now, and his voice is getting stronger. He hums as he plays, stacking blocks in tall wooden steeples. *Mhmmmm, mhmmmmm, mhmmm.* He pulls sounds from everywhere, *aaaaahh, eeeee, rrrrrr.*

At some point he's no longer a pop song, this boy, he's beyond that.

The doctor brings him clothes, an old pair of red corduroy dungarees that the boy wears without a shirt. His skin is dark with a pattern of freckles that rise and fall on his back.

"What are those?" the doctor with glasses asks another doctor.

"Notes," the other doctor says. "They look like notes."

The notes seem to blur. The doctor blinks. *Did they shift? No, they couldn't . . .* The boy in the red dungarees continues testing his voice. He sings low, *ooooooo.* He sings high, *eeeeeee.*

The doctor with the glasses talks to him.

"Ben," the doctor says. "That's my name, Tok." He gets the uneasy feeling that the boy is just listening to the sounds his words make, not the meaning. That meaning is an irritation to this boy. That raw sound is all he wants.

"Ben," the boy sings. "*Bennnnnn.*"

The doctor feels unnerved. He scribbles things down on his notepad but it's just to do something, to hold onto meaning. He feels the boy's sounds sucking him in.

"*Bennnn,*" the resonance of the boy's voice shakes his skull.

The doctor scurries away.

Tok, the boy in the red dungarees, paces up and down in between the spires he has built with blocks. Only he can see their pattern. He climbs onto the edge of his bed to get a view of their rise and fall.

Notation.

Tok, the boy, was brought into this world as a song. Now he is creating his own.

He was a pop song, ephemeral, abandoned. A song abandoned eventually disappears. A child abandoned becomes angry.

The song he is writing becomes mountainous, it is peaks and cliffs, it is high manic wailing and low keening. *Eeeearrrgghhhoooo.*

The doctor, Ben, is worried. This boy, so strange, so strange. As a doctor he thinks he should sedate him, keep him safe, contained.

But the song makes something in his chest crack, a glacier splitting. Memories pour through. He remembers things he's forgotten, things he swore he'd forget, events he would give everything to relive.

They pour through his carefully constructed defenses. He's put a lot of work into who he is, and in an instant that song sweeps it all away. He's a child again. Small, alone, one note in a vast silence.

He sits on the edge of Tok's bed and listens, tears streaming down his face. "Tok," he says. "Please. What do you want?"

The boy in the red dungarees stops singing and looks at him. "My sister. I want my sister."

All songs are connected, anchored deep in the language of sound. How do you find an angry, abandoned song's sister?

Aaaahhhhh. Meaning is superficial. You just follow. One note after another.

Ben finds himself outside of the hospital, walking on feet that are too fast. He can barely keep up with himself. The sound drives him.

Sister notes. Scales. Harmony.

In a world of sound, a sister could be anything. The sound of a car alarm ricocheting off suburban walls, two rough hands rubbing together for warmth, the mewling of a cat sluggishly nursing a fatal injury.

Ben wanders for hours, taking his shoes off so that he can feel the rhythm in the pavement, slowing down, dragging his feet, thirsty beyond anything he's ever experienced, a mystic in an urban desert begging for answers.

He knows when he is close. A record shop in a bad neighborhood. A glowing neon sign of a musical note. His burning bush.

He swings open the door and steps into the bright light.

The guy inside is tall, gaunt, and ponytailed. He takes one look at Ben and urges him to sit down.

"Tok," Ben croaks. "Tok."

"Tok, okay, man," the record shop guy says. "Tok. Yeah, yeah, man I get it." He drums his fingers on the counter. *Tok, tok, tok.*

"*Urgh,*" Ben says. "*Uhrmm.*" Meaning eludes him. He only has sound, and he can't explain it.

The record shop guy nods. "Okay, man, okay. I'm Travis. It's cool. Like, let's just listen to something, maybe? Until you feel like talking."

He walks the stacks, tapping his fingers on his chin. Which one, which one? Pulls a slim black LP from a shelf.

"This one has a story to it."

He slips the LP from its cover and places it carefully on a turntable behind the counter.

"Back in the '50s a bunch of British missionaries were in Kenya, right? And they played music on a gramophone to the Kipsigi tribe."

He raises a finger and gives Ben a smile. "These Kipsigis loved all the music, but they went wild for the country singer Jimmie Rodgers." He shakes his head. "That dude wails, man, like really wails. The Kipsigis listened to that and were like, wait a second, this isn't a man. This is a creature singing and wailing, some kind of half-human, half-antelope demigod."

Travis laughs. "They translated his name. Jimmie Rodgers became Chemirocha. And they created a song to mimic this mystical creature. True story." He lifts the arm of the turntable.

"This is the song, man. This is the Chemirocha."

When the needles hits the groove, Ben knows. He knows he's found what he's looking for. Tok's sister.

The haunting, lilting wail catches him by the hair and doesn't let him go. It wraps itself around him, a creature with horns and fur and spots like musical notes.

"Hey," Travis shouts. "Hey, man, where're you going?"

The Chemirocha has Ben in an embrace that he'll never escape. Ben knows that. The memories have all returned. He understands things that before he could only catch glimpses of on the edges of his consciousness.

That's why he was so inhibited as a teen. *That's* why he let relationships gradually dissolve. *That's why everything.*

Ahhheerggaaaa.

He returns to the hospital on unsteady feet, carrying the Chemirocha on his back.

Tok is waiting for them in his room, his hands in the pockets of his red dungarees.

Ben stops in the doorway, waiting as Tok walks toward them, slowly pushing over the block spires as he goes. Then he smiles and kneels as Tok reaches them. The Chemirocha unwinds itself from him, pulling bits of him away as it unravels. Ben lets them go for they don't matter. They're notes that don't contribute to the song.

The Chemirocha is tall, translucent, spotted with a Rorschach pattern. Tok places his forehead against its flat face. A song who became a boy, and a myth who became a song.

Ben feels the world fading into one single note.

Aaaaaaaaaaaaaaaaa . . .

CHARLIE HUMAN *is a denizen of South Africa's small but ferocious speculative fiction scene. His two novels have been published in nine countries.* Apocalypse Now Now, *his first novel, has been optioned for film—with* District 9 *co-writer Terri Tatchell writing the script. Charlie has an MA in Creative Writing from the University of Cape Town.*

. . . there were creatures much hungrier
in the forest than bears and wolves.

HONEY

by Valya Dudycz Lupescu

Outside of purposeful violence (military action, terrorism, etc.), there are few events in modern memory that inspire such horror as 1986's Chernobyl nuclear disaster in Ukraine, which released four hundred times more radioactive material than the atomic bombing of Hiroshima. The catastrophe has left a legacy of widespread fears regarding radioactive-related illness, monstrous mutations, and slow death.

And although much of the surrounding region is still officially quarantined as "uninhabitable," there are people who nonetheless make that land their home, residing in forests where ghosts are said to move through the poisoned trees... people like aging Luba Ivanova, who will not leave behind the memories of her life. Author Valya Dudycz Lupescu shares with us this plaintive tale—as bitter-sweet as the balm of a bee sting—that wishes a good life lead to the sweetness of Honey.

L UBA HAD GROWN TO LIKE THE STINGING—NOT JUST the relief it brought to her swollen, twisted hands, but the prick itself. She imagined it must be like getting a tattoo. Her husband had had his name crudely tattooed on his arm during the war. Or was it in the displaced persons camps afterward? Such details got lost, they were less important to hold onto than other memories. Happier ones.

She knelt beside her husband's grave in front of the hollowed-out log and listened to the buzzing deep inside. It was a soothing sound that reminded her of concentrating in the night to hear Kalyna's breathing when she had been a baby, a nightly ritual to make sure that her daughter did not follow her older brother into death's embrace. Kalyna eventually did, but many years later... From cancer brought on by the bright betrayal of too many sun-bleached days on the coast of the Black Sea.

Luba placed her hand atop the log and felt the soft vibration. It throbbed familiar and comforting, so similar to the feeling of resting her hand atop her husband's chest as his heartbeat slowly stopped. She had touched so much death with her hands: resting her head as a child atop the starving body of her mother while her mother's hair came away in clumps in Luba's small hands; squeezing in solidarity the hands of friends bruised and beaten at the hands of Nazi soldiers; the cold hands of corpses she helped carry into the mass graves; holding the fearful hands of wounded rebels and revolutionaries; the gnarled hands of other babas finally succumbing to old age or disease. Her time would come soon. But not yet. That was why she needed her hands, and why she loved her bees.

The steady enthusiasm of this hive was so different from her other hives. Each one had its own personality: the constant diligence of the three sister hives in the ancient wooden boxes she had inherited from her father, the wild and unpredictable energy of the hive in the birch tree in her garden, the quiet hum of the forest hives beside the river. She loved them all, and visiting them was one of the bright spots in her day. As she tended to them, Luba would talk about her day: collecting eggs from the chickens; chasing off the fox; harvesting her enormous garden full of tomatoes, potatoes, beets, and peas; foraging for mushrooms in the forest; collecting wild raspberries for jam; perhaps a visit from one of the scientists who came every few months to collect samples for radiation testing; or a rare but treasured visit from one of the other babas in the neighboring villages.

She kissed the bark of the wild hive. "Good morning, my darlings."

In many ways, a hive was more like a single creature than many individuals, working together much like her hands working with her arms working with her heart working with her imagination. Together. *When* they worked, that is. But that was why she came here for help, so that they *could* work.

Luba placed her bare hands inside the log, her youngest hive. Even without the usual sparse dusting of wormwood powder, the bees kept their distance and did not sting her all at once.

Luba began to sing to them, slowly moving her fingers to get their attention.

> *"Beloved sister bees,*
> *a few of you must surely be ready,*
> *a few of you must have lived long enough—*
> *a good life full of sweetness.*
> *Is it time to say farewell? To return to the earth?*
> *Would you gift me your venom before you go?*
> *Would you give me relief before I die?*
> *Would you trust me to help care for your sisters?*
> *Aren't we all sisters? Sisters all are we."*

She felt the first sting, and the second, but after that only heat and pressure as more and more stung her wrists and fingers. After a few deep breaths, Luba slipped her hands out from the hive. Those bees who sat atop her skin flew off, but a handful fell to the ground after completing their sting. More would get carried out of the hive to join their sisters in a small pile of dead at the base of the log.

Luba rubbed her hands to help spread the venom. Miracle creatures, they were. What kills one, can heal another—lessons learned from her father and grandfather. She watched as several dead or dying bees got tossed out to join the others on the ground. So good at handling their dead. For a moment Luba flashed back to the war, when she had been among the young people forced to dig the deep pits for mass graves. She shuddered with the weight of the remembrance.

She pulled out the bottle of *samohonka*, her homemade moonshine, from an apron pocket and poured a little onto each of the graves of her loved ones, allowing herself a small sip before closing it up and putting it back into her pocket.

"*Na zdorovya!*" she said aloud, then walked toward her house to finish the day's chores. Luba paused to pluck a few choice apples and pears off those trees heavy with beautiful shining fruit. Carrying them home in her apron, she thought about baking a nice apple cake sweetened with honey.

Tonight was the full moon, and that usually brought visitors to her house on the edge of the forest—young men in their secondhand army fatigues looking to stop someplace on their way to the *Chornobyl* Nuclear Power Plant near Pripyat. Luba wondered if they saw her as some sort of Baba Yaga, a witch guarding secrets they hoped to discover. She did not see *them* as the heroes of any folktale, and they had no idea that their "adventure" would lead them to an unhappy ending.

She felt bad about the first few, until she came to better understand their motivation. These boys were not like the young men of her own generation. No, these boys did not have war or famine or disaster to test their character, so they went looking for death in the "toxic" wilderness of her backyard. Eager to prove that they were even less afraid of radiation poisoning than of police and guards and scientists, they dared each other to drink the muddy waters and eat in the archaic cottages of one of the dozens of old babas who, like herself, had found ways to sneak back into their homes, back into the Exclusion Zone after being forced to evacuate.

Luba felt anger course through her, and she squeezed one of the apples in her newly-healed fist until she felt the skin break and juices spill out over her fingers. She and the other babas had walked on foot for kilometers, crawled under fences, and snuck through brambles to reclaim their cottages and gardens and graves. This was *their* land, not the playground of foolhardy young men eager to take advantage of their hospitality and loneliness. The boys' rebellion served no noble purpose, just a desire for the fleeting fame that came from photographs and videos of their "daring adventures."

She steadied herself against an ancient birch tree, the same one she and her sister used to sit beneath as girls. Luba relaxed her rounded back and shoulders against the trunk, released the tension in her face and neck, and closed her eyes to feel the energy of that tree, another sister in this place. She smiled. The babas knew something the young ones did not. These boys had forgotten that there were older and more dangerous things in the ground than buried radioactive buses, and there were creatures much hungrier in the forest than bears and wolves. Let them come. Nature has her own rules, stronger than the folly of these young men.

LUBA SAT BESIDE her table, the only light from a single oil lamp and from the fire burning in the stove. The table was dressed with her finest embroidered tablecloth, delicate red and black cross-stitch from the days when her fingers could more steadily hold the tiny needle and thread. Atop the cloth was a bowl of bright red *borscht* beside plates of still-steaming potato *varenyky* and *kapusta*, cucumbers and tomatoes tossed in dill, sliced *salo*, homemade pickles, and fresh baked apple cake. Everything must eat, her own Baba used to say. A hungry dog is stronger than a satisfied wolf.

She whispered, "Never let it be said that Luba Ivanova let a guest go hungry."

Outside the window the moon shone over the tops of the trees. Luba waited, hand around her teacup. She would not touch any food until her guests arrived, and if they did not arrive by midnight, she would pack up the food until the next night. It was only a matter of time. Her home was directly along the most commonly traveled path to Pripyat. One of the scientists had once told her that her tiny cottage even appeared in a popular computer game set in *Chornobyl*, making it a "tourist destination." Besides, she had seen more strange shadows than usual gathering in the trees the past few nights, and the flickering of so many glowing eyes from her window. The forest was restless. Hungry. Luba smiled and sipped her tea, waiting for the knock.

At ninety years of age, she was patient and unafraid. She had nothing for them to steal: her small pension was well hidden, her food was readily shared, and her body was too old and broken. All she had left was time and memories. And her home.

Home was why she and the other babas had returned to the land that held their mothers and fathers and children. This land was her family, and she was a part of it. They all were, and they knew that the ancestors and nature spirits would ultimately be stronger than the poison that human beings spilled into the air and soil. One by one the babas were taking their turn to feed the land, like the Motherland had always fed them. It was their bond and their promise.

The land must be loved and cared for. It was part of the cycle of life and death. For creation, there must be destruction. Sometimes the sacrifice was gentle and peaceful in one's old bed with honey on their lips; sometimes it was sudden and bloody with bits of bone and teeth left behind.

Luba saw the branches swaying with more force outside her window. The winds had picked up. Perhaps a storm? Or perhaps the creatures in the woods were getting restless, hungry? She had grown up with stories about the dangers: folk tales of hairy backward tricksters deep in the woods, tortured souls of drowned women waiting in rivers, haggard old women in huts on the edges of civilization—

Knock. Knock. Knock.

She jumped.

Knocking, again, but it was against her window, not the door. Luba crossed herself and listened to the noises increasing outside: the howling of the wolves, the owl nearby, the crying of something like a child farther off, and a faint whistling that seemed to be coming closer.

Nature had found ways to reclaim the spaces where men had built towers and fences: trees broke through the concrete, vines wore down brick and mortar, the city and nearby towns were transformed into wilderness faster than Luba would have thought possible.

She thought back to the first waves of young men who wandered into the Zone dressed in shades of green, their faces smeared with paint, their backpacks filled with cameras and video recorders. Like forest creatures come out of the trees, she thought of the first time two men came out of the trees and greeted her. Then a familiar but ancient panic as she remembered so many other young men with a similar hunger in their eyes who had also come out of the trees—when Russian and German armies marched through during the war leaving broken homes and gardens and women in their wake.

But these were not those. These boys were neither magical creatures nor monsters. They had Ukrainian faces. So much like her son.

The face in her window looked *so* much like her son Mykola that she initially thought him a ghost and inhaled sharply, crossing herself. Then as his breath made warm fog on the glass, she jumped to her feet to answer the door.

"*Dobriy vechir, Babusia!*" said the young man with a dramatic bow in her direction. "I see you have dinner set out. Do you have enough for a poor traveler?"

This one did not barge in like so many others had before him. He stood on the threshold and waited for her to invite him. He was a polite one, at least, she thought to herself. Perhaps they would have a little conversation before his imminent disappearance.

"I do, and you are welcome," she said and gestured for him to join her at the table. He took off his shoes and then came in, sitting down at the table opposite her teacup. Luba took her place across from him and began to pile food onto his plate, watching his eyes dart from dish to dish. Still he waited to eat until she had also served herself, and only then did he take the first bite. She watched him eat hungrily. It was a hungry kind of night.

"What are you doing here?" she asked in between spoonfuls of borscht. "Have you come to explore the abandoned town like so many others before you?"

"Not exactly," the young man answered, straightening his shirt and smoothing down his trousers. "I'm an artist."

"Is that so?" she asked. She wondered what kind of art. Another photographer, no doubt, trying to make new money on old images, since they all went to the same places: the ruins of the Palace of Culture, the overgrown fairground and rusted Ferris wheel, the peeling paint on the children's classroom mural, so many broken dolls with gas masks and missing limbs.

Her visitor moved like a cat, long and lean with smooth fluid movement. Luba looked at his hands that seemed rough and strong. At least he was not one of these boys with manicured nails and baby-soft fingers.

"I'm a sculptor," the young man said. "I make things with my hands, and I like to incorporate things from the world around me that I find. I like to create things that most people cannot see. I especially like to go to places that are abandoned, to find secrets there and share them with my art."

Luba nodded and pulled her shawl tighter around her as he talked about sculptures that he'd made from bark and branches, copper and wire. He had a nice voice, and she liked the way he kept looking in her eyes when he spoke. It would have made her blush when she was younger. Back then, Luba would have looked away because her mama always told her that she should play coy with boys. Thankfully she was past such games now. She held the young man's gaze and looked at the way he studied her. It made her smile.

"What are you thinking, Babusia?" the young man asked her.

She did not tell him that she was wondering what manner of beast or spirit would scoop him up after he left her house. She did not say that she hoped his affairs were in order. She never told them. She never warned them. It seemed a betrayal to the forest.

Luba was loyal to the land in a way that these young men could never understand, a promise renewed when she gratefully placed that small handful of dirt into her mouth after returning home. She was of this earth, and the forest was her family—the only one she had left.

"It is nice that you do not chew with your mouth open," she answered. "And you are very well-mannered. Your mama did a good job."

He gave her a grin that would have melted her young girl's heart. "It is nice that you are such a good cook, and you are a very good listener. Your children are lucky."

At that, she put her hand to her chest.

"They were not lucky," she said.

He frowned and reached over to touch her arm.

"I'm sorry," he said. "I didn't mean to make you sad."

She pushed his hand away. Then she reached for her samohonka. "Would you like a taste?" she asked. "For luck?"

He grinned again. "Please."

They first toasted to each other's health. With the second shot they toasted to Ukraine's freedom, and after that to family, then friends, followed by poetry, fine cheese, and the cleverness of foxes. Luba welcomed the warmth that flooded her body with each sip. It was a nicer evening than she'd had in months. The last visitors, three months prior, had been rude and gruff, two large men who ignored her completely and ate like pigs. She was not sorry to see them go, nor sad when she found strips of their shirts braided with hair tied to the tree down the path from her house. She was not sure if the bones she later saw on the riverbank and arranged in neat piles were theirs, but she suspected they were.

"It must be lonely here," the young man said to her. He had pulled a notebook and pencil out from his pack and was softly sketching something. She closed her eyes and listened to the gentle scratching sound. Soon it was joined by soft whistling from outside, still far off but carried closer by the wind.

"It's quiet," Luba said. "But that's not the same as lonely."

Neither one of them spoke for a while.

"What about you?" Luba asked him. "You choose to travel alone, to places where there are few people. Are *you* lonely?"

The young man smiled, and Luba was once more reminded of a cat.

"Like you, I appreciate the quiet," he said. "It helps me to understand that we are never really alone."

The young man sketched, and Luba listened as, all around them, the night seemed to get louder. He did not jump when the wolf howled. He said nothing when there was a crash in the woodpile, and he just kept sketching when the inhuman laughing began not far outside her door. Luba had grown used to all the sounds, but strangers usually found them unsettling at best. One young man several years ago ran out of her home and into the rainstorm leaving behind his camera and bag. She left them on the road the next morning.

"There are many still alive here?'" he asked, but it was not really a question.

"A few of us came back home after the evacuation, and many things that live here never left," she said, opening her eyes to stare out the window into the darkness. "Some have changed. A few have died off. Most I recognize, some I do not." She paused remembering her early explorations after returning home. "The worst of all is the Red Forest. A graveyard of trees stripped and stained red that remind me too much of Stalin's skeletal sacrifices during the *Holodomor*."

"I am haunted by a story I heard on a documentary when I was a boy," the young man said, "about birds living in the Red Forest who fly in and out of holes in the reactor building. I have dreamt of those birds ever since, sketched and sculpted them my entire life. Can you imagine? Such misshapen magical things able to come and go in a place both poisonous and beautiful."

Luba did not have to imagine. Many times she had watched the birds in Pripyat. In the early days she never knew when one of them might suddenly fall to the ground, dead or dying. She always tried to find and bury them, saying a little prayer for their souls—tiny victims of human folly.

He looked at her. "Of course you know."

Luba fought against her heart softening for this strange young man.

"There is something about those birds that started me on this path," the sculptor said, and Luba didn't know if he meant the path to Pripyat or his choice to be an artist, but she didn't want to interrupt him.

"I think that magical things happen in places of great tragedy," he said. Luba could not argue.

He continued, "Do you know about the large dam that Stalin's troops blew up in 1941? In Zaporizhzhya?"

Luba shook her head. She knew about many things that happened in the war, but mostly only to her and her family and friends.

"As the Nazis were making their way through Ukraine," the sculptor continued, "Stalin's police blew up the hydroelectric dam to slow their advance. But it flooded the nearby villages along Dnipro river and killed tens of thousands of people."

"I am not surprised," she said. "Stalin had so much blood on his hands." Luba looked down at her hands, wriggled her fingers, and said a tiny prayer of thanks to the bees.

"I went there and spent several nights sleeping outdoors along the Dnipro river," said the sculptor. "I like to look for things that no one else can see—legends and mythic creatures. I came home to my studio with a bag full of driftwood and wreckage and photographs, and I created a mobile of *rusalky* dancing in the air. They are terrifying and lovely, drowned souls dancing in pain and pleasure. It's hanging in a gallery in Zaporizhzhya.

"Those nights on the river continue to inspire me—I listened to the rusalky singing and weeping from my tent. I still dream of their songs."

"I think he must be a lucky boy," she said softly.

She had been in the habit of talking to herself for years, but usually only when she was alone. Luba was embarrassed when she realized that she had done so in front in the sculptor.

"I mean *you*," she said, "you must be a lucky boy."

Maybe it would be enough to save him? Maybe he would be the first? Maybe he would come back. To see her.

"And you must be getting tired," the sculptor said. "I suppose I should leave soon, so that I can reach the city."

She thought again of warning him. Would that be a betrayal? She had made a promise to protect this land and all her creatures. They were all connected, like the bees. Luba wished she could ask another of the babas, but they never spoke overtly of the strange lights that flickered in the trees, or the blood in pools at the roots, or the wreaths of hair floating on the surface of the river.

To talk about these things felt wrong somehow, so the babas hinted around them instead. They discussed new additions for their bottle trees—a suggestion from one of the scientists, who told them that sliding colored glass bottles onto the branches of a tree close to the home would entice and trap evil spirits. Luba and her friends embraced the tradition with enthusiasm and traded colored bottles the way children once traded marbles: a blue one for a green, an amber one for a red, and so on. They shared flasks of holy water, compared samohonka recipes, and remembered prayers and blessings. On one of their infrequent reunions, they might admire the colored glass gleaming so bright in the sunlight, praising each one for doing its job of trapping evil spirits, daring to ask if there were many more wild animal attacks around than usual. They spoke often about death, but in the language of symbol and story.

"You could stay here," she offered, for the first time, "tonight. My couch is soft and my home is warm, and the night is not kind to strangers." It made her a little sad to think of finding traces of the sculptor in the woods in the weeks to come, a patchwork of skin and bone.

He looked surprised. "I should go, but thank you."

He set down his sketchpad. Luba tried to take a look at what he had been drawing, but he folded his hands on top of it. "You are a most kind and generous hostess."

He grinned at her, and this time she could feel a flush warm her cheeks. Something crashed against the outside wall, and then the sound of nails or claws scratching against wood. Without flinching, he looked around the cabin. "Are you never afraid?"

"No. Not in my home. Not for myself. This place, this land, all of it—it is a part of me. It is in my blood." She poured them each a final shot of samohonka, emptying the bottle. "I was never more afraid than those nights after evacuation, when we didn't know what was happening, when we didn't know whether or not we'd ever be able to return home. Those nights, away from here, I thought I was going to die. I knew that if I stayed there, I would."

She looked into the eyes of this boy who so much resembled her son. "I am old, and I have lived a long and full life. I am not afraid of dying, but I am afraid of dying away from here. That is the only thing I fear."

The lamp on the table turned on and off. It was another sign she had come to recognize—after the loud crash and the laughter always came the flickering light. Luba stood up, feeling the weight of her years in each joint.

"Then I would not worry if I were you, Babusia," said the sculptor, stepping closer to take her arm to steady her. "I do not think there is a force in Hell that could take you from this place."

She envied him the strength and confidence of his youth, so like a tree she might lean against, so certain that he could withstand any storm.

"May I have one last slice of your delicious cake with a little honey to take with me?" the sculptor asked with a dramatic bow.

"You may," she said with a small curtsy, then she packed him a small package. Luba knew it was futile, but perhaps the birds and bears might find his bundle and enjoy the snack.

She walked him to the door and as he stood there against it, she was overwhelmed with the desire to reach over and hug him, as she had long ago hugged her own son. But she couldn't. She felt frozen to the spot, and emotion welled up in her throat and chest and eyes.

"What is it, Babusia?" he asked. "Is there something wrong? Are you hurting?"

On cue, the window rattled and the walls of her home squeaked as if under strong pressure. Luba's chest felt tight and her knees weak.

"Nothing. It's nothing," she said. They stood looking at each other, the sculptor and the baba.

Luba wondered what was out there this night, what would catch him, whether or not he would fight, if he could possibly escape. She wondered what his family would think, if he would be missed, if the world would be worse off without his art. She had a feeling it might. Some people left bigger holes than others. Her own hole would be small, so very small. The holes left by death got smaller the fewer people left behind to remember.

He leaned over and kissed her cheek, and he smelled like the woods, like smoke and wet leaves and the deep brown forest musk that leaked into everything in autumn. "Be well, Babusia. Until our paths cross again."

After that, he turned and walked past her bottle tree and down the path into the woods. Luba quickly closed the door and leaned with her back against it surveying the room. She saw a piece of paper from the sculptor's sketchbook on the table and walked to it, all the while listening for signs of struggle outside. Luba turned the page over and saw a sketch of herself, an old, tired baba sitting beside the fire, and behind her stood all manner of creatures drawn lightly to look like ghosts or shadows, their claws sharp, the teeth pointed and dripping, their fur and clothes and scales splotched with mud or blood. She could not tell if they were standing there to attack her or support her.

Luba felt cold, and the hairs on her neck stood at attention, as if their eyes were actually upon her. Someone was watching. Something was gathering around her, and she started to feel breath coming closer, a movement of air, a low breeze at her ankles. Luba closed her eyes and thought about the song she sang for the bees:

"... You must surely be ready,
you must have lived long enough—
a good life full of sweetness.
Is it time to say farewell?"

She heard whistling outside, then screaming followed by laughter, and the sound of boots running up to her threshold. Her doorknob rattled and then stopped.

Luba concentrated on her breathing: in and out, in and out, unable to open her eyes. *It's time,* she said to herself over and over. *At least I'm home. It's time. I'm home. It's time. I'm home.*

A quiet knocking on her door, but Luba did not open her eyes. She could not move and tried to convince herself that it was the sculptor, changing his mind, coming back to stay. But she knew it wasn't. Luba knew that the sculptor was gone. It was not him.

Knock. Knock. Knock.

It's time.

VALYA DUDYCZ LUPESCU is the author of The Silence of Trees *and the founding editor of* Conclave: A Journal of Character. *With her partner, Stephen H. Segal, she is the co-author of the book* Geek Parenting: What Joffrey, Jor-El, Maleficent, and the McFlys Teach Us about Raising a Family *(Quirk Books) and the co-founder of the Wyrd Words storytelling laboratory. Valya earned her MFA in Writing from the School of the Art Institute of Chicago, and her poetry and prose have been published in* Kenyon Review, Gargoyle Magazine, Gone Lawn, Jersey Devil Press, Strange Horizons, Mythic Delirium, Scheherezade's Bequest, Abyss & Apex, *and others. Valya teaches at DePaul University in Chicago, and is currently at work on a novel set during the genocidal famine (Holodomor) of 1932–33 in Soviet Ukraine.*

He looks up at the star fruit . . .

WARNING: FLAMMABLE, SEE BACK LABEL

by Marcia Douglas

Statistics of slavery in the West Indies point to some of the most atrocious conditions in the history of human trade, with an estimated 80 to 90 percent of the islands' population being slaves, and with a death rate one-third higher than any other country engaged in the practice. It's no wonder, some of the darkest ghost tales come from this region, where large plantation estates were used for the production of sugar ("White Gold") and molasses, as well as leading by its byproduct to the distillation of rum.

*Marcia Douglas, novelist and professor of Caribbean Literature, brings us this next piece, a haunting flash fiction vignette of Jamaican history and reckoning, where the past catches up to the present. Before you consume that next bottle, consider your roots, and be sure to fully understand the advisory message—*Warning: Flammable, See Back Label.

Cask N°: 14
Bottle N°: 247

YOU EMPTY THE BOTTLE OF RUM IN THE KITCHEN sink. It is an expensive bottle, given to you as a present—the label, *Old Plantation,* in gold letters—but something is not right. Nights you dream dreams filled with running feet, and in the morning you wake with an urge to run. The lime tree outside your window leans so far to the side, the branches almost touch the ground. And there is something different about the taste of sugar in your tea. You are pleased to be rid of the rum drink.

It is half-day Friday; hot-sun, but time to clean the yard. All afternoon you rake mango leaves, bird feathers, and rotten breadfruit pods. You pile them in a heap to burn later on; your arms ache. When the children begin to come home from school, they pass the fence and throw stones to hit star fruit from the tree. One boy's stone lands on the verandah. His empty right sleeve flaps with no arm. You yell for them to leave, and they all run, laughing. Their feet kick up dust and it makes a red cloud; their voices weaken around the bend.

Inside, the kitchen smell is double distilled rum. You pour bleach in the sink; boil water for a cup of tea; sink into a chair; turn on the TV, wondering at the mysteries of bad rum, police violence, rigged elections, and the price of gasoline. Long after dinner and the seven o'clock news, the kitchen still smells of plantation gold. You take the rum bottle from the bin and sniff at the neck; such 40% estate blend can take one back three hundred years to a place of cane blossom—high sun and no water; the cane grown tall above your head; overseer's boots coming toward you. Such 40% can take one to a place of noise and churning—late year, and a boy feeding cane into a mill; it is your job to stand beside your friend and quick-quick cut off his arm if it gets stuck in the machine. And, *oi*, such 40% takes one to a room of heat and boiling; where it is your job, slave that you are, to test hot sugar with your elbow; overseer said, *Let the boy do it*; for too hot, and it sticks to limb and bone-oh, and you are good for this and nothing else. Hurry, hurry. The room is furious heat and vapor; you faint, and dark molasses drips—

where, a little unsteady on your feet now, you put the bottle back in the bin, turn off the kitchen light, and head for the bedroom. The walls are moon bright as the scent of dark blend permeates from the pillow beneath your head. You close your eyes, eager to fall asleep; a lizard crawls the ceiling. Something is dragging on the ground beneath your window; a tinny metal sound. You breathe in dark spice and try to ignore it, for you are so tired now, so tired. But the sound keeps on, making a perimeter—*tin-tin jingle*—around the house. The night is humid-hot, and you throw off the covers; 40% distilled cane-press fills your nostrils, every cell of you, and when at last you go to the window it is also because you are in need of air.

What you see, in half-moon light, is a metal chain on the ground, trailing the length of the wall. You lean over the windowsill, your eyes following the iron, but it continues around the south side. Then, at the bathroom window, you see it laps still around the next corner, moving slow and *clink-clink*. You are in the kitchen when the sound stops. The heat is so thick, you can hardly breathe. The refrigerator pauses its humming. The plates in the dish rack wait.

Through a slit in the curtain, you see him—a one-arm boy with a chain and collar around his neck. He is naked, except for molasses on his face and belly. Three hundred years, and he has not aged. He looks up at the star fruit; there is noise and churning; and you look down, and you are wearing overseer's boots, and have his whip in your hand.

MARCIA DOUGLAS grew up in Jamaica. She is the author of the novels, The Marvellous Equations of the Dread, Madam Fate, *and* Notes from a Writer's Book of Cures and Spells *as well as a poetry collection,* Electricity Comes to Cocoa Bottom. *Her work has appeared in journals and anthologies internationally. Her awards include a National Endowment for the Arts Fellowship, and a Poetry Book Society Recommendation. She is on faculty at the University of Colorado, Boulder, where she teaches creative writing and Caribbean literature.*

When it's Carnival, any joke is good fun!

ARLECCHINO

by Carla Negrini

One of Europe's best known historic figures of "devilish" note is that of Harlequin, originating as a checkered servant from the Italian form of masked theatre, Commedia dell'arte. Harlequin (Italian: Arlecchino) was introduced in the late 1500s and soon became a comedic devil-stock character who is nimble, mischievous, and often undermining or outwitting those around him through trickery. For centuries the character has been lauded, loathed, imitated, and cherished, and herein Italian author Carla Negrini brings her own take... for those who hate Harlequin most, earn his greatest attention.

And especially be most cautious during Carnival, for the laughs of Arlecchino may not always be of mirth.

I am the most cunning and the most mischievous,
and the emperor of the whole Carnival;
I offend everyone and scowl
at those who grow sick of it.
It's a bad habit, you know,
to always say the truth!

—Translation of Italian Harlequin Rhyme

FEBRUARY. THE TIME OF YEAR I HATE MOST. THE reason why I'd like to erase this month off the face of the Earth dates back to a couple years ago: the fourteenth of February, 2015.

Her name was Claudia. We'd been together for two years, then. I was the affair of her life: an attractive thirty-year-old career man, owner of a wine company and a villa in the center of Bergamo. She was a model, such a perfect beauty that not even Michelangelo could have sculpted anything like that in his masterpieces. I was crazy for her. A part of me thought that Claudia cared only for my money, but the other part, the silliest part, honestly believed in that woman's love. Man, how blind I was.

On Valentine's Day, I took Claudia out to dinner in Bergamo Alta's best restaurant. Unfortunately, that year Valentine's was on the day before the historic Carnival's parade. All around the city were banners and colored streamers, while in the shops' windows mannequins were dressed as Punchinello or Meneghino, and children ran in the streets, throwing confetti while wearing their own Carnival costumes.

See, the Carnival in Bergamo cannot be compared in grandeur to the ones celebrated in Venice or Viareggio, but everybody's so happy that they don't care if the decorated wagons are small and poor, and the music weak and out of tune. One way or another, everybody finds a way to celebrate and have fun.

But if others were happy in that period of the year, I've always felt anxious and depressed. I hate Carnival, and when I was a child, it scared me to death. Let alone the crazy, vulgar costumes that my mother forced me and my brother to put on, I was frightened by the masks, those devils on the loose in the streets playing nasty tricks, those witches with their spells made of colored streamers, those clowns with their full heads of hair and their big red noses. Even super heroes and cowboys made me cower, and I'd always run from those children, with their Hulk or gunslinger costumes, with their plastic weapons or rubber fists. I feel silly now, but I was a small and fragile child, back then, and I always ran under my mama's skirt at the first sign of trouble. When she died of cancer, I was only twelve. I had to roll up my sleeves and fight my fears, and eventually I became one of the richest men in town. But my hatred for Carnival had grown with me through the years. Should I have children, one day, I would forbid them to put on a Carnival costume and make fools of themselves with all those other idiots!

Unfortunately, even the restaurant where Claudia and I were having dinner was celebrating the Carnival. Waiters and waitresses were dressed up like all the typical Italian figures: Brighella, Pantalone, Punchinello, Columbine, and many others. Claudia was talking, but I was distracted and could barely follow her words. I felt very uneasy. If it hadn't been Valentine's Day, I would have already asked for the bill and got out of that damn restaurant. I would have sought shelter in my villa, turned on my PC, chosen a piece by Verdi or Rossini from YouTube, cranked up the volume, and relaxed on my sofa listening to that wonderful music. That was the only way I could calm down and forget what was happening outside my mansion's walls. But that evening I could not run. I wanted to give Claudia her gift, and I didn't want to back away, despite the mood around us. Thinking about it all, I kept fidgeting with the little red box in my pocket that contained an 18-karat diamond ring.

We were just having our appetizers when I decided to end the meal and give her the ring without waiting for the main course, the dessert, and the champagne. I couldn't bear that noisy and garish place anymore, and with my grand gesture I would have justified my sudden impatience; I would have made her happy and we would have been free to run away from the restaurant and take shelter under the sheets, where to make love until the next morning. I put the little box on the table and then froze, as if turned to stone by the face of Medusa. My stupor, however, was not due to that mythological creature, but to a creature of Bergamo: *Harlequin!*

Actually, he was just a waiter with the typical leather mask of Harlequin, covering his face from brow to nose. But it was like I'd seen the Devil himself, or a monster come to chew on my insides. When I was a child, that was the Carnival costume that scared the shit out of me more than any other. It was my Uncle Marco's fault. The first time Momma brought me to celebrate the Carnival out in the squares, my uncle had a Harlequin costume on, and he played a horrible trick on me by leaping from the shadows and pretending to be a Harlequin-devil; he chased me through alleys, waving his wooden cudgel and laughing hysterically just to hear me squeal. Months after, I had terrifying dreams where Harlequin-masked demons blocked me in a corner and beat me with huge cudgels, even though my uncle had later told me it was all "just a joke for fun!"

The Harlequin-waiter poured red wine into my glass, then walked to the next table to do the same with other guests. I was speechless for some time staring at that scarlet fluid in my glass that looked like blood. Should I drink it, I wondered, or should I throw the wine in that monster's face?

I was snapped out of my reverie when Claudia started yelling she'd had enough. I tried to calm her down and tell her I was sorry for my odd behavior. I blamed that period of the year, so hard on my nerves, and the Harlequin-waiter who'd distracted me.

But Claudia was unexpectedly furious.

It was not just for my present mood. All evening, she had tried to tell me that our relationship was coming to an end, but I hadn't been listening to a single word she said, just smiling and nodding casually. She said we were growing distant, and that she'd taken to seeing another man. I wordlessly stared at her. What kind of person leaves their partner on Valentine's Day?

Claudia got to her feet and walked out. I ran after her, grabbed her by an arm, and tried to make her change her mind with words that came out only in sputters. I squeezed her harder, meaning only for her to know how much she meant to me . . . She slapped me and walked out of my life forever.

When I came back to our table, the other customers were glancing at me with pity in their eyes. I was desperate, but also furious. When I calmed down, I decided to go home, get drunk, and offer the ring to Rosita, my maid. I would fuck her all night long, without stopping even if she begged me to. But when I looked for the ring on the table, I noticed that the little red box was missing. I didn't search for it, because in the same moment out of the corner of my eye I saw the Harlequin-dressed waiter sneaking away. I was sure he'd stolen my ring.

In a blind rage, I followed him into the alley behind the restaurant while he spoke on his cell phone. When I got to him, I grabbed the phone from his hand and threw it on the pavement. I heard its screen crack and laughed at the joy I felt with that brutal act. I couldn't celebrate much longer though, because Harlequin punched me in the face! If I was in a rage before, then I completely lost control. I kicked him in the groin and took him down; I matched his punch with my own, grabbed a fistful of his hair, and started slamming his head onto the concrete pavement, one, two, three times, and then again. Blood ran from his nose and ears, splattering the sidewalk.

When I stopped, he was dead.

I started going through his pockets, searching for my ring, but didn't find it. Suddenly, I heard the howl of approaching sirens: the police.

I panicked and ran without looking back. I hid in another alley and stayed there for what seemed an eternity, my heart pounding and my initial elation fading, leaving room for doubt and confusion. *What had I done?* I'd just killed a man. What was wrong with me? But then I also tried to justify myself—he *deserved* it. He'd stolen my diamond ring, and if only I hadn't panicked because of that damn police siren, I would have surely found it.

And further, an elated part of me thought, I had obtained a childhood revenge: I'd killed the monster who had haunted me since I was six.

But I needed to remain realistic, so decided to go home and call my lawyer. I was lost in thought when I heard a laugh ringing in my ears. I looked around, but saw nobody. I was alone with my stupid face, there in that alley.

An icy gust of wind ripped the air. I hugged myself and started walking home, trying to walk casually, to look innocent and calm. Around me, groups of masked youngsters swore and listened to loud music with their iPhones. They looked like so many evil spirits. They glared at me and sniggered. I knew they were making fun of me, of this hollow-eyed man with the word *ASSASSIN* carved on his face.

I'd not gone much farther before I heard that laugh again . . . I turned, and it was like a boulder smashing onto my shoulders—before my eyes I saw a figure illuminated by the streetlight: Harlequin!

I knew he wasn't the man I'd killed, but the one who haunted my dreams, with his multicolored costume, black shoes, white hat, and wooden cudgel in hand. The mask covering his face was horrendous, more than the waiter's, like a monster had descended in Hell, flayed the Devil himself, and made that mask with his own demonic skin.

At his sight I ran and didn't look back, but the more I tried to get away, the more I felt him nearing. I heard his cudgel cracking everything along the way, grinding against metal fences with a grating and irritating sound, and I heard him laugh at my desperation at the top of his lungs. When I was finally out of breath and my spleen felt on the point of exploding, I stopped and hid behind a dumpster. I thought I'd managed to lose him, and felt a short moment of relief. I was slumped on the pavement, my eyes closed from the exertion of running. But when I opened my eyes again, I realized I was just a plaything of the monster... On the dumpster and the walls of the buildings around me were dozens of Harlequin faces made with spray paint, and under each of them was writing: *When it's Carnival, any joke is good fun!* I felt every hair on my body stand up in fear, my skin covering in goosebumps.

That mischievous laugh slowly returned, ratcheting up in volume, and I saw Harlequin's monstrous shadow on the wall near my hiding place, approaching. My eyes fell on a metal bar underneath the dumpster. I grabbed it and charged him.

My enemy yelled something I didn't comprehend. I hit him, and kept on so, shouting all sorts of obscenities. I didn't want to stop. I needed to get rid of him once and for all.

An arm wrapped around my neck and hands grabbed me all over, brutally pulling me back. I didn't understand what was happening until someone punched me in the stomach and the metal bar was yanked from my hands. Three men forced me to my knees, while a fourth helped up my assailant. I yelled out to be careful, to finish off that monster before he could kill us all! One of the strangers struck me in the face, shouting that I was nuts. When Harlequin was back on his feet, I couldn't believe my eyes. I was looking at a kid who couldn't be more than sixteen years old. He wasn't even wearing a costume, but just had on a patched-up jacket that could vaguely resemble the costume of the monster I'd run from.

Then the cops came. During the investigations, many witnesses said they saw me running like a madman through the city streets, but no Harlequin monster was ever seen following. As they handcuffed me, an officer went through the pockets of my Armani suit and found that little red box. I hadn't realized I'd put it there myself, back in the restaurant. I laughed, and when I heard the sound, I recognized it as Harlequin's own.

It's been two years since they locked me up for murder, and I won't get out of this cold cell for a long, long time. Worse, since being behind bars, Harlequin has found delight in haunting my nightmares again, making every day his own Carnival. There he whispers in my sleep, *Ah, the jokes to come, the jokes to come!*

CARLA NEGRINI was born in 1990 and lives in Italy. During her years of education, she attended the Art Institute, graduated in Graphic Design & Art Direction at NABA, and finished her studies at the School of Comics. During her studies at the School of Comics, she began writing thanks to the course of scriptwriting and creative writing. So she wrote stories and took part in literary competitions, especially within horror genres.

In 2014 and 2015 she was among the winners of the Scrivere la paura *competition and published work in the* Horror Maximo Tales *anthology. In 2016 she won two* Letteratura Horror *competitions and published a story in* Z di Zombie *anthology and another one in* Orrore al Sole *anthology. In 2017 she published a short story of erotic genre in the anthology edited by Milena Edizioni. In 2018 she published her first horror novel edited by Astro Edizioni:* Il Confinato. *Since 2016 she's been a member of the Horror Writers Association Italy.*

She took the wine to the man at table nine...

THE MAN AT TABLE NINE

by Ray Cluley

I've been fortunate enough to work before with English author Ray Cluley, and I hope to continue doing so, for he's one of those writers who, quite simply, can do no wrong. Ray's stories are always engaging and his characters just have this quality of insightful honesty, regardless how bizarre or outlandish their circumstance. Following is a quiet, subtle tale, perhaps more Weird than Horror, although, I suppose, that will be dependent upon your interpretation of it.

Having worked for years as a waiter while in college, I can attest there are certainly all manner of "normalized" horrors in a restaurant, and often those are related to the dining patrons. After a while, you feel you've seen it all, and you develop this ability to size up a customer at first glance, although nothing is certain, should that customer be The Man at Table Nine.

NIKOLA WINCED AT THE HEAT OF THE PLATES AS she loaded them onto her arms, gripping one with the crook of her elbow and balancing the other two on her palms. She backed away from the counter to avoid Carla, though Carla said, "Careful," anyway before calling for her order. Nikola glanced at her meals—beef, chicken, risotto—and was relieved to see she hadn't taken Carla's accidentally. Two weeks in and she was still making mistakes, only a few of them language-related.

Edwin raised his eyebrows at Nikola as she left the kitchen. "Table four are—"

"It is here," she said. "I have it." She knew her grammar sounded clumsy but at least she was reducing her accent.

Edwin nodded and stepped aside in an overly theatrical way for her to pass. He was all right. Not as bad as some of them. Nikola weaved her way to table four, pausing for an elderly woman and sidestepping a child, spilling gravy onto her fingers both times. "Chicken?"

"That's me," said one of the men. Nikola set the plate down.

"Did you have to catch it yourself?" the other man asked. The woman with him said nothing but at least she looked embarrassed.

Nikola ignored the comment, telling 'chicken' to be careful of his plate because it was hot. "Beef?"

"Bring it all the way from Russia, did you?"

She put it down but spared him the same warning about the plate. If he burned himself it would serve him right. The risotto she placed in front of the woman, admiring her dress briefly and then complimenting her on it. Maybe it would improve her chance of a tip.

"Lucky I like it rare," said 'beef,' poking at his meat as if afraid it might move. It looked fine to Nikola but the man added, "A good vet could bring this back."

Two weeks and already she felt like she'd heard it all before. She smiled politely, leaving him to decide if she was appreciating the joke or apologizing, and asked if there would be anything else, suggesting the usual condiments. She took an order for more drinks, wished them a pleasant meal, and headed back to the kitchen.

"Bar first," Edwin said as she approached.

Idiota. How many times had she done that this week? "Sorry."

She took the drinks order to Mark. He was her favorite of the barmen because he was the only one who didn't try to flirt with her or sneak a look at her cleavage (though perhaps he was simply more discrete about it). Her uniform was the standard white and black combination, but the blouse was tight and the skirt short. As far as she could tell, the waiters didn't have the same problem with their shirts and trousers. The other girls joked that their clothes led to better tips but these were tips they had to share, which didn't seem fair to Nikola.

"Scale of one to ten?" Mark asked, tilting a glass beneath one of the beer taps. "Need me to spit in any of these?"

Nikola smiled. "I am okay."

"You are okay. So what's that, about a seven?"

Nikola tilted her hand back and forth, then held both up to show, "Six." Mark laughed. She said again, "I am okay."

But she wasn't okay. She was tired, and her feet hurt, and fitting these shifts around her other job and classes was exhausting. She didn't tell Mark this, though. She didn't want to complain. She would work harder.

She took the drinks to table four, removed the empties she should have taken earlier, and headed back to the kitchen. Edwin gave her a friendly nod as she passed, then busied himself with two new customers as Nikola pushed her way through the swing doors and—

—into Carla.

The woman tried to back up from the doors but she wasn't quick enough. One of the dishes she carried tipped back against her chest, spilling mashed potato and a slop of gravy down her blouse. The other dishes crashed to the floor.

A cheer rose from outside in the restaurant. Someone delivered the ever-popular line about firing the juggler.

"*Gówno!* I'm so sorry!"

Carla wiped curls of fried onion from her clothes before looking up to direct the full intensity of her stare at Nikola.

Graham, one of the chefs, came over with a cloth. "Whoops," he said.

"Yeah," Carla said. "*Whoops.*"

"I am *sorry.*"

Edwin was suddenly in the kitchen. "What's going on?" He assessed the mess quickly and said, "Graham."

"On it."

"Table twelve?" Edwin asked.

"Yeah," Carla said, "and I still need to prep nine."

"Nikki can do it."

"Yes, I can do it, of course. Carla, I am—"

"Sorry, yeah, you said."

Edwin told the chefs, "Two new sausage and mash, Caesar, and medium grill." He looked at Carla and she confirmed with a nod.

The mixed grill would slow them down. Nikola almost apologized again but Edwin turned her around by the shoulders and directed her back out onto the floor. "Prep nine," he said. "Wipe it down, make sure it's not still wet when you're done."

"Of course."

"No cutlery."

"No—"

"Go, go, go."

Nikola could feel she was still red-faced when she emerged into the restaurant but nobody was paying any attention. They were busy with their meals, their drinks, their partners and friends. She grabbed the squirt bottle and cloth from behind the *Wait Here to Be Seated* greeting stand and made her way quickly to table nine.

Nine was one of the more private tables. A small two-seater just off from the windows, it was tucked away at the end of the booths. Nikola sprayed it with cleaner and wiped, although apart from a spill of salt and a smudge of ketchup it was quite clean. She straightened the menus in their narrow wooden holder.

When she glanced up from her work she saw a man outside, staring in at her. He was in his fifties perhaps, well dressed but lacking any kind of coat despite the cold, and he wore a satchel over one shoulder. He nodded. She thought of the view he must have had as she leaned to rub the table clean and put a hand to her chest, palm at the area her blouse didn't cover. She was about to wave him away, maybe even make a ruder gesture, when she noticed Edwin standing with him.

"Nikola? Is the table ready?"

It was Edwin's voice but it came from behind her because—of course, *idiota*—what she was looking at was a reflection in the glass. There she was as well, a ghost she hadn't noticed.

"It is ready," she said, turning. "I just need to set the cutlery."

The man shook his head, and Edwin said, "No need, Nikola, thank you." He pulled the chair out for the man to sit. "There you are, sir," and said again, "Thank you, Nikola."

Nikola realized she was being dismissed, that Edwin was preparing to serve the man himself, but before she could go, the customer said, "No, Edwin, let the girl serve me this evening."

Edwin looked at her.

"I can do nine," she said.

"Splendid," said the customer. He smiled at her and set his satchel on the floor. "A glass of your finest red wine, please."

She noted the order and was surprised to see that not only had Edwin lingered but he even bowed slightly before departing with her.

"Be polite but not chatty or he'll keep you from your other tables," he said as they headed back. "Don't ask him anything except to take his order. And try not to stare."

"Is he someone important? Is he famous?"

"He owns the restaurant—owns a few restaurants, actually—and he pays our wages. We want that to continue, don't we?"

"Of course."

"Good. Now take him these, then fetch his wine."

He gave her a pair of scissors. She looked at him with a question but he didn't give her the chance to ask. "Just take them," he said. "And be careful, they're very sharp."

The man at table nine was looking at the menu when she returned. He had the satchel on his lap.

"Sir? These are for you."

"Thank you." He took the scissors from her and set them on the table. "You're a delightful young thing, are you new?"

His glance at her seemed cursory but she thought of the view he'd already had of her cleaning the table; he may not have been outside looking in, but the view would have been just as provocative from behind. Still, she tried to smile. "Yes, I am new."

"Where are you from?"

"I am from Gdańsk. It is—"

"Ah, Poland. Coming over here to steal all our waitressing jobs, eh?" He smiled. Perhaps it was a joke.

"Are you ready to order, sir?"

"My drink?"

"Sorry, yes. One moment."

He smiled at her and returned his attention to the menu.

At the bar, Mark told her, "Cabernet sauvignon," as he handed her the wine. "If he asks, which he probably won't. He never drinks it anyway."

"He does not drink it?"

Mark shrugged. "So long as he's happy. He tips well, so do what you gotta do." He winked, but Nikola didn't think he was entirely joking.

She took the wine to the man at table nine. He was opening his satchel. Nikola recognized what he retrieved from it by the design; it was the same type of camera her father had owned. Not a sleek digital model, nor something expensive and professional with a removable lens, but rather a squat and clunky square shape with a rainbow stripe on the front. A Polaroid. An old one.

"Ah, here she is."

"Your wine."

"Set it just there, please. Thank you."

As Nikola watched, he brought the camera to his face and directed his view at the glass of wine she set before him. He photographed it, and the *click, clunk, whir* of the process was loud enough to attract the brief attention of the neighboring tables. Nikola expected to see him shake the picture—that was what her father had always done—but he clamped it under his armpit instead.

"Are you ready to order?"

The man put his camera aside and raised the menu. "Yes. Garlic mushrooms to start," he said, pointing to the text in case she didn't understand, "and then the spaghetti bolognaise."

Nikola wrote it down. "We have excellent garlic bread, or maybe—"

"Just the mushrooms and spaghetti for now." He smiled at her briefly, surprising her with, "*Dzięki.*"

Thanks.

He withdrew the photograph from under his arm and leant it beside the glass of wine. Nikola saw its reflection appearing in the clouded square. She'd seen plenty of people take pictures of their food before, of course, using their phones to capture the image of a loaded plate or fancy meal—she'd even done it herself a few times when she'd first arrived in England—and while some did occasionally photograph their drinks, usually it was because they'd ordered an impressive-looking cocktail or a long line of shots. She wondered what he intended to do with the photo. It wasn't like he could put it on the internet or anything.

She found out when she returned with his starter.

By the time Nikola returned to the man at table nine he'd cut the photograph so that all remained was the wineglass. No table background, no nearby napkin or menu: just the glass of wine. It rested against the actual glass of wine as a smaller twin. The rest of the photograph had been discarded, white edges crushed into a loose ball beside the scissors.

"Your starter," Nikola announced, delivering a bowl of pungent mushrooms and thick creamy sauce. She had to wait to put the food down because the man chose that moment to reach for the scissors and his photograph. He leaned away with an apology and she placed the steaming dish before him.

"*Dzięki*," he said again.

"*Proszę bardzo.* You're welcome. Be careful of the dish, it is very hot."

He didn't appear to be listening, but instead cut a section from his photograph, trimming a thin strip of red wine off the top of the glass. It curled alongside the blades of the scissors.

"Would you like anything else?"

He shook his head, said, "No thank you," and popped the sliver of photograph into his mouth.

Nikola began to say something but abandoned the words before they could come out as the man took another mouthful of photograph. He made no effort to disguise the action. In fact, he seemed to savor it.

He looked at her. He waited. "Yes?"

"Nothing," Nikola managed after a moment. "Enjoy your meal, sir."

He smiled and dismissed her with a nod but she lingered long enough to see him raise the camera to photograph the mushrooms. He leaned in close, surely *too* close to capture all of it, and took the shot as she walked away.

Click, clunk, whirr . . .

When she glanced back he was repositioning the bowl for another photo, and when she glanced back again before losing the table entirely from view he was cutting another piece of wine from his picture-glass, a selection of Polaroids poking out from the clench of his armpit.

BETWEEN WAITING ON OTHER TABLES, Nikola saw the man at table nine cut up and devour all of his wine photograph (except for the glass) as well as all of the pictures he'd taken of the mushrooms. The actual wine, the *real* wine, remained untouched, and his dish of mushrooms went cold without him so much as putting his fork to them.

"Spaghetti," Graham announced when Nikola returned to the kitchen.

"He has not eaten the mushrooms."

"Who?"

"Table nine."

Graham smiled. "Yeah, he never eats anything. Well, nothing we send out anyway. Just bring it back in here and take the spaghetti."

"What is he doing?" Nikola asked.

"Well, my guess is he's taking photos of his food."

She nodded. "He cuts them up and he eats all the pieces."

Carla scraped plates into the bin. She had a clean blouse on. "Table nine?"

Nikola said, "Yes. He eats the photographs."

Carla laughed. "Yeah."

"It is a joke?"

Graham said, "Whatever, his spag bog's ready. Bring me those mushrooms, yeah?"

"And don't forget to scrape those plates," Carla said, nodding at the stack Nikola had only just put down.

Nikola grit her teeth. She knew already to scrape them without Carla's scolding.

"Don't mind her," Graham said when the other waitress was gone. "She's not a fan of foreigners, that's all. We get through a lot of them."

"Oh," Nikola said, pushing wasted food into the bin. "Yes. Welcome to England."

She went to fetch the mushrooms.

The man at table nine was cutting a final strip from what was left of his photographed wine. He put it into his mouth as Nikola asked, "Was everything okay with your meal?"

"Delicious, thank you."

He seemed very comfortable with the lie; the starter clearly hadn't been touched since she'd brought it out. The sauce had begun to congeal.

"What's your name?" the man asked. "*Nikola?*"

"Yes."

"Nikola . . . ?"

"Gomolka."

A scattering of Polaroids littered the table, each with a shape cut from it so that all that remained was a bit of dish or table background, nothing of his food. Nikola moved to take the mushrooms away but paused to ask, "Would you like to take another picture first?"

"Excuse me?"

"The mushrooms?"

"*Oh.* No, dear, thank you, they're cold."

Nikola put her hand to her chest. "I am so sorry. I shall bring you some more. I don't know how—"

"No, they were hot enough when you brought them out, don't worry. But they're cold now. You can take them."

She took the food as he swept the photo scraps aside and with a final smile she returned to the kitchen.

"Everything all right?" Edwin asked as she passed. He was on the phone but he'd covered the mouthpiece to ask her anyway.

Nikola shrugged. "He didn't eat anything."

"But was everything all right?"

Nikola shrugged again but said, "Delicious."

Edwin smiled. He looked relieved. He gave her a thumbs up, then waved her back into the kitchen as he returned his attention to the phone.

Nikola swapped mushrooms for spaghetti. Graham took the mushrooms to the microwave. "What's it like out there," he asked, "quieting down yet?"

"A little." She looked at the kitchen clock—watches weren't allowed on the restaurant floor—and saw she still had over half an hour left of her shift.

She took the spaghetti.

"Oh my," the man at table nine said when she returned. "Very saucy."

Nikola couldn't be sure, but she thought maybe he'd glanced down her blouse as she lowered the food. He smiled at her, and she tried to smile back but by then he was turning the dish this way and that, admiring the long loops of pasta and its thick meaty topping. "Fork?"

"Sorry?"

"May I have a fork, please? I don't usually ask, only—"

"Of course. Yes." She handed him one from a nearby table, expecting to see him eat this time, but he only used it to tease out the spaghetti from beneath the bolognaise, making a pattern of it on his plate.

"Perhaps you would be liking another glass of wine?"

The man at table nine nodded, aiming his camera at the food.

"Would you like something different this time?" Nikola pointed to the full glass he hadn't yet tried.

He shook his head. "No, the same will be fine, thank you. Take this one back with my thanks."

She felt like she'd made another mistake in asking and said, "It was a cabernet sauvignon," by way of compensation or distraction, adding her best smile as she took the glass.

He looked at her exactly as her uniform encouraged and returned her smile with an enthusiasm he'd so far only shown his food. "Full bodied," he said. "My favorite." Yet he hadn't taken so much as a sip, as far as Nikola could tell.

She took it back to the bar.

"What a waste," Mark said, tipping it away.

"Maybe we could send the same one back next time?"

"No, you don't want to do that. One of the others tried that once but the guy must've been watching or something because he complained." Mark poured a fresh glass. "I think Edwin fired her, actually. Be careful. The foreign help don't tend to last long around here."

"He is a crazy person?"

"Edwin?"

Nikola smiled. "*No.* The man at table nine."

"The man at table nine is rich," Mark said. "That makes him eccentric." He handed her the fresh wine with a broad smile. Nikola didn't know the word 'eccentric' but she knew it was a joke so she laughed. She would look up the word later.

By the time Nikola returned to nine the man had cut up four pictures of spaghetti. He had a little pile of pieces before him and was picking at them as she approached. Nikola thought about the chemicals—didn't those kinds of pictures use chemicals?—but she didn't say anything. She'd been told not to ask questions.

He popped another piece into his mouth.

Eccentric, she remembered.

She left him photographing his fresh wine.

IN THE KITCHEN, Carla was arguing with Graham.

"But those mushrooms are *swimming* in garlic sauce," Graham was saying.

"Hey, I'm just telling you what they said."

"What is wrong?" Nikola asked.

"Twelve sent their food back."

"Oh."

Not her table, not her problem.

"Try it yourself," Carla said to the chef. It was an unnecessary response as he was already spearing mushrooms with a fork. He took a large mouthful as Nikola picked up another order and moved to the door, but as she turned to bump it open with her behind she saw Graham spit the mushrooms back out into the bowl.

Carla crossed her arms. "See."

"What is it?" Nikola asked, pausing in the doorway.

"Nothing," he said. He licked at some of the juice on his lips and wiped the rest away with his hand. "I mean, they taste of nothing."

He looked at Nikola and she knew without him saying anything else that they were the same mushrooms she'd brought back from table nine.

Carla carried a new order away and said, "Watch out," to Nikola as she passed.

Nikola followed her into the restaurant, longing for her shift to just finish.

THE MAN AT TABLE NINE asked her to wait once she'd brought the bill, counting money from his wallet directly into her hands. His table was a litter of Polaroid scraps. Some tiramisu remained in a few of the photo fragments. All of it remained in the dish. The camera itself was away in its satchel.

"Keep the change," the man said, passing her the final note. It was a good tip, Nikola thought, surprised he paid at all if he owned the restaurant. He took her hand and closed her fingers over the money.

"Thank you, sir," she said, waiting for him to release her. He did so by waving her comment away as if it were a fly that bothered but evaded him. He seemed a little drunk. Perhaps he always had been. It would explain his strange behavior.

"Did you enjoy your meal?"

"I did, I did. And the service was *wonderful*. You work so very hard, don't you. That's why I like you lot. Poles, Czechs, Slavs, whatever. So hard-working. And nobody notices."

He took her hand again before she could leave and pulled her down to him. "You're a beautiful girl," he told her, his breath rank with a mixture of wine, garlic, and coffee. "Yet nobody notices any of you."

Nikola pulled free and backed away abruptly.

The man at table nine held up his hands. "Sorry," he said. "Sorry. I've embarrassed you."

Nikola glanced over at the bar. Mark tilted his head in a way that asked if she was all right.

Perhaps the man at table nine saw some of this. He lifted his bag to his lap and asked, "Could you fetch my coat, miss? I'd like to go now."

Nikola nodded but when she took the bill and payment to Edwin she told him, "He wants his coat," and pushed her way through the doors into the kitchen. She collected her own coat from the tiny staff room at the back and retrieved her bag, tucking the extra money the man had left as a tip into one of the pockets. She checked her phone. There was still ten minutes left of her shift but she didn't care.

The staff had their own bathroom but it was a grotty cramped space so Nikola always used the ones provided for customers. A couple of girls were using the bathroom mirror to take photos of themselves, preening and pouting and giggling, phone held high, so she hid herself away in one of the cubicles and waited for her shift to end, trying not to cry. She took a few sheets of paper from the dispenser beside her and dabbed her eyes and nose, hoping the girls outside couldn't hear her sniffling. By the time she came out from the cubicle they were gone and her shift was officially over. She fixed her makeup in the mirror and left.

THE NIGHT WAS cool but not cold, pleasant after hours of rushing between tables and a hot kitchen. Nikola left her coat undone, glad now to have the open blouse and the short skirt. She was so tired. So very, very tired. She felt like one of the plates she took back to the kitchen, the best bits gone and everything else scraped away. It was so hard over here. She thought of quitting, of going home like so many told her to do. It was all so exhausting. The work. The comments. The way people like her were treated, and the way people like her tolerated the treatment.

"Miss?"

She barely heard him behind her. Only when she heard her name as well did she turn.

"Nikola?"

It was the man from table nine. He stood a short distance away, camera already up at his face. "Cheese," he said, and then—

Flash, click, clunk, whirr . . .

"*Wypierdalaj!*" Nicola gathered her coat shut and scowled. "Hey!"

But the man from table nine only smiled. "Just a little something for later," he said, tucking the photograph into his trouser pocket.

He licked his lips.

RAY CLULEY is a British Fantasy Award winner with stories published in various magazines and anthologies. Some of these have been republished in 'Best Of' volumes, including Ellen Datlow's Best Horror of the Year *series and* Nightmares: A New Decade of Modern Horror, *as well as Steve Berman's* Wilde Stories: The Year's Best Gay Speculative Fiction, *and Benoît Domis's* Ténèbres. *He has been translated into French, Polish, and Hungarian, with a Chinese version of his award-winning "Shark! Shark!" due soon and German translation of his novella,* Water For Drowning, *rumored to be in the works.* Probably Monsters, *his debut collection, is available from ChiZine Publications. You can find out more at* probablymonsters.wordpress.com.

Out from the underground rise the creatures, the *Mamu* . . .

THE MANTLE OF FLESH

by Ashlee Scheuerman

Penning horror and science fiction from Perth, Australia, Ashlee Scheuerman writes in a magnificently rich and sophisticated voice, suggestive of somebody seemingly far beyond her youthful age. I even had to crack open the dictionary while reading her work in order to look up some unfamiliar vocab, which is a rare thrill these days. And she enjoys occasionally discussing insects with me, suggesting that entomology and high intellect must correlate (right, insect lovers?) . . . or, at the least, it leads into the following selection.

For one man's family line pits him against the Mamu, demonic creatures that live in burrows underneath a hard-packed desert, and to survive, he must nurture a demonic creature of his own. Tragic, dark, and epic, this one has it all: Terrible is The Mantle of Flesh.

Emu Field, Great Victoria Desert, South Australia
October, 1953

GLASS-CRUSTED SAND RUMBLES WITH THE STIRRING of something beastly. This tremor of the earth could signal more explosions in the sky aloft the Emu Claypan, the next round of Project Totem's atomic testing, but Murray knows otherwise. He pauses climbing into the cab of his Land Rover, arm extended to the grab handle overhead, prepared to head east along the dirt track which comprises the Anne Beadell Highway. He'll have to consult his holy books when he returns home.

And the stars, if the black nuclear mist has cleared by then.

Coober Pedy, Stuart Range, South Australia
Decades Later

BLOOD WELLS UPON my sliced fingertip, glistening with a color so vivid that I've become enamored. It distracts me from the incessant itch of my beard's regrowth and the ever-present background shrieking of a Judas Priest album playing on repeat. For a drawn-out moment, my focus has narrowed down to nothing but scarlet. Compared to the khakis and grays of my clothes, the black of my hair and nail polish, the cream and sun-dulled terracotta orange of sandstone all around me, this swelling bead of blood is hyper-bright. Like it's the only thing in this pocket of reality to still have vibrancy.

I cradle my wounded digit to preserve the color. If the blood spills to the dark gray couch cushion, or the light gray floor of my caravan—my mobile home—I know the wool and nylon will soak up the brilliance and leave a sad, muted brown-red. The cut is crisp from nail to knuckle on account of my pocket knife being kept *very* sharp and my right hand palpating the surrounding skin, coaxing resistant fluid to the surface. In this desert, I'm always thirsty.

I reach over the funnel affixed above the glass bottle terrarium, and turn my hand over, fingers draped with a careless grace. The blood tickles on my fingertip, and the falling droplets seem to suspend mid-air above the white plastic cone. The Malaysian cricket living inside moves from under dried leaves with too-fast demonic trickery to impossibly, miraculously, catch the drips as they fall into its cage, clutching my perfect red in its palpi. I leave my hand to hemorrhage into the funnel while I lean closer. The jewel-like, spring green of the vampire insect's revealed body is lovely. As bright as my blood. A true marvel. A commodity. My hope for the future: the supernatural cricket summoned for my salvation.

At least the woman who smuggled it here had promised the insect would safeguard me. She read my skepticism and desperation as she took payment and provided simple care instructions. *Keep the creature in glass. Feed it my own fresh blood every month, always from the same finger, always on the full moon.* Pictures of the eerie cricket fill three flash cards, and half the space on my digital camera's internal memory. My photography hobby has become a lonely obsession over these years of isolation. I will print a selection of significant images at the Community Library to stick between handwritten notebook pages under the title of *Pelesit: An immured spirit which does little except chirrup and drink my fluids.*

When the time comes to combat the threat underground, to defeat the sharp-toothed, cannibalistic crawling horrors where they hide, filling the tunnels below Coober Pedy, I will open the glass top of the Pelesit's terrarium and bid my insect to strike.

My grandfather Murray had brought me to the mouths of the opal mines before, where deep pits and hand-hewn shafts plunge down through sandstone. Granddad resisted the rise of the ancient beasts, keeping them below ground after the government's bombs brought them up in a cloud of dust, rage, and radiation. He experimented with lives and loss to appease the old gods, these bad spirits called *Mamu* by the local mob, giving them the meat of humanity in spiteful offering.

He recalled protruding eyes gleaming by torchlight. Sacrificial bones glittering, too.

Granddad hadn't wanted me to know the extent of his understanding, of his bequeathment, just as he withheld the whole truth from my father.

But, firstly, I survived. Twenty-eight and older now than my dad, who died before seeing twenty-five. Perhaps Granddad would have made his halting, manic speech to my father if Dad reached my age, instead of wasting, thinning down to a walking skeleton, held together by skin and sinew and cancerous cells as they blossomed and spread—lungs, thyroid, stomach, bowel—an infestation, just like these vermin in the deepest tunnels. Just like the monsters, hoping to claim the world.

And, secondly, I *believed*.

The description of oversized insects deep underground inspired Dad to argue for radioactive mutation of Australia's already-large invertebrates. Granddad, outraged, called that comic book fantasy. Dad thought the other explanation to be superstitious drivel.

Granddad knew them as vengeful spirits, an Occultist through and through, with his notions reinforced by local myth. I trusted his word even before I saw those terrible worms, those legs and pincers and impossible wings the size of my car, paper-thin and rattling. Before they stood on hind legs and morphed into man-shaped beings with fangs and long hair.

Shape-shifters, he said. *Humanoid one moment, insectoid the next. They'll change bodies to confuse you, boy, and leave you unsure of what you're facing. A* Mamu *might coalesce toward a familiar form, only to flicker into something new and more unsteady.*

It had been years before his warnings were proven to me.

I now carry the memory of my first encounter with the *Mamu* to add to my grandfather's recollections, which he passed to me through rambling stories as an inheritance of wisdom and wariness, of witchery and otherworldliness. And in my pocket, the rainbow-and-flame of an opal, his talisman of scales and spirit.

And blood.

Always, back to blood.

I thumb my camera on and take a picture of the fresh wound to add to my growing grimoire.

Tufi Test Site, Maralinga Tjarutja Lands, South Australia
Three Years Prior

GRANDDAD LIVES at the center of the sun.

The roads laid across the clay face north of Maralinga map out a giant sunburst shape in white, marking where the military intended to suspend another balloon hundreds of meters above the ground and detonate a thermonuclear device. With the end of Operation Antler, this site remained clean. Stark and brilliant, when seen from above. A place Granddad has no authority to be living, but he hides well and no one bothers him.

I've known my grandfather views the marked location as a kind of sacred grove, a place of potential, and a link to our family through graves and grief. He's invited me here in pilgrimage.

I leave my caravan on firm ground around a klick out from my destination, where it's safe from getting bogged down in the red sand. I walk the rest of the way with a cautious exactness, edging between saltbush and spinifex, taking my time to photograph the landscape around me. The spiny tussocks, upraised sticks, and bull ants scurrying, gleaming in the sunlight as they patrol around their mounded homes.

I follow Granddad's directions, hiking the history of higher gods, better beings than those we resist, until I reach the burial sites, so sacred, so beloved.

One for my grandmother, the first to keep the monsters down with the cost of our family blood, one of the only human sacrifices available in this remote place, whose death would go unremarked by any authorities.

Another grave marker for my infant aunt, the second, following close behind Grandma. Then Granddad's sister, all dead for human survival, lest the *Mamu* stay risen and scour the lands. Spilling carmine, sangria, scarlet, to dye the already-red dirt to new hues. After these bittersweet successes, Granddad has grown evermore assured that we are special, and ours will be the lineage to defeat the monsters older than time. I find myself trusting his belief more and more, as though we are heroes and demigods ourselves.

Father's body was too diseased. Too riddled with plague and blight, too much like our enemy, so he couldn't be brought here and laid out in offering, couldn't *bleed* to help our cause. Granddad and I tried to understand the ire of the universe, that his son, my dad, would be the one struck down within a year of anyone knowing something was wrong, but we couldn't puzzle out the reason for such a punishment.

My grandfather is here to meet me, his Land Rover parked between tussocks and perpendicular to the obvious shrine. It sits dead center. I snap a string of photos from behind, capturing the essence of this place in a rapid-fire burst, then tuck the camera in my cargo pocket for the final approach.

I thought I was braced, prepared for the weight of this truth. To see the names, *Anna Marie, Georgina Anne, Carrie Eloise Morgan,* and know what Granddad did to repel the bad spirits, but all my reassuring self-talk vanishes in the explosion of emotion I feel at finding another name carved into the memorial wall: *my mother, Isabella Mandy.* The day's sunlight is cast away by a black mushroom cloud in my head, unreal wind buffering against my body, the grasses, the stunted trees around me.

"What the *fuck?*"

Bad enough to lose Dad to cancer when I was five and worshipped his every word and action. Lightning crackles through my internal storm. "You said she died in a car accident!"

Granddad is unfazed, spindly arms leaning across the dusted bonnet of his vehicle as he weathers my eruption. "She did. Brain-dead at the hospital. It wasn't my intention to use her, boy, but waste not, want not."

As though my beautiful, radiant, laughing mother was *fucking leftovers* to be put to use. Scraps of meat to throw to the dogs.

Granddad adds, "The *Mamu* are cannibals, not scavengers. They won't take someone who's been long without a pulse, no cold bodies, nothing touched by decay, but it's not as though they need brain function to be calmed."

Another detonation occurs inside me.

Later, I'll wonder how my grandfather got her dead-but-breathing body brought out here to the mines. How he stole her from the hospital, and how he orchestrated her funeral without her remains. Because, surely, her bones are here, collected once the flesh was entirely devoured by the grim and hungry spirits. They who withdrew back to dormancy, sated with Isabella's sacrifice.

Later, I will want to know so many answers to questions I render unaskable. Later, I will feel both regret and grudging admiration for my grandfather's insights, wisdom, and ingenuity.

Not now. My muscles flush with heat and tension, then a skin-prickling cold of fury. My vision is fragmented. The peripheral blurs, becoming hazy and darkened, while other details remain hyper-focused. As my awareness picks moments to fixate on, time stops and starts. I don't notice him back away from the four-wheel-drive or my forward stride, but I see my hands bunch in the faded blue plaid of Granddad's shirt front. First like claws, next as fists. The sudden heave as I propel Granddad's frailing figure sideways is a flash of rewarding release, using all the strength in my hateful body, an exothermic reaction.

He yelps. He collides with the side of his ancient Land Rover, feeble neck crunching to a deadly angle. Flakes of rust tumble down from the oxidized corner of his car door. I hear nothing more, nothing at all, yet catch the mist of blood which sprays from between his lips. The ruby dewdrops land in the dark gray wire of his beard.

Sound returns to me in an unearthly shriek screaming out of my tight throat. I have no control over the wailing, high and piercing, on and on.

At some point, I fall to the ground.

Rough grains of red clay press and cling to my body where I lay sprawled on my side, staring sightlessly across the space to where Granddad's corpse drains its various fluids in the shadow of his vehicle. Not even the low roar building from below rouses me.

Flies crawl across my face, but as the earth beneath me begins to tremble in earnest, they take flight and withdraw to other nourishment, leaving me to exist alone, utterly alone, in this remote and hellish place.

Except, of course I am not forsaken. Out from the underground rise the creatures, the *Mamu*, the spirits Granddad had appeased for so long. All twelve of them.

My mind seeks the familiar in the approaching beings. From a distance, their stance reminds me of dogs stalking closer with snarling teeth and huge pairs of reflective eyes. But they move on far too many legs, and once closer, I can see the limbs are insectoid with many segments and prickly hairs. The painfully dry air catches in my throat as I witness them shapeshift. Their forms are like jittering smoke, some moments transitioning smoothly from insect to animal, then other times snapping from image to image, as though the sequence is seen through a camera shutter. Once the spirits stand biped, their extra limbs shrink into long, waving hair.

I push myself backward across the scorched sand, away from my mistake and the horror of our family shrine serving its purpose once more.

The only features to remain constant are the large, round eyes, which seem to melt into place on their changing faces, and the long, long fangs filling their mouths. With each confusing shift, I can't decide if the *Mamu* are all forms at once and my poor mortal mind is just struggling to make sense of their appearance, or if the spirits truly change physical manifestations to suit their own enigmatic purposes.

Alternating between scurrying and striding, depending on their shape, and looming higher than the Land Rover's roof rack, the great creatures fixate those bulbous eyes upon my grandfather's corpse and make their unwanted arrival into the desert grove.

I'd gotten into my head the idea they were only unrestricted at Coober Pedy, where we humans had carved into the land and made holes and tunnels toward their dominion. Foolishness and arrogance on my behalf. The gods of old wouldn't need manmade pits to emerge in their own territory. That was a falsehood I'd accepted to give myself the impression of safety, an illusion of control. As though I could guard myself from their long cannibal teeth just by avoiding the mines.

Maralinga could not be inexplicably safe from their presence, here where the *Mamu* were angered enough to rise in 1953 by atomic blasts. And this murder, this involuntary offering, would show me first-hand the nature of Granddad's sacrifice.

Coober Pedy, Stuart Range, South Australia
Present Day

THE PELESIT GROWS and learns its purpose, the way I was taught: with blood and blades on my flesh. Veins tracking and branching, ley lines of the body, acting as paths of atonement and sabotage. Blood, which carries cancer from one organ to the next. Blood, tying me to a place of ochre, sandstone, and desert. Blood, feeding my weapon, nourishing the salvation of the world. One small, insignificant man, bleeding for all of mankind.

Years past, in the aftermath of my grandfather's demise and witnessing the *Mamu* feast on his broken form, I resolved to not suffer his legacy. I couldn't take up his mantle of parricide, lacking a ready pool of relatives to choose from, or the will to offer more flesh to the hungry ones. I read, researched, and drew forth a means for inflicting profane deicide instead.

My little vampire cricket turns on its leaf and begins to stridulate, observing me through compound eyes as it sings. Full moon feeding day is upon us for the last time and my skin hums with anticipation. The partially-healed scars of my fourth finger catch the moonlight through old lace curtains and shine. I take photographs of it all.

I pray to the higher gods for a death far beyond here, out in a lush, wet wild, somewhere remote and teeming, full of other life. For when the world and its obsession with mortality finally cash in against my subsistence and reclaim the stardust of my body, I want to succumb to wholesome bacteria and bugs. Not lay crumpled in this desiccating desert, barren of soaring tree and forest, and hellishly hot to suit its population of evil. I hope to be granted the opportunity to destroy the *Mamu* before the time of my passing, mostly to prevent myself from becoming *their* unnatural, cannibalistic dinner.

This stretch of land is an inhospitable place, made palatable through the glimmering riches of opal and gold. Harvesting and selling the scales and veins and crystalline remains of things beneath.

The bottle holding my Pelesit is the first item slid with reverence into my tattered backpack, zippered in the foremost pocket with steady hands. Packing my digital camera and several spare memory cards happens automatically. I slide my canteen of water, a handful of AA and D batteries, and a Mag-Lite torch the length of my forearm into the main compartment, behind the frayed badges of heavy metal bands, political statements, and faces of cartoon characters. The backpack has seen its fair share of rainy days, and more recent, dry. The metal pins are touched by rust and they stain the fabric with their ochre, so much like the color of dirt and dried blood.

I heft the heavy, sagging bag and let the aluminum door crash shut behind me, rattling the cladding and filling the night with an echo I interpret as decisive and final.

I'd parked my mobile abode in the pitted terrain south of the township in defiance for my fear of midnight visitors sneaking out of the underground. It wouldn't happen. Granddad's sacrifice still holds. Down in their lairs, sated on the flesh of my flesh, the *Mamu* will maintain their present docile state, regardless of how much I have to bleed nearby.

My grandfather had offered so much more than any one man ought. He gave beyond what anyone could ever ask, even at the last, sacrificing.

Sacrificing.

I extend a climbing rope from the tied anchor point on my 4WD's roo bar, down into the nearest pit laying shadowed against the gleaming white of the landscape. I lower myself into this opening, descending in a stop-start, slow when I require caution, quick when I forget and forge ahead. I've never come this far below, yet it feels easy and familiar.

The peak of the lunar cycle is due at 1:55 a.m., so down I go, phosphorescent watch hands signaling twenty minutes before my goal, Pelesit, knife, and holy justice ready to bring to collision Australian and Malaysian myths, and to rip apart reality.

I release the rope when my descent becomes a gentle slope and stalk unhindered down the sandy, stony passage carved into the land. These places are rough and rounded like warrens as they burrow through the white-red-banded sandstone in search of the blue-red-green glint of precious opal. I'm aware the depths should be consumed by darkness at this hour, yet I'm able to see enough of my surroundings to leave the Mag-Lite untouched.

The pale lime bars glowing on my wristwatch spin closer to the designated time. I halt in the next cavern and swing the backpack from my shoulders. Pelesit removed from one pocket, knife withdrawn from another, I give a final precise gash to my scarred finger and run rivulets of red around the bottle's opening.

Do I announce the cricket's release? There were no words taught to me, no grand ritual. The *bomoh* had little warnings to offer regarding the Pelesit's other form, an essential part of my plan, but she didn't give me much advice on *enacting* these final steps.

So I remove the stopper and turn the bottle up, as though the gem-green vampire is a fluid to be poured, libated, consecrating this soon-to-be hallowed ground.

There is no obvious movement. No theatrical flow of spooky mist or gelatinous goop to herald its escape. The cricket is gone from the glass vessel in my hand, and a young and feral-looking child crouches on the sandstone ground instead.

Black hair, straight and hanging over eyes and ears, like my own. A small, jutting chin and defiant button nose protrude in warm olive tones. Its gender, if it has one, is indeterminate under simple gray clothes, another similarity. Bare hands and feet appear normal, slightly grubby, like any child.

It has accusatory eyes the color of spring, unlike me.

I possess hundreds, maybe over one thousand photographs of the cricket from its months in my care, every conceivable angle and lighting captured in compressed image files, yet it feels wrong to take a picture now. I obey my misgiving, leave the camera untouched, and offer an impassive expression to gaze upon the Pelesit-in-human-shape. The child parts its petulant mulberry lips, and vivid crimson gushes out.

At first, I believe it's regurgitating the blood I've fed it for months, though the illogicality of such an idea is almost immediately apparent at the freshness and sheer volume of liquid pouring from its open mouth, soaking into its shirt, far outweighing the scant drips I've given. From somewhere behind its little pearls of tooth is a darker sanguine stump. Whatever nub remains.

True to myth, the wise woman had bitten out the demon's tongue to enslave the summoned shadow.

The bleeding child begins to cry, a convincing sound of terror and pain. An instinct deep within me twitches, tenses. I find I don't want to do this, this sacrificing. At least not with a young, helpless human, and the Pelesit's current form is impossible to tell apart from the real thing. The wet, gurgling wails make my insides cringe and writhe with trepidation. I want to rush to fix whatever harms this little one. To soothe it and offer comfort. And, in equal measure, I'm shocked by my reaction. Is this what I would feel as a father? If I survive, victorious, if I dare let myself seek out the trappings of having my own family, would I be overcome by a protective wisdom, all righteous fury, when something causes my offspring distress?

I quash the musings and try to ignore the sobbing child and how much its sounds move me. I have to rationalize away my emotional response. This is the same creature I've held contained in a bottle and fed my vital fluids. Not some five-year-old, lost, alone, hurting. Not a little boy with shaggy black hair whose daddy just went limp on a hospital bed, who has been hustled out of the stark, stinking ward, made to sit by himself in a barren waiting room, whose chest feels like it's caving in around the sudden absence of its hero, its father, its rock, comedian, protector . . .

Then the dozen cruel *Mamu* arrive.

They glide into my limited range of vision with their protruding eyes fixed on the crouched Pelesit. My pulse stutters, adrenaline rushing to keep me alive and fighting. The cannibals' shapeshifting is etched into my memory, but here in the underground I discover their bodies glow maroon in the darkness, emitting an illumination so red and dim that my brain is unconvinced there is light at all.

I fully understand why Granddad felt so compelled to sacrifice, to appease their wrath. They emanate power, like a scent, a whisper on the stale air.

The child's shrieks of horror renew as continual blood loss from its severed tongue makes the Pelesit grow visibly weaker. It topples to its side and tries to crawl away from the approaching monsters with skinny arms. Blood and mucus and tears wash down its young face.

I can't help the Pelesit, nor can I stand and watch. Its panicked eyes glitter peridot, small, grubby hand outstretched toward me. Its bloodied mouth shapes words of beseechment I will never hear. I want to leave. I need to turn away and escape while my poisoned bait lures in the enemy. My body is wracked with tremors of indecision. Here is the terrific culmination of my work. It's nearly over, and I've surely won. I can make my father proud by daring to subvert the murderous destiny Granddad had tried to foster onto me. Yet Dad would not have let anything hurt a child and I'm aghast at the disgrace of my present weakness.

The *Mamu* strike, and my options are stripped away. The unhallowed spirits fall upon the human-bodied demon with a low, grinding chuckle in approval of my offering. The child's heart finds more blood to pump from its bitten and torn body. Its whimpering softens, then fades, replaced now by squelching and lapping. I'm frozen in place. The *Mamu* fossick around in the spilled guts, pulling long strings of intestine up like floss between their vicious teeth. Clods of darker organ meat patter to the sandy tunnel floor as they chew, falling out of open mouths in ragged pieces, only to be snuffled back up before they plunge their shifting faces into the child's cavity. They crowd in, they chew, they rumble to each other in voices too low for me to fully hear.

They strip every available shred of flesh and meat from the child's bones, cleaning brain and gristle from the skull last, then sit back on their varied haunches to lick and groom away the remnants of gore from their faces, muzzles, mandibles.

Moments of slavering pass before they turn to me, altering their appearances into the uniform bodies that Granddad most often described. The static-frizzed hair and bulbous eyes, long claws and longer teeth.

I turn to run, but the dark glow from the *Mamu* has changed my night vision and the tunnel is black against black. I remember my entrance to these tombs, but the electric terror is making everything disorienting and alarming, too chaotic to navigate as I shamble forward into the darkness. I flail over my shoulder for the zipper pull and extract my Mag-Lite as though unsheathing a sword. The torch glares warm white light down the carved tunnel.

I feel the *Mamu* pursuing, a gusting heat on the back of my neck, and the sound of many feet and snapping teeth always just behind. I don't look back, not even once. My strides lengthen. The violently bobbing light shows my way is clear. My legs burn with the flood of lactic acid, muscles unused to such strenuous athletic efforts. I struggle against the tightness in my chest, knowing as long as I can get out of the underground, I will be okay.

A fierce bellow makes me startle hard enough to almost drop my light. One of the creatures at my back is falling. I hear the scuff of its stumbling, the grunt and expulsion of air as it collides with the hard stone wall, and feel the ground shake when it collapses in a heavy heap.

I don't try to stop myself laughing, as wheezing and difficult as it is. My plan is working! I sense others go down behind me, two and three at a time. I give a victorious whoop. Joy floods me. There are no more signs of pursuit and I can see the bright tail of my climbing rope splayed across the floor ahead.

Safe and exultant, I now glance over my shoulder, and see one of the slain *Mamu* prone on the ground. Ridges of loose, cream sand bulge up around its face and bushy shoulders. I have no urge to check any closer for the surely-absent signs of life, content with its motionlessness and akimbo limbs telling me the bad spirit, the plague, the infestation is poisoned and gone.

I return my torch to my bag and have a grateful, celebratory gulp of water before rising out of these accursed tunnels.

The *Mamu* have been a looming threat for as long as I remember thanks to Dad and Granddad's frank discussion in my presence as a little boy, then, after, my grandfather deciding far too early on to keep me peripherally aware. In the years since his first confession, then the fatal reveal, I had dedicated so much emotional and mental resources to the dangerous existence of evil spirits and other impossible beings. To the reality of "magic."

What would I do with myself now?

Some part of me always believed they would get me. That this mad play with the Malaysian Pelesit would fail, end tragically for me. The rapturous triumph is almost too much.

I'm greeted above ground by the perfect, luminous disk of my precious full moon riding high overhead. So instrumental in my success. It lights this strange new world with its reflected glow, showing the rise and fall of the landscape. Coober Pedy to the north sleeps on, unaware how close they'd all come to being consumed.

The Universe itself commemorates my euphoria with a breathtaking show of shooting stars, more meteoroids than I can count blazing across the sky in brazen magnificence.

I dance in place, feet scuffing and batteries clattering together. The slight sound reminds me of the digital camera stowed in my backpack. Now is the *perfect* time for a photograph. The moment of my supremacy. I can document my glorious ascension to Unknown Hero. *Savior.*

I unpack the camera and flick the dials to *On* and *Auto*, positioning myself toward my caravan trailer to have the vast, mounded field all speckled with pits in the background and point the lens at my grin-stretched face. The device gives an electronic whirr before its flash shatters my sights. I answer the rush of discomfort with a string of colorful swears and fumble the settings off *blinding* to snap another, far less jubilant, shot.

The miniature screen glowing from the back of the camera displays the most recent image. I squint down at my pale likeness, and despite the mishap with the flash, my eyes still show a crinkle of delirious joy, and moonlight shines off my exposed teeth. I hit the zoom button with my thumb and find spots of similar luster in the scenery behind me. Bone-white vertical lines, like long teeth. Pairs of bold orbs above each elongated grimace. Looming forms which shouldn't be rising from the sandstone . . .

I try to tell myself it's the light of falling stars caught in digital stillness, and maybe trees I never noticed.

My gaze flickers up to survey my surroundings, searching for the inconceivable presence, knowing the lie I'm feeding myself. Even the lunar brightness cannot defeat the temporary nyctalopia of the camera flash then staring into its illuminated screen. I can't see details in the distance.

But there aren't tall trees in my vicinity, only shrubby mulga. Shadows are rolling toward me from all sides, black beings low to the ground, matched by gloomy, clotting vapor blotting out the silvery moonlight. Goosebumps erupt as something booms.

I recall the old tales, the sounds of explosions and the air filled with black mist.

I silently plead for this tremoring sound to be a storm, or an earthquake, or a meteorite collision. The rumbles are sub-bass, felt more than heard, refreshing my fear in a cold wash.

I refuse to believe more evil spirits can exist. I killed them. I won. Granddad confirmed their numbers multiple times. There were only around a dozen *Mamu*, he said, all of which are lying poisoned and accounted for down the closest pit, felled by their hunger and my cleverness. In his decades of obsession, he only ever proved a handful existed, *and I destroyed them!*

I cling to that information. A life preserver in my time of need. It's unforgivable arrogance to have never considered there are more *Mamu* than the rare few seen by Granddad. His feeding them might have removed a limiting factor on their population and caused them to multiply.

If the *Mamu* have bred, they now awaken *en masse* in true vengeance for an offense brought against their kind instead of being placated by another generation of blood and sacrifice.

The terrain I'd parked upon rises in a slight plateau above shallow basins of rock and sand hills, evidence of excavation left by miners, all reds and whites and drab olive greens in daytime. An ideal stage on which to turn, to discover my fate, to meet my end.

I pray the blackened clouds bring rain.

ASHLEE SCHEUERMAN is the author of the dark fantasy novel, The Damning Moths, *and its looming sequel. Her short apocalyptic fiction is published in the award-winning and acclaimed horror anthologies,* Surviving the End, Qualia Nous, *and* Lost Signals. *Ashlee resides in Western Australia with an excessive collection of pine cones, a medley of pets, and her family who forgive her for taking too many photos of bugs, clouds, and sunsets. You can visit her website at* www.AshleeSch.com.

AUTHOR'S NOTE: I acknowledge the Indigenous People of this land as First Australians, and I recognize Elders past and present. I appreciate the importance of storytelling within Indigenous culture, and understand how intrinsic it is to their identity.

He saw his shadow ahead of him, growing in length . . .

THE SHADOWS OF SAINT URBAN

by Claudio Foti

When it comes to sub-genres or tropes of horror, my vote for Number One Scariest has always been Religious Horror: For if the Devil exists, by his very nature he is the champion of monsters, and all things horrific are in some way of His arrangement... it's really very emotionally devastating. The idea, the prospects, the insidious battles waging in subtle ways in all aspects of our life is terrifying, or at least just damn creepy.

So when I began to read Claudio Foti's submission, I immediately braced myself: There it is... a Catholic Professor on mission from the Pope to investigate strange occurrence within the church itself, and who better to tell such a tale than an actual horror author living in Rome?

What lies in the shadows around us, the world of darkness that is constantly emerging, shifting, following us? Find out with Professor Michele Bergorio as he steps into The Shadows of Saint Urban... *and remember to leave the lights off at the door.*

*A*T THE CENTER OF ROME, JUST BEYOND THE *Aurelian Walls, there is a green park called Caffarella. Quite old, wild, and rich in history, this park still is one of the most important treasure chests in the Eternal City, filled with its lore and legends. It's a place where dreadful ghosts still wander restlessly and disquieting things occur . . .*

PROFESSOR MICHELE BERGORIO parked his car in Via della Caffarelletta and strolled toward the park, enjoying the fine spring day. He'd parked farther from the appointment place than needed, but he knew that at his age—almost sixty—and with his girth, a nice stroll "in the countryside" would be good for his health, or at least that's what his physician had recommended during his last check-up.

He crossed a small wooden bridge surrounded by rushes and gnats and walked at a brisk pace across a wide field. It was midmorning and hot already. By the time he left the field behind and reached the long vat that had been a drinking trough of the Vaccareccia, he carried his jacket under his arm, and a lock of his gray hair stuck to his sweaty forehead.

Perhaps I overdid it, he thought, removing his glasses to clean them.

It would have been far easier to park in front of the church, but he was almost there now. He took a moment to catch his breath.

"Here, in front of the Vaccareccia," a voice lectured from behind, "we have this drinking trough, once graced with the Torlonias' coat of arms and a large gargoyle. The first was stolen in the 1970s, the second destroyed some twenty years later, during the excavations to lay an electric cable . . . "

Bergorio turned to see a plump lady using her telescopic cane to indicate the trough to a host of elderly people, all equipped with gloves, shorts, T-shirts, and canteens, standing around like feral beasts ready to pounce, leaning on their trekking poles.

Bergorio walked on with a smile, envisioning that host of Nordic walk fanatics as they trekked all over him. Ahead was the Caffarella, which he knew well, because he was from the area and as a young man had often gone hiking there, at a time when monuments and historical remains weren't fenced and everything had a wilder, more natural look.

As he turned left, he was surprised by the shrieking of Brazilian parakeets flying above. He knew of the existence of that colony, and of the legend according to which the original parakeets had escaped from an aviary and then reproduced safely and abundantly in an environment free from natural predators. He smiled at the thought that those parakeets had adapted far from their tropical climate of the Eternal City, and he thought of what else might do the same.

He walked under white cedars, pedunculated oaks, cornelian cherry dogwoods, elms, and white willows, full of pollen that covered the ground like snow, passed by some mulberry trees, and finally reached the small, long iron bridge stretching in front of the Nympheum of Egeria. There he lingered for a moment to look at what was left of the statue of the god Almone before tackling the sun-drenched uphill path that led to the Sacred Wood.

He finished that uphill climb, panting, and grabbed onto the drinking fountain by the church where the appointment was. He cleaned himself up as well as he could, trying to look presentable again, then entered the wooden enclosure, heading for the front door, where a plump man trotted forward holding a set of long keys.

Bergorio took a moment to look at the church of Saint Urban. It certainly was one of the best Roman architectural works that had survived through the centuries, mostly due to its transformation into a Christian place of worship. He ran his hands over his long gray hair, trying to comb it some, and settled his glasses to better examine the inscriptions. He'd always felt attracted by the place, but it was usually closed to the public.

"It is well preserved, that's true," he said to himself, "but who knows how many times it was desecrated and robbed, since it stands on the Appia Pignatelli, outside the Aurelian Walls."

"Are you interested in this church's history, Professor?" the keeper asked, his tone almost rude.

"Just curious. I've often gone by, but it's always locked. I've never been inside."

"We generally keep it closed to the public for reasons of preservation. It became a church only in the sixth century, when it was built over the remains of a temple to Bacchus, which in its turn had been built over a temple to Ceres and Faustina Major," the keeper replied, a mischievous wink in his watery blue eyes.

"Ceres is the goddess of plenty, but who was Faustina?"

"She was Antoninus Pius' wife, who was deified the very day of her death. The church was later consecrated to Saint Urban, bishop and martyr. Once inside, you'll be able to see the Roman structures, perfectly preserved and adorned with frescoes added to the inner walls when the church underwent renovation by Cardinal Francesco Barberini, in the seventeenth century," the keeper explained. Bergorio thought the man had to be about fifty, but time had not been kind to him.

"Very well, but why am I here?" Bergorio asked, while the keeper's pudgy fingers fumbled with the keys, trying to open the church doors. "Or, better, who is it so important that I meet?" Being a member of the Department of Psychology of the Pontifical Gregorian University had virtually forced him to look into this case.

Bergorio held a prominent position at the Department and dealt only with theoretical cases, but when the letter from the secretary of the Pope was delivered to his study, he could neither refuse nor stall for time. According to what the Pope's personal secretary had written, the Holy Father wanted him to look personally into the case of the church of Saint Urban.

"This way, Professor, come. Be careful, the floor is rather slippery here," the keeper said as he ushered him inside.

Bergorio stared for a moment at the square interior of the church, dimly lit by the sunlight filtering through few openings. The air felt humid and sacred. He could see the frescoes only when the keeper turned on the lights.

"But . . . there's really somebody who lives in here?"

"Oh no, not nowadays, or at least that was the case up to some time ago." The keeper stared at him with his large—and bored—blue eyes. "In the 1960s, however, a keeper lived here, who had adapted the ancient pronaos and made it his home. Then, in 2002, the municipality of Rome bought the building and entrusted its management to the diocese of Rome," he said, shaking his balding head. "And the diocese opened it to worship again in 2005, as church rectory in the parish of Saint Sebastian outside the walls. If only they gave me a house, too, as they used to do in the past!" He added under his breath, opening his eyes wide, "Keepers must learn so many things . . . "

"I'm told someone does live here now," Bergorio said curtly, pushing back the usual, unruly lock of hair that kept falling across his forehead. "So *where* is this person?"

"He doesn't live *in* the church, you see. We keep him underneath, in the cellar," whispered the keeper conspiratorially, "in the most absolute darkness, because light gives him anxiety and tachycardia. He's been here for a few months now, since he had a stroke during afternoon Mass. Another stroke like that and he'll be a goner, if you want my opinion. The problem is, since that day he never came out again."

The keeper added, narrowing his eyes suspiciously, "Who knows why . . . "

"What?"

"He never came out again," the keeper repeated, nodding. "He's clinging to the gloomy cellar under the church, in the darkness . . . "

"Until the Vatican—"

"He'll stay there forever, I suppose."

"Why is that?"

"He used to be the parish priest," the keeper said casually, as if it were public knowledge. "Careful now, those marble stairs are slippery. Over here, behind the altar. That's the way down."

The words seemed to echo in his ears as Bergorio slowly climbed down the stairs into the darkness, his arms extended in front of him to avoid bumping into anything.

"Can't we have any kind of light?"

"No. Not anymore," the keeper answered, two steps ahead of him. "Come on, toward me . . . this way . . . now take hold of this waist-high rope on your left . . . did you find it? Good, now follow the rope and it will take you to him. I suggested repeatedly that they highlight the way with a phosphorescent line, you know what I mean? Like those you have on planes. That kind of light shouldn't bother him, but who knows? For now this is the only safe way to keep your bearings in this darkness."

"All right . . . "

"By the way, Professor, down here the crypt is very small, an underground chapel with a beautiful painting of the Holy Mary and the Child between the Saints Urban and John Mary. It's a strange painting, if only you could see it."

"Can I not see it?"

The keeper seemed to ignore his question and went on. "As I was saying, the Holy Mary is portrayed with a stance typical of eleventh century Byzantine paintings and seems to be standing because there is no throne. Her hands, however, rest on the Child's shoulders and he is sitting, instead, so that he seems to be floating in the air."

"Why am I not allowed to see it?" Bergorio asked, feeling himself pushed aside. The keeper was moving past him, returning back up the stairs.

"Saint John and Saint Urban are to her right and left. The first, who wears a pallium and a tunic, holds in his left hand a gem-encrusted Gospel; Saint Urban wears priestly garb and offers the Child a holy book which is encrusted with gems, too."

"Yes, but why can't I see it?" Bergorio asked again, annoyed.

"Ah, for the same reason why Don Pierini chose to hide down there," the keeper finally answered as he reached the altar level.

"I'm sorry, I don't get it?"

"The painting represents the Redeemer within a cross-shaped halo, barefoot, wearing a long-sleeved tunic, his hand raised in blessing. Rough and rigid in its lines, the whole painting is completely devoid of life or expression. The fresco can be dated back to the tenth century because of its rigid frontality, and has the peculiarity of lacking any shadows. Those same shadows Don Pierini is hiding from! That's why he has shut himself up down there, in absolute darkness.

"By the way," the keeper added after a pause, "the back of the underground chapel is divided from the rest by a gate made of iron bars, and that is where you'll find Don Pierini."

"Did you lock him up?" Bergorio asked incredulously.

"No, no, *he* locked himself up. The lock is quite ancient and he has the only key. He did it so he could not be dragged out of there. We informed the Vatican, but up to now you're the first they've sent."

They said nothing more.

Following the rope that, as far as he knew, led straight down to Hell, Bergorio advanced slowly through the dark, one arm still extended out.

"Don Pierini!" the keeper shouted so suddenly from above that Bergorio almost lost his footing. "There's a visitor for you, Professor Michele Bergorio. Let him hear you!"

In the next instant, Bergorio's extended hand met the cold metal of the cell bars, and he sighed in relief. He felt extremely uncomfortable in that gloomy nothingness, when something touched him, and he gave another sudden start.

Cold fingers intertwined with his own through the bars, holding them tight.

"Don't be afraid, Professor," said a weak, wretched voice coming from the cell. "It's not me you must fear, for far greater horrors present themselves to your eyes every day without you even noticing them. But they are there, Professor, no less insidious from going unnoticed."

"Don Pierini," Bergorio began, struggling to find the right words. He knew nothing about this case, so he had to make do as best he could. He opted for a conversational approach that could shorten the gap between them. "They want me to get to know you so that I can understand what is tormenting you."

A long silence followed his words. The priest drew back his hand.

"Don Pierini?" Bergorio called, waiting for his eyes to adapt to the absolute darkness of that place.

"To begin, I already told *them* what is tormenting me, Professor. The Vatican knows, which is why they allow me to live *here*," Pierini said, emphasizing the last word. He was silent for a while—a silence Bergorio didn't dare break—then went on. "Some of them don't believe me, but it is their problem. They are the sick ones, the ones who don't want to see, just like yourself, I'm sure. What kind of help can I get from somebody like you, Professor?"

"First, please explain why you're here. Why do you refuse to leave the cellar of this church?"

"Because I am safe here." Pierini's voice echoed in the crypt.

"Safe from what? How can the church of Saint Urban save you?" Bergorio asked, straining his eyes to see anything.

"I'm sorry to gainsay you, Professor, but this is not a church."

"Really?" Bergorio was amazed. "What is it?"

"It's a Roman temple."

"Ah, yes, of course, the temple of Ceres and Faustina."

Silence.

Bergorio finally asked, "Then how can Ceres and Faustina help you?"

"For starters, there are many things you don't know. Ceres is not just the goddess of the earth, of fertility, maternity, and harvests. She is bound to the world of the dead as well, through the *Caereris mundus*, a pit that was opened only on three specific days, August 24, October 5, and November 8. Those are the days I'm waiting for."

"But it's only May now!" Bergorio exclaimed. "Do you really wish to remain down here till the end of August?"

"I have no choice."

"But why?" Bergorio pressed him, while he pulled his cell phone from his pocket. It was the only source of light he thought to use to see something in the darkness.

"Because on that day, the pit between the world of the living and the underground world of the dead will be opened. The opening of the *mundus* is a delicate and dangerous moment, but not for fear that the dead might leave the underworld to invade the world of the living. On the contrary, according to Macrobius it is dangerous because the *mundus* draws the living into the world of the dead . . . "

"Is it there you want to go, then?" asked the professor while he turned the cell phone on, pointing its screen first at the floor, finally managing to glimpse something in that underground crypt.

"Yes."

He lifted the phone, and through its dim light looked into Don Pierini's protruding eyes. They were full of anticipation that turned to terror as soon as the light touched them.

"Turn it off! Turn it off!" he screamed like a maniac. Bergorio quickly did so, jamming his cell phone into his pocket.

"No shadows! There cannot be any shadows down here!" The voice of the parish priest was frightened, cracking with anxiety.

"Okay, I just had to make sure you were fine," Bergorio lied to make him calm down.

Pierini only huffed.

"You were telling me you want to get into the *mundus* . . ." Bergorio prompted, waiting some time for a response.

"Yes, to find a solution."

"A solution to what?"

"To the shadows," the priest whispered back.

"The shadows?" Bergorio repeated dumbly. "But how can Ceres help you in this?"

"Professor, are you *cerritus*?" Pierini asked suspiciously.

"What, please?"

"Of course, I must explain this, too. *Cerritus* means 'possessed by Ceres' spirit.' I am, you know. Yes, yes." Pierini's voice wobbled, as if he nodded frantically. "When I tell you *cerritus*, do you understand what I mean?"

"Possessed by Ceres?"

"Yes, Ceres is also the *mater larvarum*, the mother of ghosts. The ghosts have no shadow, so they are the ones to help me," Pierini went on.

"But how can they help you?" Bergorio insisted. "And why fear shadows? What do you see that we cannot?"

"I see not just the shadows, Professor, but the monstrosities hiding within their dark, porous surfaces. They are everywhere, and their numbers grow. I don't know for how long they have been among us, but they grow stronger, they are more . . . solid. Have you never noticed?"

"I still don't understand."

"Here, do you see? You're in denial, pretending not to know, and perhaps at a conscious level you really *don't* . . ." The parish priest paused for a long time, then went on. "But I believe you do know, deep down. If you had not met me, perhaps you would have managed to hide the truth from yourself forever, but now you will have to come to terms with it, now you won't be able to procrastinate for long. Now you will see, with all the consequences, what your fragile mind will have to face."

"What should I see? What is hiding in these shadows?"

"Monstrous beings. I don't know how they got here, but I know they aren't like us, they are different from any known living organisms but cannot survive if exposed to direct light, which is why they take shelter in the shadows, where nobody can see them . . . unless one should look very carefully."

Shaken in spite of himself, Bergorio looked around, trying to see anything, but his efforts remained in vain.

"These . . . beings you speak of, you say they do not tolerate the light. Why then does light frighten you?" Bergorio asked in his most reassuring tone. "Wouldn't it be enough to stay outside in the sunlight or, at night, in a well-lit room, to be safe from them?"

There was a deep, almost asthmatic, sigh, then Pierini answered, "Haven't you listened to what I told you? They can't reach into total darkness, they live only in the shadows. And wherever there is light, there are shadows as well. The more numerous the sources of light, the more numerous and insidious are the shadows. Yes, yes, they *flow*, Professor. Going home, today, you just look at your own shadow, notice where it blends and flows with the others over and over again: the long thin shadow of a lamppost, the awfully twisted one of a huge tree, and so on."

"They *flow*, you say?"

"Yes, they trickle, percolate, flow, crawl, slide, advance, and follow one another from shadow to shadow . . . " Pierini said, his voice beginning to take on a sound not unlike a hideous cackle.

"From shadow to shadow," Bergorio repeated dubiously.

"Pay careful attention and you'll see them too. You will see them flow, always following the contours of the shadows, and you will realize that every time your shadow crosses another, something evil flows into it to infect it. Once it nests in your shadow, it will start feeding off you, becoming more solid, more real."

Bergorio decided he'd had enough of the session, as the parish priest was surely influencing him with insanity.

"Don Pierini, this short conversation allowed me to begin to get a clear idea of your problem. You must understand that I want to help you, which is why in a few days I'll return with others to speak with you again.

For now, however, I have to go." In saying so, Bergorio extended his arm to shake hands, but Pierini grabbed his arm instead and forcefully dragged him forward until his face was pressed against the bars isolating the back of the crypt.

"Dusk is the time of day they like best," hissed Pierini in his ear, his tone almost vicious. "That moment when the sun has already set but there is still light in the sky, when even the most insignificant object has a longer shadow, and all the shadows form such a complex network that *they* can reach anything, anyone."

Bergorio wrenched himself free, then searched frantically for the rope leading upward. He left the crypt with all the speed that dark, infinite world allowed, followed by the disquieting voice still hissing from behind, "The light is not your friend. Avoid the shadows, Professor Bergorio, now they know that you know, that you can see them!"

THAT SAME DAY, after eight in the evening, while the sun slowly disappeared to the west beyond the tops of trees that seemed to pierce through it, Bergorio saw them.

They moved (or better, flowed) like black flat snakes endlessly altering their own shape, dreadfully laying in ambush behind every wall, every tree, every *thing*.

Bergorio came outside in a cold sweat as the hissing words of the mad priest echoed in his mind. He gritted his teeth and shivered while every fiber of his being screamed silent warnings. He did not want to give in nor to believe: The rational part of his brain that fought the irrational was already seeming to be losing ground.

He pushed back the unruly lock of hair from his forehead and quickened his pace, but he could not run. He sought only to get back to his car, while at the same time to head north to avoid the shadows.

His own shadow fell to his right and he could barely take his eyes off it. As he walked along the path and through the fields, he tried to prevent it from getting in contact with any other shadows, but it was an impossible task, and at each new contact his black shadow would blend with another, the shadow of a branch, a tree, a passing jogger. Something moved then, and afterward his shadow turned darker, more ethereal, but also . . . thicker.

Beyond the small bridge he had to turn left. He saw his shadow ahead of him, growing in length. He changed direction, and his shadow fell behind him. It followed him, never leaving, but all he could worry was that no longer it seemed just a shadow, but something demonic and hungry, as that Pierini had spoke of . . .

Bergorio felt weak, a weakness that grew by the minute. He wanted to run home, lock the door and the windows, shutting out even the weakest thread of light, so as to find again the welcoming darkness he had experienced only a few hours before, but he had no strength left.

His mind barely registered the shrieking Brazilian parakeets as they flew above. The world lost its colors, and a grayish fog began expanding at the edge of his field of vision. Bergorio fell to his knees and had to support himself against a tree not to hit the ground with his face. He could not move anymore, not even when his feet started tingling, when the tingling turned to pain, and he knew for sure that something was nibbling at him like a host of termites gnawing at a piece of wood, consuming it.

He knelt like that while more shadows enveloped him, and when everything turned gray and disappeared, over the shrieking of the Brazilian parakeets nesting in the tree he leaned against, madness finally claimed him.

Epilogue

"FOLLOW ME PLEASE, but mind the steps. They're slippery and it's quite dark down here that it'd be easy to step the wrong way and break your neck. You'll certainly be wondering why it is he's kept here in the cellar and why there isn't any light, not even a candle. The fact is, Professor Michele Bergorio cannot stand the light, he doesn't tolerate it . . . what I mean is that he's quite insane. Mad as a hatter, if you get my meaning," the keeper said, staring down with his watery blue eyes.

"You see, we had a similar case a few months ago with Don Pierini, who used to be the parish priest in this very church and sort of became unhinged as well. Professor Bergorio was a psychologist and should have treated him, but instead..." He paused for a moment. "Well, Don Pierini is now dead... one of the volunteers carelessly left the trapdoor to the crypt open one day, and a little light reached him. That was enough, and I found him stiff the next morning." The keeper's voice was filled with equal parts sorrow and disgust. "Ah, what an awful scene: He was there, stilled, with absolute dread in his swollen eyes, and the bars of the cell seemed to carve him into many little pieces.

"The physicians thought it might be something contagious, but the autopsy gave no such results. For sure, the fact that Professor Bergorio is suffering from a mind illness identical to Don Pierini's, who was his patient, is a real mystery. Is it possible that his patient perhaps infected or influenced him? Who's to say. In any case, you just be careful not to end up the same way, for goodness sake. I'll wait for you up here. You can reach him following the rope to your left.

"And... good luck to you."

CLAUDIO FOTI, writer and essayist, was born in Rome in 1967 and produces a constant stream of short weird stories. Major novels published include: Dobb e gli adoratori di Fenrir *(Elsa Morante Prix, 2000),* Ombre su Campo Marzio *(Ex J.R.R. Tolkien Prix, 2006),* Il Grande Orso *(2008),* Gli Occhi di Adanedhel *(2012),* Nereolie *(2013),* Romagick *(2014), and* Voynich 2017 *(2017). Major essays published include:* Il Codice Voynich *(Eremon, 2010),* Le Defixiones *(Eremon, 2014),* Il mito del Windigo *(Parallelo45, 2014),* Il Dio Anfibio *(Fenix, 2016),* I Segreti del Necronomicon *(Enigma, 2016), and* Guida alla Barcellona esoterica e magica *(Mursia, 2016).*

"Not enough," she says. "Never enough."

WARASHI'S GRIP

by Yukimi Ogawa

The following tale is a strange one, and I say that with the highest of praise. Author Yukimi Ogawa brings us her take on the Zashiki Warashi, a youthful yōkai-child often believed in legends to bring fortune to those whose houses it haunts.

As a bit of context, yōkai are the classification for all monsters, demons, and spirits inhabiting Japanese folklore, whether their alignment be good or evil, or with elements of both, which, as with most mythology, is generally the case, used for purposes of parables or cautionary tales.

So it is with the Zashiki Warashi, for its good intentions are bound, its beneficiaries unappreciative, and the fortune it's expected to bring comes, perhaps, at a price.

Haunting, beautiful, and complex: Woe to those fortunate in Warashi's Grip.

U P. OR DOWN. I CAN NO LONGER TELL.

In the flow, the tide, I will my arms out, away from me. I know fortune when I see it. Some tug at that fortune, those rare beings that can feel my presence, trying not to lose *it*. But I cannot afford to let anyone succeed.

Down, or up, I drag myself back. Into the house where, without all the flow, the push, I still pant as she takes *it* from me. As she swallows *it* so easily, the thing I managed to obtain after so much suffering.

She looks at me, me still shaking, panting, never recovering from the fall, or the surge. "Not enough," she says. "Never enough."

I pant more, and wonder about the end of all this.

AGAIN AND AGAIN. Yet again.

The first time, I still remember: She was as small as me, me who is still small, forever small. She looked so sad and lonely, and I *had* to give her something to pull her out of that sadness. So I pushed on against the tide, this harsh, relentless tide of eternity, of providence, my not being able to breathe hindering not a bit.

That first time, I could only snatch a tiny piece of fortune out of a small animal's paw. Prompted by this fortune, though, a neighbor came to the house when My Girl's mother—the old woman—was out. The neighbor gave My Girl a tin full of biscuits, which she soon hid from the old woman.

My Girl smiled then. She did. That was the only reward I needed for the drowning, that day.

Or, maybe, even today.

SHE GREW, but her mother didn't pay attention; My Girl needed more food every day to keep growing, and the old woman didn't give it to her. So I snatched bigger pieces from bigger animals or more of the smaller ones, when I had to. Soon though, My Girl wouldn't smile that easily. She would save her smiles, as if smiles were exhaustible.

So I started to snatch something even greater, pieces from people.

And of course fortunes such as those required more of my strength, more of my suffering. Even though I never grew, nor did my hands get bigger to grab more.

"MOTHER," MY GIRL SAID one day to the old woman. "I need a costume for the school play."

The woman looked at her once, looked away and sighed. "School play. In my time, in my place, there was no time for such leisurely things. I never had enough to wear. Now you want costumes?"

"Mother—"

"In my time, nothing was enough. Such leisurely thought—" the woman babbled on, without even looking at My Girl.

My Girl retreated to her room where I was, and she looked straight down at me, those eyes that never said anything, yet were so ablaze with demand.

But I was still panting from my last push. *Soon*, I thought, *I'd drown*. But if I drowned, who'd bring My Girl those small pieces of fortune she needed? What if my *not returning* threw her into more troubles? Her life full of troubles, as it was.

I hauled myself back into the flow. With an effort I opened my eyes. But something was wrong with my vision—it was too blurry, and that made it look as though everything in the tide was too fast, too violent, and there was nothing my small hand could hold. I was drowning! I frantically looked around; it took too much just to keep my eyes open, even—

—In my desperation I saw a girl who looked about the same age as My Girl. Around her, as if time had stopped or was extremely slow, the tide was calmer. I approached her.

She looked up, and our eyes met. Such empty eyes, without any fire, without demands; they asked for nothing. They somehow reminded me of My Girl—but that was impossible, of course. My Girl's eyes were always full of fire.

I grabbed at a piece adrift above this little girl, and plunged back into the tide.

IN MY HAND the other little girl's fortune pricked at my palm, just the same way My Girl often felt to me. I looked up, gagging for breath, and My Girl looked at me. Then snatched the thing out of my hand.

My head ached. If I hadn't been able to find that small girl, this time it might have been the end of me. Really.

Why had that other girl been so indifferent? Why let go of a piece of fortune with no resistance at all? For she had seen me, I was sure.

I shook my head and focused back on my surroundings. These days, the way My Girl devoured the things I brought back, she looked very much like a savage beast. She licked her lips and looked about, as if, for a moment, she couldn't quite remember where she was.

Once her eyes had unfocused and then focused back on me, she licked her lips again. She looked like an animal or like a monster that was far worse than me.

She stood. Left the house, without glancing at her mother once.

I HAVE NO IDEA where she got the dress or how. But she knew how to use the stolen pieces of fortune well, and she turned them into whatever shapes she wanted. Some years later she said to the old woman, "Mother, you need to talk to my teacher."

And the old woman looked halfway up and frowned. "Why?"

My Girl looked halfway down, and their eyes never met. "You. We. Need talk about my future. My high school."

The woman looked back down at her own hands. "High school? I never got into high school."

She didn't make a sound.

"In my days, we had no choice. We girls—"

The woman went on babbling like always, and faded into silence when My Girl said or did nothing. When she stopped speaking completely, My Girl said, "You need to go talk to the teacher. Otherwise he'll come visit. Do you want him to come visit?"

The old woman hugged herself and shook her head. "No."

Without another word My Girl came back into her room. These days, I dreaded meeting her eyes. But how could I look away?

She looked into my eyes, savage fires in both of her own.

BEHIND ME WAS a wall that was her fire. I inched closer to the flow until my feet were swept away from under me. I screamed a voiceless scream as the tide closed around me. I looked for that little girl, rather than her fortune. I had more chance that way.

And I found her.

Or did I? The little girl seemed to have grown, or shrunk, I couldn't tell. But she had those empty eyes, and I didn't have enough time to stare and decide. As soon as my fingers were around something, I was pulled away, back into the tide. Back into the room where My Girl devoured the thing I had stolen for her.

And somehow, she turned it into high school.

WHY DON'T I simply walk away? That just isn't my nature, after all. I am a monster that's so closely attached to a house, with an insuppressible impulse for making the house's residents happy. In the old days people were satisfied with simpler things, like better cultivation or better health. But My Girl, this beast, is never happy.

And soon, I'm looking again for that empty-eyed girl from the flow.

Sometimes she looks smaller, sometimes older. I don't care. I cannot afford to care. Every time I find her, she lets me take from her. Soon, there isn't even the sense of guilt.

Back home, My Girl turns things into a career and then into a man. The biggest smile comes when she tells her mother that she would never come back to the house again, and when the old woman clings to her and begs not to leave her behind, My Girl shakes the old woman off, as if trying to get rid of a foul bug buzzing about her. She then half-looks at me, never meeting my eyes. And I realize, she no longer has the savage fire in her eyes. Perhaps she feels guilty. Probably not.

I realize I am more relieved than sad.

The old woman cries and cries for days. I spend days just lying, having nothing to do. But then my instinct starts to buzz.

And then there is no suppressing it.

I am a monster attached to this house, and the house now belongs to the lone old woman.

It doesn't look like she can see me. But I sit beside her, anyway, rubbing her old, bent back. "What do you want?" I ask her.

She says, "My Girl . . . My Girl . . . "

So I throw myself back into the flow.

THIS TIME, the empty-eyed girl looks so small, so vulnerable.

Those empty eyes, just like always, wanting nothing. I rip a piece off her, tiny and fragile, with a sting of guilt in my chest. But I return to the old woman without looking back.

"Here," I say to her. "This is yours."

I make her swallow it by putting it into her tea.

A FEW DAYS LATER I hear loud voices and footsteps. I recognize one of the voices, and before long, My Girl is in front of me, clutching my throat.

"What did you do?" she hisses. "What did you do?"

Behind her the old woman is chanting "My girl, my girl . . . " and a man looks back and forth between her and My Girl. He looks horrified as he asks, "Who are you talking to?"

My chest aches, just like when I am about to drown. My Girl throws me sideways, almost banging me into the wall.

She says to the man, "I'll stay here till the baby's out."

"What?" The man blinks, and he looks so stupid. "But I thought . . . you said . . . "

"Just till I see the baby safely out. I need it."

"You need what?"

"You won't understand."

I watch them as they exchange more words, huddled and shaking in a corner.

AS SOON AS she's carried her things back into the old house, she crouches over me, pinning me down to the floor. "You bring me whatever you can find," My Girl says above me, her eyes wide open and beginning to burn anew. "Whatever that can make her condition better." And she pushes me into the flow.

Up. Or down. Did that thing I brought back for the old woman draw My Girl back? Did I *want* her back? What do I want (but does it matter)? I search for the empty-eyed girl. I have to tear whatever I can off her, whatever might make My Girl happy.

There she is, old or young, small or tall—

—I reach my hand out—

—And a girl turns around, looking half-up at me, fires kindling in her own eyes. She grabs my wrist that I extend toward her, and pulls me down to her side, out of the tide.

Wrong girl!

I fall to the solid ground. I look around stupidly; I didn't even know it was possible to be out of the flow, outside the house.

The other girl sits down on the ground and makes me sit up. I'm still panting, but the girl's lips are so pale and I wonder if this girl, too, just almost drowned. "Who are you?" she asks.

Who *was* I? "I don't know."

"Why do you take things from me? I'm always weak and ill, is it because you are taking from me?"

My eyes sting. So this is not the wrong girl. "Sorry," I say after a moment.

"You have reasons, right?" She shifts and looks into my eyes. "You always look so frightened."

"Sorry," I say again. "I took so many things from you. More than I can count. I shouldn't have."

"So many? Only a few, as I remember, but many enough to make me weak."

I say nothing to this. Sure enough, every time I took a piece of fortune from an empty-eyed girl, she—or they—looked somehow different. Were they a few different girls who looked like each other?

"I'll forgive you if you become my friend. I don't have a friend. My classmates are all frightened of my mom."

Friend. I swallow. I haven't heard that word for decades. "Okay."

She smiles. *Smiles.*

I look around. I cannot see the outlet that I came through, or the tide behind it. Did I manage to escape? Just like that?

We start to play and talk. Just like two small girls. Without my trying to snatch pieces from her, she looks happy, all the while, until she says goodbye for the day.

SO AFTER THAT, every day after school this little girl comes to meet me. One day she asks, "Where do you live?"

I've been spending nights in various places, under this tree, or in that toilet booth. Which has caused no problem because most people cannot see me. "Where do *you* live?" I ask her to avoid answering.

"Just over there." She points. And then, "Maybe I can show you, Mom's out right now."

She takes my hand and leads me to an old, small house.

Oh yes.

Of course, I had never seen the house from the outside. I had rarely even been out of her room. But I know that smell. The smell of unhealthiness, the smell of my own panting. So I didn't escape, after all. How could I believe otherwise? We reach her room, and the girl, unaware of my shallow breathing, pulls a flat cushion for me to sit on.

"Is this your room now?" I ask.

"Now? This has always been my room."

I examine the room. The tatami mat looks new, with different linings. But there are scratches and stains on the wall that look familiar. She goes to the bookshelf and traces the spines of a few files. She says, "Do you want to see my photo albums?"

I nod.

She pulls the albums out of the shelf and lays them in front of the cushion. We sit down and she opens one of them.

"Look, this is me, when I came home with Mom from the hospital."

She points at one with My Girl holding a baby in her arms, the man smiling into the baby beside her. I point at the man. She answers my silent question. "My father? He's gone."

"Where?"

"I don't know. Mom says 'the house betrayed us,' when she talks about him, or about my health."

The house betrayed us ... Did I? But how could I have known? That old woman. My Girl. And now this little girl. All the empty-eyed girls that I took from. No wonder I could never tell up or down. I've been both, future and past.

I hear the door open, and then her voice, My Girl's voice laden with years, calling the little girl. I cannot look up. Beside me, the little girl is saying, "Mom's back!" My eyes are still fixed on the photos—

—and then her hands are on my throat. The little girl is screaming. But I knew this would happen. I am even glad, in a way, that what I knew would happen happened after all. This is the way of us.

"Where have you been," My Girl says to me, she hisses. "Husband's left and Mother's weak, and look at my girl! You didn't come back, and she's still ill! Why didn't you come back! Why did you betray us!"

"I ... you ... "

"Mom! She can't breathe!" The little girl screams.

My Girl glances the little girl's way, and her hand loosens ever so slightly. I pant, and vaguely wonder how not-panting was ever possible. "That was all yours. All of them." I cough. I gag. "I'd been taking from you three, bringing back to you three. It's always been a zero sum."

But I swallow the next words, *Because you all somehow let me.*

Her hand on me loosens a little more for one second, before tightening back the next. She seems to be thinking hard. There must be a bell ringing in her head, because of course I've taken from her, too, in those years when her eyes happened to be empty. "So for my daughter to be healthy," she finally says, "one of us would have to be unhappy."

I nod.

She looks in the direction of the room in which the old woman must be laying.

"No," I hastily say. "I cannot choose where I turn out. And I cannot tell you three apart when you don't have fire in your eyes. And I'm not strong enough now to go for someone entirely unknown to me . . . "

When she looks back at me, the fire is there, in her eyes, while only the moment before there'd been none; now it burns so cold that I choke on my own shivering. She says, "Why don't you take yours, then?"

"W—what?"

"Yours." Her grip goes even tighter, if that is possible at all. "You little fortune-bringing monster. Why do you keep thinking you can take from some to give to others? Why don't you take from your own self, and make us all happy?"

Why? *Why?* Because that is what I do. How can she assume happiness is something endless, something that never drains? But how can I say that to her? How can I simply refuse to go back to the days when I had to almost drown just to scrape a tiny, coarse piece of happiness from someone or something else?

So instead of all that, I say, "Me . . . "

"Yes, you."

"You want *me* to take from me."

"Yes."

Slowly, her grip loosens to nothing and I sit up. I decide to try not to imagine what would happen if I do that; it doesn't matter to her, what I imagine anyway.

So I fall. Not up, not down, just into the nothingness of my own.

THE CHILDREN IN THE NEIGHBORHOOD call it the horror house these days. It looks as though it is leaning, with the roof tiles falling away, some of its wood rotting as it stands. The grandmother is a mad woman, bobbing up and down on the languid river of her own mortality. The little daughter never gets up anymore, her illness slowly but steadily eating her away in a slow trickle. The mother tries to take care of them both, and fails, her own strength seeping away too.

None of them have any fire in their eyes now.

I watch them all from my corner. My own strength is draining, I can feel, but once I started I cannot stop taking from *me*. My happiness is for her to be happy. I take from me, which means she is unhappy, and her unhappiness makes me take more—it's an endless, downward spiral. And this will last until one of us is dead. Perhaps I'm the first to go, but by then, everything would be far too late for her, too.

And it feels so much better than drowning, anyway.

YUKIMI OGAWA lives in a small town in Tokyo where she writes in English but never speaks the language. She still wonders why it works that way. Her fiction has appeared in such places as Fantasy & Science Fiction, Clarkesworld, *and* Strange Horizons.

"Alvarenga's life ended badly," she said. "You may
say he was overtaken by his sins . . ."

THE WHITE MONKEY

by Carlos Orsi

So like tragic memories do the ghosts of slavery haunt us, do they revisit with vestiges of past horror, barbarity, and pain, tainting the land, and tainting, too—even generations later—the descendants of those involved.

Acclaimed Brazilian author and reporter Carlos Orsi brings us this account of Professor Leoni who travels to a São Paulo university in the tropical savanna of the Cerrado in order to give a lecture on Biological Science. What he unexpectedly finds is a mystery of ancestry and revenants of hatred, and, as circumstances often dictate, it may be he, the teacher, who learns a lesson, and that is to beware The White Monkey.

O F COURSE, THE TAXI DRIVER GOT LOST ONCE WE arrived on campus—he couldn't find the Biology building where I was supposed to make my presentation. In the end, I just alighted at some random point, close to an open area that looked like a food court for the students. It was lunch time.

I couldn't, in good conscience, call the long hours of travel that had got me there a "nightmare," but the whole process had been increasingly annoying, Chinese-torture-wise: more like an itch you cannot scratch than real, up-front pain. With a sigh and a crackling from the taxi's plastic seat cover, I got out, feeling disgusted by the perspiration drenching my armpits and neck.

There were long lines at almost every food stall, so I ended up with a sausage roll and a can of some local soda that tasted like frozen bubble gum. Then I texted the careless professor who was supposed to be my contact here, telling her I was already on campus and please, could someone tell me where I should go, or could somebody come for me?

They'd invited me to speak to the Biological Sciences undergraduates. I'd accepted with a mixture of vanity and curiosity—sins for which I'd been paying dearly since the departure from Sao Paulo, some five hours ago. After a cramped flight and the bumpy taxi ride from the airport, the hotel they'd booked me in couldn't process my check-in, due to a computer problem or whatever, so I'd come directly to the university. All I wanted was a decent bath and some air-conditioning.

I wasn't going to get any of that anytime soon.

I'd never been in the Brazilian Midwest, never seen the Cerrado, that haunting composite of gnarled desert trees and savanna that the soybean plantations and beef farms were destroying at an alarming rate. Although, as far as I knew from tales told by a great-aunt, ancestors of mine had been slaves somewhere close by, hundreds of years ago, so I had hidden roots here.

And it was then, thinking about things hidden in plain sight, that I noticed the monkeys.

Capuchin monkeys, the size of big rats or small cats. There were not many, and they were somewhat shy—but they were certainly *there*. Mischievous, sometimes outright perverse, monkeys played an important role in my great-aunt's stories, and I instinctively moved to protect my meager meal.

The food court was a long corridor, a stone-paved trail on the short grass, covered by a white plastic cupola. This cupola was supported by metallic trusses, chock-full of vines and creepers. You could see the monkeys running up and down, sometimes dangling, briefly, from a horizontal truss above one stall or another. I saw signs: *Don't feed the monkeys: They get all they need from nature.* The campus was virtually continuous with the surrounding Cerrado. There was just a thin wire fence dividing the university from the open country.

Mostly, the students and the food vendors did their best to ignore the animals. Here and there someone tried to get a snapshot of them. I believe I saw one or two people disingenuously letting small bits of bread fall to the ground "by accident." Then, the cutest thing: a little monkey timidly raising a white ball of bread in its tiny, beautiful, nervous hands.

Or, at least, I knew, intellectually, that it *should* be cute—the whole scene, I mean. That I ought to find it all very quaint, very touching.

But I didn't.

The court's plastic cover made the air trapped inside, in the shade, stuffy, and moving outside put me under the ruthless midday sun. Perhaps it was the combination of weariness and discomfort, perhaps the memory of some old story, but to me the capuchins seemed slightly repulsive, with their open, baffled mouths, all-black eyes, dust-dirty fur, and almost-human faces.

While I ate, I kept my backpack propped against my right leg. I felt immediately, then, when one of the capuchins tried to grab it. The attempt was ludicrous, of course; that piece of luggage weighed more than the animal. I should've smiled and laughed.

Instead, it was as if every single frustration of the last hours finally found a focus; I'm ashamed to say that I turned on the monkey as if it were the very soul of evil, aiming, with a snarl, a fierce blow at it. The soda can was my intended bludgeon.

A few things happened. First, the can, slick on the outside, twisted in my sweating hand as I brandished it. My thumb got caught in the opening. I felt a little pain, which imparted some extra violence to the move. Secondly, the capuchin jumped when it saw the blow coming, but with the can slipping in my grip as I bore down, the trajectory misaimed, and the little primate got the metal smack in the jaw. The blow sent it cartwheeling in the air, screaming.

The third thing was, of course, that everybody turned to stare at me. Hurting a monkey was a big no-no there, I could see.

So I grabbed the backpack and marched out, looking for shade elsewhere. I found it some fifty yards away, a whitewashed wall in the middle of an area delimited by a circle of red bricks. A bronze plaque declared that this was the last remaining wall of an ancient house from the seventeenth century, made of rammed earth, and that there lived and died the infamous *capitão do mato*, or bush captain, Amadeu Teodoro Alvarenga.

I knew about bush captains: They were commanders of small mercenary groups employed in hunting down escaped slaves and in waging war against the *quilombos*, free villages built in the jungle by such slaves. These were wars of extermination, with women and children butchered to serve as example. I asked myself how the students allowed the wall to stand: I could understand its historical value, and remains of rammed earth buildings from the seventeenth century are exceedingly rare, but the thing might easily be construed as a monument to the memory of a monster.

Well, I told myself, *now this monster's work is keeping me in the shade, so I presume I should thank him, even if some great-grandparent of mine had suffered in the hands of his ilk.*

Touching the wall lightly, I noticed that the whitewashing was somewhat recent. To preserve the construction from the elements, surely, but also perhaps to cover some indignant graffiti? Then I saw that my thumb was bleeding—my clownishness with the soda can had left a straight cut over the joint, not deep, but . . . some of the blood stayed on the wall.

I shrugged. If the university didn't want people to interact with the thing, they should've removed it to a museum. So I sat on the grass, propped my back against the wall, and enjoyed the view. The campus was large, sprawling. Most of it was grass and flowerbeds, everything well-tended. The buildings were the usual modernistic fare, flat slabs of concrete at odd angles to each other, interspaced with steel tubes and glass. The color scheme was of white, yellow, and red.

"Hi there! Mister Leoni? Sorry about . . . "

The girl coming toward me wore blue jeans and a T-shirt reading *BIO-SCI SYMPOSIUM: ORGANIZATION*. I called her a "girl," but she was, of course, a woman: Doctor Melissa Pereira, my contact. I've been working with science and scientists for more than two decades, but I still get a little disconcerted when I find people in their late twenties who have doctorates, or even post-docs, something that is becoming more and more common. Dr. Pereira was young enough to be my daughter.

I groaned, my knees complaining as I stood, and offered my hand.

"No problem," I lied. "Pleased to meet you."

"I called your hotel," she said. "They told me your reservation is still valid, and that you can make your check-in anytime today."

"I'm glad to hear it." I'd mentioned the hotel problem in the text message. "You have quite a piece of history there," I said, pointing over my shoulder to the wall, as we walked away.

"Yes, it is," she agreed. "This whole campus was built on what used to be Alvarenga's farm. He bought the land after retiring from . . . well, from what he did. He raised cattle."

"This place here was far from civilization at the time, wasn't it?"

"In a way, yes. But it happened to be a sort of crossroads on the path between the sugar cane plantations, to the northeast, the gold mines to the south, and the Araguaia River, which was an important waterway back then. Drovers would stop by to trade in livestock, get some rest, buy fresh horses."

I saw that we were mercifully moving toward a car—one of those American monstrosities, a SUV, with stripes in the university colors on its doors and top. I'm sure I couldn't have walked much more under the sun. Dr. Pereira—Melissa—had taken my backpack from me, and I'd allowed it, my old-man-of-the-world self-sufficiency, rugged masculine pride be damned. I asked, "Is it not a little controversial to keep that wall?"

"Controversial?" She seemed puzzled.

I explained my view that it might be seen as a monument to a slave hunter and killer. Melissa laughed. "Yes, I guess so. But here, people quickly learn the whole story."

Now it was my turn to be puzzled. "Whole story?"

"Alvarenga's life ended badly," she said. "You may say he was overtaken by his sins. His place was busy during summers and springs, but he wintered mainly alone. One spring the drovers came by to find the house burned to the ground, only one wall standing—that wall—and his eyeless, jawless, half-vulture-eaten corpse nailed there with heavy iron spikes. Everybody supposed it could only have been payback, from a *quilombo* posse or even from local Indians. So, in time, people started to see the wall as a symbol of resistance."

Revenge more than resistance, I thought, but kept the distinction to myself.

She added, "Not that this was the original interpretation, of course. When word got out, a poet wrote an epic with Alvarenga as the tragic hero and the wall as a final boundary between civilization and savagery, but nobody reads that shit anymore. And then it all became..."

She stopped in midsentence, her arm half-stretched to open the driver's door of the SUV. I noticed she was looking over my shoulder, toward the wall.

"That's curious," she muttered, her mind seeming to run in a different track.

"What?"

"A monkey on the wall. They usually avoid it, people here have all kinds of theories about why it's so. And it is... oh, it can't be..." She squinted, raised a hand to protect her eyes from an excess of sunlight. "Yes, it is. It's licking something there..."

WE DROVE TO the Biology building, and once inside she led me to the auditorium. After a brief stop on the way to wash my face and brush my teeth, I went to meet the audience.

I have an academic degree in Brazilian Literature, but life—"that which happens while we are not looking," etc.—turned me into a somewhat popular writer of science books for the general public. My first work, *The Facts of Evolution*, had been published some twenty years before, and since then I had written about Mathematics, Astronautics, Astronomy, and, in partnership with a well-reputed physicist, Particle Physics. Last year I'd returned to Biology with *The Price of Knowledge*, about the importance of doing research in living animals. It was a controversial topic, to say the least, and the reason I'd been invited here to address the Biological Sciences Symposium.

I like to believe that my approach to the subject is both rational and compassionate. The whole point is that animal experiments are sometimes necessary, to advance knowledge and to save human lives. This was the gist of my presentation.

The auditorium wasn't much more than a glorified classroom, really. It wasn't full, but it was less than half-empty—a victory, as far as I was concerned. Not bad for a second-rate guy.

Melissa gave a little introductory speech, graciously mentioning the fact that my books were available at the campus bookstore, and then I talked a little about myself before dimming the lights to start the slide presentation. We were a few minutes into the semidarkness when one of the double doors of the room opened—the light from the outside flooding in from behind the students' heads, making me squint—and someone stood there. I could see only a dark human figure, all black space with a dim contour.

"If this is so important," said the human-shaped void, "we should spare the nobler animals and do the research in the filthy niggers."

And it was gone. The door closed.

I confess it made me speechless for more than a moment. Racial abuse was nothing new to me, of course—after the publication of *The Facts of Evolution*, bad jokes about my skin color and the "descent from apes" became common currency among some strident fundamentalist preachers, and I usually had a good-humored, even if barbed, response ready. But the thing at the university was so gratuitous and unexpected.

Then the lights were on and Melissa was standing up and apologizing, asking me if I'd like to stop the lecture, if I'd like her to call campus security to find the offender. But I just smiled graciously and said that I'd prefer to go on. Lights out, I completed the presentation in my own time and without further ado. There were questions, which I answered, and more apologies from the students. Then a sophomore made a sophomoric little speech about racism on campus and how ashamed everybody was . . . People applauded, and that was that.

The next event in the symposium was a teleconference with a Brazilian astrobiologist working at NASA who'd talk to the students directly from the U.S. I decided to attend, out of politeness and because I didn't have anything else to do. The idea of steaming in a taxi all the way back to the hotel was not appealing. And everybody else was going to the teleconference.

To follow the crowd is always the easiest way.

Afterward, Melissa offered me a ride back to the hotel. "The SUV is air-conditioned," she said.

I accepted, gladly, but kept my mouth shut most of the way. She may have thought I was chagrined by the racist rant during the lecture; as a matter of fact, I believe I was experiencing some symptoms of a mild form of sunstroke. Anyway, when we were arriving at the hotel, Melissa asked me, in a tone that was half friendly and half apologetic, if I would like a drink.

"There's a new bar in town," she said. "They have a lot of new beer labels, microbrew stuff. What do you think?"

"Yes, it would be nice, thank you," I answered. "Just let me check-in and leave the backpack in the room, and off we'll go."

I GOT BACK two hours later, slightly drunk. Don't remember if I invited Melissa to my room; she was young enough to be my daughter, but she wasn't. My daughter, I mean. She was a little plain, and too thin around the hips for my taste, but I was touched, after all. Anyway, if I did invite her, she declined. Fair enough.

Got into the elevator and to my room, without inflicting any further damage to my dignity: slightly drunk, but still capable of keeping proper balance and looking serious enough.

My room was cold, freezing cold, just as I hoped; when I'd been there earlier, I had turned on the air-conditioner and left it running. Now it was pure bliss. The place was small and nondescript, walls painted white, white plastic furniture, off-white bed sheets that were this close to threadbare. I took a bath, went to bed . . . and couldn't sleep.

With my eyes open, I felt just as I already said, slightly drunk; but as soon as I shut them, the world seemed to spin on all three axes at once. My stomach lurched, but that wasn't the worst. The worst was the fear.

I cannot explain it, but the sudden sensation of movement made my skin clammy. I felt as if I were tumbling in a void that wasn't really a void—it was the vast, voracious, empty belly of something dire: Canny pools of glistening acid hid there, I felt, just waiting for me. I knew I was trapped; an imaginary sound, a delusional scream—an apish screech—brought me back.

Eyes open, things went back to normal with a jerk—or almost. The all-white décor had become upsetting; now it suggested the hospital or, worse, a room in a mental ward. I went into the bathroom (off-white towels) to splash water on my face and try to shake the dread.

It almost worked.

So, back in bed, eyes wide open, I took the laptop, hoping that the internet would help me to kill time until my body had finished with what I believed to be aftereffects of alcohol and hops. The hotel had a barely useful Wi-Fi network—not strong enough to allow streaming video, but okay for some web browsing.

In the bar, my conversation with Melissa had drifted here and there, until we'd finally got to the subject of Alvarenga's wall. We'd talked about bush captains—how they went from heroes in their own lifetimes to pariahs from history, an embarrassment not even mentioned in most high school textbooks.

Then I recalled she'd said something about an epic poem. The Literature Major in me couldn't help but to feel tickled.

"Oh, I don't know much about it," she'd said. "The author was some exile from Portugal, I think, but, as I said, nobody reads it anymore."

It had to mean that the poem ought to be especially atrocious. The number of people writing Portuguese poetry in Brazil during the seventeenth century was so small that any production from the period should've become canonical, just for existing. And I'd never heard of a text like the one she was describing.

So, I Googled it.

It wasn't easy—the only keywords I had for my search were the bush captain's name—but I finally found the so-called epic, tucked into a forgotten corner of an almost-forgotten public-domain-content website. The author's name was Basilio Nuno Gonzaga, and, yes, he'd been a well-educated man exiled to the colonies, becoming a drover. There was precious little information about his life and work. His year of death was given as 1712. The first widely known Brazilian epic was from 1769, more than a generation after Gonzaga's passing. It was amazing.

The poem, called "The Last Stand," was relatively short for a narrative piece, having less than five hundred lines. The versification seemed almost haphazard, with little attention to metric—there were verses from five to ten syllables, with no discernible pattern—and even less consistency in the rhyme scheme. One might, with a little charity, call the style baroque. The man was clearly an incompetent poet, but there was an expressive power in the verse, conveyed more by brute force than by subtlety.

The theme was the final siege of Alvarenga's farm by an alliance of natives and escaped slaves. For the author, it was a mystical prefiguration of some future "Last Stand" of Christianity, and civilization against savagery, paganism, and barbarism. According to Gonzaga's broken verse, the bush captain had fought for his life under a heavy storm, with sudden flashes of lightning revealing the well-muscled naked bodies of howling cannibals and blood-crazed man-apes, all armed with heavy, gnarled clubs and razor-sharp, yellowed bones.

The Alvarenga character had one, and only one, friend and companion: a white monkey that trod upon his shoulders, like a pirate's parrot, and that fought by his side, gouging eyes and drinking deep from lacerated necks.

What could this animal stand for? "Pure" nature, unsoiled by man? "Tame" Indians, who allowed themselves to be subdued and Christianized? *What?*

I read it with a mixture of awe and revulsion. It was no surprise, I saw, that the poem had been forgotten in the nooks and crannies of literary history, despite its chronological importance. But, as I said, there was a brute force element in the writing that almost made me hallucinate blood seeping out of the page—or screen, in this case—at one time or another. However, even these forceful moments were more grotesque than artistic. The thing was engrossing, but it would not help me sleep.

What made me stop reading—and re-reading—was the clap and clash of the windows rattling with a sudden wind and rain.

A storm had broken outside.

Curiously, there was no thunder. But when I raised my eyes from the laptop, I had to shut them; the white walls were suddenly too bright, too glaring. I reopened them slowly, cautiously, before my world started spinning again . . . I didn't want back into that monster's belly. The white flare endured, but I saw I could tolerate it by squinting a little.

Somehow feeling soiled and demeaned, I decided to have a bath.

I WAS NAKED and soaped when it happened. The tap-tap-tap of the bathroom shower fused with the roar of the rain and wind outside, and something ruffled—a towel, or leaves on a branch? I had the bathroom lights dimmed, to avoid the glare effect I'd suffered in the bedroom, and now the brownish shades and shadows around me, projected from the outside on the dim surfaces of the milky-colored shower stall had gained a new quality—a new depth, just as the noise of the water falling on me mixed with the music of the rain outside. These qualities of sound and light made the stall feel like a capsule in an infinite expanse. I was sure I could see the silhouettes of branches, to listen to water dripping from leaves.

Padded feet trod on the other side of the stall. Something wrapped in white fur jumped in—the wind propelling a towel? I tried to think so; but then it screeched and bared its teeth. I scrambled back, screaming.

I slipped and tumbled backward, breaking through the plastic stall, falling on . . . the bathroom floor?

No. Dead leaves. Wet grass. The scent, the texture of rainwater and wind-propelled dribble, so different from shower drops. Blue lighting, far away. And the taste of blood. My lips, smashed, bled.

I felt my heart jump to my throat, there to become a ball of ice. Incomprehension mingled with dread, and before I could deal with the confusion, the white animal was at me, vying for my neck.

It was a monkey, fangs dripping a pink mixture of rainwater and blood, small, hard nails crisscrossing my hands with tiny tracks of broken skin that slowly filled with red from underneath. The critter was strong and quick. The onslaught, staggering.

"Is that the slave? The one we saw stalking our house? Who bloodied it with its filthy ichor?"

It was a bass, masculine voice. There was something curious about the diction, but I only thought about it much latter. At that moment, I had other things on my mind. The voice, however, seemed immediately familiar. The monkey had relented and jumped away at hearing the man.

He came nearer. Amid the shadows, all I could see was his outline—and then I knew where I'd listened to that voice before.

"Why were you skulking around my house, boy? Are you hungry? You would steal a calf, wouldn't you, you lazy bastard? By God, it's been a long time since I last hunted down the likes of you, but if you come around to steal my meat, you can be sure I'll get yours. I'll brand you, gut you, give your heart to the ants, and then I'll feast on you, boy."

The talking outline had something shiny in its hand—a machete. I froze. The night was hot and rain, lukewarm, but the ice in my heart spread to the rest of the body. I was frozen in place. All I could do was to chitter, uncontrollably, like a monkey myself

The atmosphere changed suddenly. Somehow, the vastness I felt all around disappeared. There was a sense of closeness: A group of forms now surrounded us.

"Our great-grandson did a good job bringing him out," said one of the forms, addressing, as far as I could tell, me. "Go home, child. We'll take it from here."

There was an echo of screams as the grass under me turned into tiles, and the night darkness exploded into fluorescent light. Melissa was kneeling by my side, along with a hotel clerk.

"Leoni? Are you all right? Lord, you're burning!"

I felt the fever, then. There was water all around me, but my mouth was parched. I looked up—there was a splitting headache—and I saw the shower stall, the aluminum shafts twisted, the plastic surfaces splintered like thin glass. I'd fallen right through it.

I NEVER KNEW WHY Melissa came back.

I spent a few days in the university hospital. The diagnosis was fungal infection, probably from the cut on my thumb. The doctors explained that there are some fungi, especially found in bird droppings, that can wreak havoc in the brain when they enter the bloodstream. It's a rare kind of infection, but... *Bad luck.* I'd probably acquired it when I touched the Alvarenga wall.

It didn't explain the cuts and bites on my hands—someone said something about plastic splinters, and I dropped the subject.

After returning home, I reread the poem, searching, but it's silent on the fate of the white monkey.

For since, I've seen it. Glimpses only: a white tail, fleetingly, among the shelves of a bookstore, or behind the bottles of a bar. Little ivory fangs, shinning on my face, when I look toward the sun. White fur under my fingernails when I wake up. The echo of a screech when I go to sleep...

I don't know if I brought it back with me, or if it has always been here—only, until now, unnoticed. I think it cannot harm me anymore, in this day and age. But I am not sure.

Not quite sure.

CARLOS ORSI is a Brazilian writer of mystery and speculative fiction, with two novels and three short story collections published in Portuguese. He is a two-time winner of the Argos, the most important Brazilian prize for science fiction and fantasy, in the best short story category. Internationally, his work has appeared in the anthologies Tales of the Wold Newton Universe *(Titan)*, War Stories *(Apex)*, Swords v. Cthulhu *(Stone Skin)*, and Rehearsals for Oblivion *(Elder Signs)*, and in the magazines Ellery Queen Mystery Magazine *and* Mystery Weekly Magazine. *When not creating fiction, he works as a reporter and essayist, writing news articles and opinion pieces on science and culture for magazines and newspapers. Carlos lives in the state of Sao Paulo with his wife Renata and Violet the Cat.*

. . . the effect was to make the castle look as though it
were permanently besieged by the island's geology.

THE WEST WIND

by David McGroarty

Unfortunately, if you were to search for Scottish author David McGroarty's fiction writing, you'll not yet find a lot of it. But what there is, is always powerful and haunting, dark and imaginative, with a particularly sublime literary sensibility.

So as I have for each of my prior anthologies, I've selected a piece that I feel will close out this book on a powerful and memorable note, something to leave a lasting impression in the reader's mind. This anthology's choice is: The West Wind.

Take a moment before you proceed; this tale isn't one to skim lightly. For there is a wind that blows west, and an island slip you should not roam, and there are places you and I don't go together.

I N EIGHTEEN YEARS OF GROWING UP ON THE ISLE OF Aransay, Neil Corrigan had never ventured onto the Fitzroy Estate. As a teenager, he had gone as far as the park gates—ugly, frightening things that they were—but even then, in his little gang, with their propensity for wandering the island and flouting convention, he had not crossed over. It was a strange thing, then, to be returning to the island in his forties, for those gates to be gone, and to pass through like a ghost, unchecked and unchallenged.

Perhaps stranger to Neil was knowing that his childhood friends were waiting for him on the estate, and that one of them had lived there for years. He'd rolled off the ferry into the town of Tarbert that afternoon feeling invisible. People he had once known well failed to acknowledge or recognize him as he walked up and down the streets. The impression that came over him then was that he'd slipped out of phase with life on the island in his years away—that, maybe, to these people, he had never existed as an islander. That feeling took root in his stomach as he entered the estate, and he found himself imagining that when he arrived at his destination, his friends would turn him away as a stranger.

He found the old groundskeeper's cottage at the end of a long drive along a circuitous track that split from the estate's main avenue. Although Fitzroy Castle had passed out of family ownership, its grounds had been maintained in the Victorian fashion with blazing rhododendrons and palm trees. All of this was stubbornly pretentious in the shadow of Bheinn Mhor, the island's only mountain, which stood over the estate, rugged and dark. Whoever had designed the estate might have thought that they were bringing the best of the British Empire to this far corner of Scotland, but the effect was to make the castle look as though it were permanently besieged by the island's geology.

In contrast to the castle and its grounds, the cottage looked as though it might have been lifted in one piece from any town in the Western Isles. It was squat, functional, and square. Its walls were red sandstone and its roof was black slate. When Neil arrived, a thin woman in a baggy jumper sat on a wrought iron bench at the foot of the garden path, legs crossed, tapping on her phone. He saw her from the car as he approached and knew her on sight. Although he'd spoken to Rhona on the phone the day before, he had not seen her for decades. It was shocking how little she had changed. Her face had not gained a line or a wrinkle, and she was still just about managing to contain her wiry hair in a loose bun, although the hair was starting to gray, and locks were escaping here and there. Neil was suddenly conscious of how badly he had aged.

She did not acknowledge him until he was out of his car and standing over her, and even then, looking up, she only lowered the handset to her side, did not switch off the screen.

"You came," she said.

"I did. Where's Michael?"

Rhona blinked, turned away. "He's inside."

It had always been the three of them—Neil, Rhona, and Michael—and there had never been a time when Michael did not need looking after in some way by the other two. Neil had been friends with Michael before school, when Rhona was known to them only as the silent, curly-haired girl who lived at the top of the street with her gran. Even then, Michael was a singular boy. Neil's mum said he was touched, which, as a child, Neil understood to mean touched by God: a blessing, a gift. But, as with many religious folk on Aransay, there was something older and far more colorful beneath the veneer of Neil's mother's Catholicism. That sort of regimented faith had come relatively late to the islands, and people still talked not of the spirit, but of spirits, and not of the Devil, but of devils. As an adult, Neil understood that his mother probably thought that Michael had been touched by something far worse than God. There were times when she'd almost seemed afraid of him.

Michael had been late to talk, and had not been much of a speaker even then. There was a thing he would do, which Neil had thought nothing of at the time. He would press his forehead hard against another person's temple, sometimes as a greeting, sometimes in lieu of speaking. He did this to Rhona's grandmother once, climbed onto her lap and held her head in his hands and performed this strange kiss. She went berserk, screamed him out of the house. But it was her response, and not his behavior, that most disturbed Neil, and he left Rhona at home, ran after his friend, and the two of them paddled in the burn that afternoon until Michael's parents came for him.

Neil had not seen nor spoken to Michael for near-on two decades. "How is he?" he said.

Rhona frowned, and although she was as estranged from Neil as their mutual friend, she took one of his hands. "He's gone, Neil," she said. "He died this morning."

IT WAS RHONA'S IDEA that she and Neil should walk up to the Slip together, after the doctor was gone and the body dealt with. Neil understood. In his years away, he had dreamed of Bheinn Mhor and the Slip: the hidden pass on the western face of the mountain where he and Rhona and Michael had spent time as teenagers. In the dreams, he'd most often been with his two friends, and he had always been young again.

There was a bothy, a little stone cabin, up at the Slip. On the face of it, there was little need for such a shelter—the peak of Bheinn Mhor was only a three hour walk from Tarbert, even going around the Fitzroy Estate—but the place had a reputation. People found themselves disoriented up there, became lost. The farmers who had built the bothy had tales of restless spirits marching up the vale. People had died, and parents warned children not to go, even though the terrain was gentle.

As teenagers, unconcerned by all of this, Neil and Rhona and Michael would trek up Bheinn Mhor on a Saturday morning. They'd bring cold food, weed, and if they couldn't get weed they would bring wine. Often, they'd stay in the bothy overnight, and walk home early in the morning. Whenever Neil imagined returning to the island, he saw himself at the bothy. Even when Rhona called to tell him that Michael was terminal, and he made the decision to return, he found himself going back to the Slip in his mind. He would only ever be orbiting until his path took him back there.

In the end, it would need to wait until the next day. Doctor McLeod came later than expected, and there would be no time after he left. Neil had expected the doctor to be the cold-fingered old man who'd examined him as a child. It was only when a much younger man arrived that it occurred to Neil that the old doctor would have been dead by now. This man was in his forties, and Neil thought he remembered him from school: a cocky brat who had been a few years below him. The doctor completed some paperwork, said some sympathetic words, and made his excuses.

"Is someone coming to collect the body?" the doctor asked at the door.

"I've called Jon Crumlish," Rhona said. Neil had no idea who Jon Crumlish was and, by the time the doctor had gone, he started to feel quite redundant, almost invisible, and to question his own memory of having been invited. While Rhona hummed around the small house with purpose, he stood in corners with his hands in his pockets, or paced the hall, sticking his head through doorways.

He noticed quickly that there was nothing about the house to suggest that a life had been lived there. The furniture—what little of it there was—was the sort of flat-pack fiberboard junk Neil once used as a student. There was nothing personal on the walls, and the shelves were filled with dusty books that had not been touched in decades.

Finally, Neil wandered into the front room, where Michael's body still lay, on the sofa, with a red tartan blanket over it.

Michael's arm hung down from underneath the blanket. It was only on seeing the hand dangling, palm up and open, fingers curled inward, that Neil started to feel something like grief. It was the realization that all Michael had ever experienced—everything they'd done together and whatever had happened in the years since—had been to this end, as if none of that mattered more than this. That hand poking out: pathetic, like a beggar's bowl.

He quickly tucked it back under the blanket and then wiped his fingers on his trouser leg. He thought briefly about pulling back the blanket to look at Michael's face, but an image of what he might see came into his mind and he thought better of it.

It was dark in the room. The curtains were thick pulled across the bay window. It seemed suddenly to Neil that there was no air. He went to the window and reached for the curtain.

"Don't!" Rhona came into the room with a bottle of malt and two glasses. She ran to the window, put the bottle down on the floor, and grabbed Neil's forearm. "Sorry," she said, still holding onto him, with him still holding onto the edge of the curtain. "It was my Granny's thing.

When someone dies. To keep the spirits out."

In university, Neil had gone out with a Jewish woman who had covered every mirror in the flat with tea towels when her uncle died. She'd told him at the time that this was because the void left behind by the departed soul was an attractor to dark spirits, which might otherwise be seen gathering ghoulishly in the mirrors. Long after the relationship ended, he'd read that the tradition was more prosaic, and was in fact about avoiding the temptation for vanity at the time of mourning. But he had considered that there might be something between these explanations—that maybe the real dark spirits were the bereaved, and that it was the terrible face of their own grief that they had to be protected from witnessing in the mirrors. Neil understood the islanders' tradition of protecting the newly departed from the restless dead, who might sweep into a house of mourning on the west wind like a flock of birds to steal souls away, but he wondered whether, by following the tradition, there was something more earthly from which the living sought to protect themselves. He let go of the curtain.

"Still drink whisky?" Rhona said.

He said yes, and followed her to the kitchen. He did not tell her that he drank far too much of the stuff, and that Clare had been trying, and failing, to get him to cut down. He felt his hangover fighting back through the ibuprofen and codeine he'd taken on the ferry. They sat at the counter by the window and Rhona poured.

Neil held the glass of whisky up to the light from the window—an old habit. Several of the trees in the garden outside were dead. What leaves they had were a year old, crumpled and pale. "How long had Michael been living here?" he said.

"Ten years or so. He inherited the cottage when the old estate manager had a stroke and moved to Glasgow. It came with the job."

"Not bad," Neil said. Rhona shot him a dark look. He swallowed some of the whisky and swirled the remainder around the bottom of his glass.

"How was he?"

She shrugged. "He wasn't good. He'd get up in the night," she said. "Wander around. Talk . . . more shit than usual."

"But he was lucid. I mean . . . "

"He asked for you. He didn't have anyone else, you know. I came up to see him once in a while, and more after he got sick."

The image of the white hand protruding from under the red blanket forced itself into his thoughts, only now he imagined that it was reaching out to be held. Reaching in vain. Acid surged up into his throat.

"I'm sorry I left," he said.

"Don't say you're sorry when you're not. Anyway, nobody blamed you for leaving, Neil. It just broke his heart that you never came back."

"You don't seem all that happy about it yourself."

"Well, I could have done with having you around."

"Sorry."

"Stop saying sorry."

"Are we still friends?"

"Oh, we were never properly friends, Neil. You don't know the first thing about me."

"What is the first thing about you?"

She gave him a smile that he knew well from when they were young. It always seemed to him that he and Michael were beneath her somehow, that her interest in them was intellectual rather than emotional. When he had been wistful and impatient, and Michael had been tempestuous and strange, Rhona had been steady and, at times, aloof. He imagined that she could have done better than them, and wondered often why she never did. That smile, condescending, almost maternal, said, *there are places you and I don't go together*.

So they talked instead about Michael, about their new lives and their new families, until it was dark and Neil was flagging. Rhona took him upstairs and showed him to the spare bedroom, which was cramped and filled with boxes and piles of magazines, and left him there.

Before turning off the light, Neil spent some time looking through the contents of the room. He supposed that he might find some traces of Michael's life: waypoints with which to chart the spaces between the boy he had known and the middle-aged body under the blanket downstairs. The boxes were filled only with what must have been the affairs and belongings of the previous groundskeeper, trashy novels and letters from banks, but there was a pile of loose papers on the floor that did seem to relate to Michael. Among them was a large notebook, marked sparsely with Michael's handwritten words.

Neil sat with it on the bed, turning over its pages. Much of the notebook was blank, and what was written seemed for the most part to be *aide-mémoires*, names, and phone numbers, but here was something of the connection he had been looking for with the man he'd not known, and, while it might have been to do with the drink, he felt the burn of tears in his eyes.

Having flicked through the jotter for a minute, his heart gave a cold flutter when he saw his own name. But where he might have hoped to find an unsent letter or diary entry, the page was filled with nonsense. It read as though Michael had written it in dialogue with himself. There were questions, to many of which he had provided his own answers, although they were impossible to interpret without context. *Going up the sleepers. Will there be time?? Yes! Don't eat. Drink water only. Let me go.* That phrase appeared in several places. *Let me go.* And then, what had caught Neil's attention: *Neil came back.*

Neil had to pause, his hand shaking, when farther down the page, he came across the words: *Neil came back and it was too late.*

He turned over several more pages, feeling sick, almost ghoulish now, as he imagined Michael toward the end of his life, struggling to stay lucid in the middle of his illness: the unrelenting thing growing in his brain that he knew would finally kill him. The last few pages were scattered with disconnected words, every one of which seemed horrific to Neil—*cold, blinding, worse today*—and that phrase again. *Let me go. Please let me go.*

The last page with anything written on it said simply: *Up on the west wind.*

THE BED SAGGED in the middle, and a smell of damp came from the foam mattress, but Neil was drunk and tired, and fell asleep almost immediately. Sleep was fragmented and eventually broken altogether by three disturbances in the night.

The first disturbance was the sound of Rhona's voice coming from

somewhere in the house, whether through the walls or the floor he could
not tell. The tone of her voice was low and urgent, and something in her
cadences gave Neil the sense she was not speaking English. He
remembered Rhona had spoken Gaelic with her grandmother as a child,
but it didn't sound like that either. Neither did it sound as though she
were speaking to anyone else. There was none of the stop-start that might
have suggested a phone call. All of this was impression only.

He drifted, grasping with fingertips to consciousness, and soon fell
into sleep again, becoming aware as he did of a change in the light and air
in the room: darker, cooler, as if a storm had come down outside.

The second disturbance was of his own making. He'd been dreaming
fitfully of home: Clare and Alice kneeling by the coffee table, cutting
paper shapes. In the dream, he had been watching this scene and had
become suddenly aware of his own absence in it. Not only was he not
there, but there was no gap where he should have been. He did not
belong, and was not missed, and with the realization of this came a deep
and paralyzing horror. He observed as though on a screen, remotely,
unable to impinge or to influence. And he saw that behind his wife and
daughter was a sofa that should not have been there. There was a red,
woven tartan blanket on the sofa, from under which a limp arm, a white
hand, hung down.

He woke from this dream to a silent room and a cool draught across
his face from the window. He rose, felt his way to the door, and through
to the landing where there was more light. He descended the stair, turned
the corner to the front room where Michael's body lay. He knelt beside
the body, pulled back the blanket, pressed his forehead against Michael's
temple. He did all this half-believing that he was still dreaming, and
when—kneeling there, eyes closed—he saw in his mind
incomprehensible flashes of imagery, they were seamlessly joined to the
same dream: immense flocks of black creatures swirling in over the sea
like a storm cell; corpses, naked and bloated beyond recognition, washed
up on a beach.

He opened his eyes, unsure if he'd been sleeping and for how long,
but overwhelmed with tiredness, and returned to his bed. This time,
sleep was black and deep, and came upon him instantly.

The final disturbance was the dawn, which in the summer, in the Western Isles, comes late in the night, rather than early in the morning. This time, the little house seemed alive with movement. Floorboards rattled. The wind shook the window frames. And downstairs, there was the sound of shuffling feet and something being dragged, the sound of the front door latch and the door being opened. Outside, a crow took off, crying in alarm. Neil could hear the beating of its wings. He got up and stood by the window.

The sun was not yet clear of the hilltops. The light was dim and diffuse, almost like a mist: the kind of light that can't be trusted to tell the truth. Rhona was dragging Michael's body onto the lawn by the ankles. The blanket was still over his legs and torso, but had slipped away from his head.

Rhona dragged the body to the foot of the birdbath in the middle of the lawn, rearranged the blanket so that it covered Michael's head. She glanced up to the window where Neil stood, and he backed away a little. She watched the window for a moment, then turned from the house and walked off and up the road, into the trees.

IT WAS ALMOST thirty years since Neil moved to the mainland with his parents. On the night before he left the island, he walked down to the harbor wall where Rhona was waiting with Michael, and the three of them wandered around the back of the town and up the hill in the direction of Fitzroy and Bheinn Mhor, until they were out of reach of the light from the streets. They stopped and sat, just above the level of the rooftops, on a rocky patch by the side of the track that was clear of thistles and bracken.

It had been a year since the end of school. Neil was bound for the University of Glasgow. Michael had been spending more and more time on his own. Rhona had a job on the mainland, and it seemed to Neil that she was positioned between him and Michael like someone straddling two rafts, and that she'd eventually need to go one way or the other or fall into the water.

Michael opened a bottle of whisky, took a gulp, and passed it to Neil.

They talked in a faltering way about work and school and mutual friends. After a while they stopped talking and just drank.

"You'll miss this," Michael said, eventually.

"This?" Neil said. "We haven't done this for months. Years."

"Months," Rhona said.

"Tell you what. I won't miss that place," Neil said. He nodded in the direction of the town. "All those wanks in their GTIs driving up and down Castle Street every Friday night. Church every Sunday. All those decrepit yellow bastards drinking in the Anchorage."

"Someone has to live and die here," Michael said.

"Why?"

Michael stared at Neil for a moment. He seemed to be searching for something. After a few seconds, he shook his head, got up, muttered, "Fuck you, Neil," and walked off.

When he was out of sight, Rhona said, "You know it wouldn't actually kill you to tell him you love him."

"He's going to be all right."

"You don't know that any of us will be all right." Rhona grabbed the whisky from Neil. "He goes up Bheinn Mhor on his own. Up to the Slip. He's gone for days, comes back cut and bruised. He said to me that he belongs up there with the lost souls." Then she laughed and added, "My granny won't have him in the house."

He laughed too, but he'd known for a long time that Michael was heading for a crisis. The gulf that had grown between him and Michael was not a result of any natural, adolescent divergence of interests. Neil had created it because he did not want to be there when Michael went over the edge.

"I'm going to miss you," Rhona said. And then they sat, not saying anything to one another, until the whisky was gone. When they returned to the town, she hugged him tight and said in his ear, "You'll come back to us."

RHONA WAS GONE. There was no note, and no indication of when she might be back. She'd left Michael in the garden, Neil supposed, by arrangement with whoever had agreed to collect the body. As much as it seemed undignified to him, he did not feel it was his place to move the body back into the house. Instead he sat in the kitchen for hours until a van pulled up outside and two young men got out and lifted the body into the back of it. He watched the van drive away, and then made himself a cup of tea.

He wanted badly to return to the Slip. He still felt invisible, even alone in the house, and he thought returning to that hillside might reconnect him with the world somehow. He supposed that Rhona might have gone there ahead of him, had perhaps not wanted to wake him, but he did not much care now. He only wanted to be there.

The most direct route up Bheinn Mhor was on foot. He filled a bottle of water from the tap, and managed to eat some toast and some cold meat from the fridge. Once he was outside of the Fitzroy Estate, the way was simple, but far slower than he remembered, perhaps because he remembered it, for the most part, from his dreams, in which he had glided up the hillside like a bird. The track was where it had always been, but between the more familiar points of reference—outcrops and old trees—were long, featureless trudges of which he had no memory at all. He found that he was in poor shape, and the incline brought him out in an alcoholic sweat, and made his head throb at the temples.

The attraction of the Slip became stronger, the higher up the hillside he climbed. What he'd experienced at home in Perth as a curiosity to return was now a desperate longing. He would be incomplete until he got there. When he saw the shape of Bheinn Mhor's peak through the clouds in front of him, he turned westward, down a narrow gully that seemed to go nowhere, until it opened up, revealing the mountain's western face. Here, finally, was the Slip, and Neil was blasted by the full force of the west wind.

There was something Michael had said once that came back to him now. They had been fifteen, sitting on the grass at the Slip, looking down to the sea, and Michael had been talking about how the island had played a part in the war, as a launch point for sorties across the Atlantic, bombing German submarines, and how thousands of people must have died in the waters to the west. "If it had been anywhere else," he had said, "they might have got home."

Neil thought about those young men, dying in the cold and dark water, and realized suddenly that he had forgotten where home was.

The bothy was about two hundred yards ahead. It was smaller, dirtier, than he remembered, but what was more jarring was that it did not appear where he expected to see it. Instead of sitting on the crest of an incline, it was below him, nestled at the bottom of a scree-covered slope. He wondered briefly how he could have been remembering it so wrong for so long, and at what point had the memory become corrupted. But even as he did so, the corruption seemed to spread. As if the bothy were casting long shadows, and everything that fell into shade became strange and wrong, one by one the details of the Slip became unfamiliar. The clouds were around him, soaking his clothes. It dawned on him that this was the Slip that he had been warned away from as a child. He was seeing it for the first time in his life: a place where people lost themselves. In all of the years he had been coming here with his friends it had never chosen to show itself to him, and it had only now let him in.

Through the narrow pass of the Slip, Neil could see all the way down to the island's coast. Gray figures, dozens of them, walked out of the sea and over the beach, where the wind carried them like a mist up the hill. Above, black shapes wheeled in the thickening clouds.

There was light in the bothy, flickering: a candle.

Neil walked down the slope toward the bothy. He was cold now, and he could imagine that the fire would be lit and that his friends would be there again. He'd forgotten where he came from, and knew only that he had been trying to get here for a long time and had finally arrived. Through the window he saw his friends, Rhona and Michael. They looked well. They were laughing and drinking, and he felt that he should be with them, but when he tried the door, he found it was locked. He put his face to the window, and Rhona turned. Only she seemed to see him there. She shook her head slowly.

Neil turned away from the window. Around him, faceless figures took form on the mist and glided up the hill on the wind, and he followed them, because he did not know where else to go.

As he went, he looked back at the bothy. He could not see Michael now, but Rhona stood at the window. She smiled at him. It was a familiar smile.

It said: *There are places you and I don't go together.*

DAVID MCGROARTY's fiction has featured in the anthologies Rustblind and Siverbright, Sensorama, Caledonia Dreamin' *(Eibonvale Press),* Astrologica *(The Alchemy Press),* Strange Tales V *(Tartarus Press),* Wordland 5 *(The Exaggerated Press), and* The Five Senses of Horror *(Dark Moon Books). He is a Scottish writer of Hebridean and Irish descent, who grew up near Glasgow and now lives in Islington, London, with his partner and two children. He is a member of Clockhouse London Writers. David can be found online at* www.davidmcgroarty.net.

Indie publications are often a neurotic enterprise . . .

ACKNOWLEDGEMENTS

T HANK YOU TO ALL WHO INSPIRED OR SUPPORTED
this anthology, or who recognize the value of fostering diverse
voices from around the world.

Indie publications are often a lonely and neurotic enterprise for
creators, taking upon oneself all aspects of a book and hoping that the
massive enterprise doesn't fall off immediately into some void of audience
indifference.

But for your interest and hopefully (by this point!) enjoyment, it's all
been worth it.

Particular thanks to:

Alessandro Manzetti for recommending to me Carla Negrini and
Claudio Foti

Lauren Beukes for recommending to me Mohale Mashigo and
Charlie Human

Max Booth III for recommending to me Ashlee Scheuerman

Michael Sebastian for recommending to me Thersa Matsuura

Simon Strantzas for recommending to me David Nickle

Thanks also to the Horror Writers Association, who have been an
immense resource of technical information, guidance, and insight,
especially my local friends in the Los Angeles chapter, who, monthly,
vitalize me with awe and encouragement.

Enormous thanks to illustrator Steve Lines for his remarkable
artwork.

And, lastly, thanks most of all to the authors included within for
being a part of this project, and to you, dear reader, who I hope have
found some meaning or delight reading this all!

With sincerest thanks . . .

EDITOR'S REQUEST

DEAR READER, FAN, OR SUPPORTER,
It's a dreadful commentary that the worth of indie authors is measured by online 5-star reviews, but such is the state of current commerce.

Should you have enjoyed this book, gratitude is most appreciated by posting a brief and honest online review at Amazon.com, Goodreads.com, and/or a highly-visible blog.

With sincerest thanks,

Eric J. Guignard
Editor, *A World of Horror*

ALSO FROM ERIC J. GUIGNARD AND DARK MOON BOOKS:

Hearing, sight, touch, smell, and taste: Our impressions of the world are formed by our five senses, and so too are our fears, our imaginations, and our captivation in reading fiction stories that embrace these senses.

Whether hearing the song of infernal caverns, tasting the erotic kiss of treachery, or smelling the lush fragrance of a fiend, enclosed within this anthology are fifteen horror and dark fantasy tales that will quicken the beat of fear, sweeten the flavor of wonder, sharpen the spike of thrills, and otherwise brighten the marvel of storytelling that is found resonant!

Editor Eric J. Guignard and psychologist Jessica Bayliss, PhD also include companion discourse throughout, offering academic and literary insight as well as psychological commentary examining the physiology of our senses, why each of our senses are engaged by dark fiction stories, and how it all inspires writers to continually churn out ideas in uncommon and invigorating ways.

Featuring stunning interior illustrations by Nils Bross, and including fiction short stories by such world-renowned authors as John Farris, Ramsey Campbell, Poppy Z. Brite, Darrell Schweitzer, and Richard Christian Matheson, amongst others.

Intended for readers, writers, and students alike, explore *THE FIVE SENSES OF HORROR*!

Order your copy at www.darkmoonbooks.com or www.amazon.com
ISBN-13: 978-0-9988275-0-6

ALSO FROM ERIC J. GUIGNARD AND DARK MOON BOOKS:

Death. Who has not considered their own mortality and wondered at what awaits, once our frail human shell expires? What occurs after the heart stops beating, after the last breath is drawn, after life as we know it terminates?

Does our spirit remain on Earth while the body rots? Do the remnants of our soul transcend to a celestial Heaven or sink to Hell's torment? Can we choose our own afterlife? Can we die again in the hereafter? Are we given the opportunity to reincarnate and do it all over? Is life merely a cosmic joke or is it an experiment for something greater? Enclosed in this Bram Stoker-award winning anthology are thirty-four all-new dark and speculative fiction stories exploring the possibilities *AFTER DEATH* . . .

Illustrated by Audra Phillips and including stories by: **Steve Rasnic Tem**, **Bentley Little**, **John Langan**, **Lisa Morton**, and exceptional others.

"Though the majority of the pieces come from the darker side of the genre, a solid minority are playful, clever, or full of wonder. This strong anthology is sure to make readers contemplative even while it creates nightmares."
—*Publishers Weekly*

"In Eric J. Guignard's latest anthology he gathers some of the biggest and most talented authors on the planet to give us their take on this entertaining and perplexing subject matter . . . highly recommended."
—*Famous Monsters of Filmland*

"An excellent collection of imaginative tales of what waits beyond the veil."
—*Amazing Stories Magazine*

Order your copy at www.darkmoonbooks.com or www.amazon.com
ISBN-13: 978-0-9885569-2-8

ALSO FROM ERIC J. GUIGNARD AND DARK MOON BOOKS:

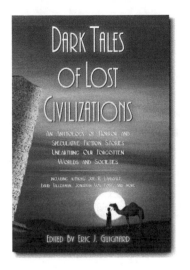

Darkness exists everywhere, and in no place greater than those where spirits and curses still reside. In **DARK TALES OF LOST CIVILIZATIONS**, you will unearth an anthology of twenty-five previously unpublished horror and speculative fiction stories, relating to aspects of civilizations that are crumbling, forgotten, rediscovered, or perhaps merely spoken about in great and fearful whispers.

What is it that lures explorers to distant lands where none have returned? Where is Genghis Khan buried? What happened to Atlantis? Who will displace mankind on Earth? What laments have the Witches of Oz? Answers to these mysteries and other tales are presented within this critically acclaimed anthology.

Including stories by: **Joe R. Lansdale, David Tallerman, Jonathan Vos Post, Jamie Lackey, Aaron J. French**, and twenty exceptional others.

"The stories range from mildly disturbing to downright terrifying... Most are written in a conservative, suggestive style, relying on the reader's own imagination to take the plunge from speculation to horror."

—*Monster Librarian Reviews*

"Several of these stories made it on to my best of the year shortlist, and the book itself is now on the best anthologies of the year shortlist."

—*British Fantasy Society*

"Almost any story in this anthology is worth the price of purchase. The entire collection is a delight."

—*Black Gate Magazine*

Order your copy at www.darkmoonbooks.com or www.amazon.com
ISBN-13: 978-0-9834335-9-0

ALSO FROM ERIC J. GUIGNARD AND DARK MOON BOOKS:

Exploring Dark Short Fiction #1:
A Primer to Steve Rasnic Tem

For over four decades, Steve Rasnic Tem has been an acclaimed author of horror, weird, and sentimental fiction. Hailed by *Publishers Weekly* as "A perfect balance between the bizarre and the straight-forward" and *Library Journal* as "One of the most distinctive voices in imaginative literature," Steve Rasnic Tem has been read and cherished the world over for his affecting, genre-crossing tales.

Dark Moon Books and editor Eric J. Guignard bring you this introduction to his work, the first in a series of primers exploring modern masters of literary dark short fiction. Herein is a chance to discover—or learn more of—the rich voice of Steve Rasnic Tem, as beautifully illustrated by artist Michelle Prebich.

Included within these pages are:

- Six short stories, one written exclusively for this book
- Author interview
- Complete bibliography
- Academic commentary by Michael Arnzen, PhD (former humanities chair and professor of the year, Seton Hill University)
- . . . and more!

Enter this doorway to the vast and fantastic: Get to know Steve Rasnic Tem.

ALSO FROM ERIC J. GUIGNARD AND DARK MOON BOOKS:

**Exploring Dark Short Fiction #2:
A Primer to Kaaron Warren**

Australian author Kaaron Warren is widely recognized as one of the leading writers today of speculative and dark short fiction. She's published four novels, multiple novellas, and well over one hundred heart-rending tales of horror, science fiction, and beautiful fantasy, and is the first author ever to simultaneously win all three of Australia's top speculative fiction writing awards (Ditmar, Shadows, and Aurealis awards for *The Grief Hole*).

Dark Moon Books and editor Eric J. Guignard bring you this introduction to her work, the second in a series of primers exploring modern masters of literary dark short fiction. Herein is a chance to discover—or learn more of—the distinct voice of Kaaron Warren, as beautifully illustrated by artist Michelle Prebich.

Included within these pages are:

- Six short stories, one written exclusively for this book
- Author interview
- Complete bibliography
- Academic commentary by Michael Arnzen, PhD (former humanities chair and professor of the year, Seton Hill University)
- . . . and more!

Enter this doorway to the vast and fantastic: Get to know Kaaron Warren.

ALSO FROM ERIC J. GUIGNARD AND DARK MOON BOOKS:

Exploring Dark Short Fiction #3:
A Primer to Nisi Shawl

Praised by both literary journals and leading fiction magazines, Nisi Shawl is celebrated as an author whose works are lyrical and philosophical, speculative and far-ranging; "...broad in ambition and deep in accomplishment" (*The Seattle Times*). Besides nearly three decades of creating fantasy and science fiction, fairy tales, and indigenous stories, Nisi has also been lauded as editor, journalist, and proponent of feminism, African-American fiction, and other pedagogical issues of diversity.

Dark Moon Books and editor Eric J. Guignard bring you this introduction to her work, the third in a series of primers exploring modern masters of literary dark short fiction. Herein is a chance to discover—or learn more of—the vibrant voice of Nisi Shawl, as beautifully illustrated by artist Michelle Prebich.

Included within these pages are:

- Six short stories, one written exclusively for this book
- Author interview
- Complete bibliography
- Academic commentary by Michael Arnzen, PhD (former humanities chair and professor of the year, Seton Hill University)
- ... and more!

Enter this doorway to the vast and fantastic: Get to know Nisi Shawl.

Order your copy at www.darkmoonbooks.com or www.amazon.com
ISBN-13: 978-0-9989383-4-9

THE CRIME FILES OF KATY GREEN by GENE O'NEILL:

Discover why readers have been applauding this stark, fast-paced noir series by multiple-award-winning author, Gene O'Neill, and follow the dark murder mysteries of Sacramento homicide detectives Katy Green and Johnny Cato, dubbed by the press as Sacramento's "Green Hornet and Cato"!

Book #1: DOUBLE JACK (a novella)

400-pound serial killer Jack Malenko has discovered the perfect cover: He dresses as a CalTrans worker and preys on female motorists in distress in full sight of passing traffic. How fast can Katy Green and Johnny Cato track him down before he strikes again?

ISBN-13: 978-0-9988275-6-8

Book #2: SHADOW OF THE DARK ANGEL

Bullied misfit, Samuel Kubiak, is visited by a dark guardian angel who helps Samuel gain just vengeance. There hasn't been a case yet Katy and Johnny haven't solved, but now how can they track a psychopathic suspect that comes and goes in the shadows?

ISBN-13: 978-0-9988275-8-2

Book #3: DEATHFLASH

Billy Williams can see the soul as it departs the body, and is "commanded to do the Lord's work," which he does fanatically, slaying drug addicts in San Francisco...Katy and Johnny investigate the case as junkies die all around, for Billy has his own addiction: the rush of viewing the *Deathflash*.

ISBN-13: 978-0-9988275-9-9

Order your copy at www.darkmoonbooks.com or www.amazon.com

ABOUT EDITOR, ERIC J. GUIGNARD

ERIC J. GUIGNARD IS A writer and editor of dark and speculative fiction, operating from the shadowy outskirts of Los Angeles, where he also runs the small press, Dark Moon Books. He's won the Bram Stoker Award (the highest literary award of horror fiction), been a finalist for the International Thriller Writers Award, and a multi-nominee of the Pushcart Prize.

He has over 100 stories and non-fiction works appearing in publications such as *Nightmare Magazine*, *Gamut*, *Black Static*, *Shock Totem*, and *Dark Discoveries Magazine*. As editor, Eric's published the anthologies *Dark Tales of Lost Civilizations*, *After Death...*, *+Horror Library+ Volume 6*, *The Five Senses of Horror*, and is soon to release *Pop the Clutch: Thrilling Tales of Rockabilly, Monsters, and Hot Rod Horror*. Additionally he's created an ongoing series of primers exploring modern masters of literary dark short fiction, titled: *Exploring Dark Short Fiction* (*Vol. 1: Steve Rasnic Tem*; *Vol. II: Kaaron Warren*; *Vol. III: Nisi Shawl*; *Vol. IV: Jeffrey Ford*).

Read his novella *Baggage of Eternal Night* (JournalStone) and watch for forthcoming books, including the novel *Crossbuck 'Bo* and the short story collection, *That Which Grows Wild: 16 Tales of Dark Fiction* (Cemetery Dance).

Outside the glamorous and jet-setting world of indie fiction, Eric's a technical writer and college professor, and he stumbles home each day to a wife, children, cats, and a terrarium filled with mischievous beetles. Visit Eric at: www.ericjguignard.com, his blog: ericjguignard.blogspot.com, or Twitter: @ericjguignard.

ABOUT ILLUSTRATOR, STEVE LINES

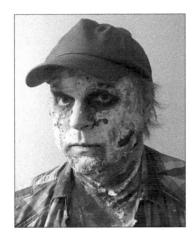

STEVE LINES IS A musician, artist, editor, and occasional writer, and runs Rainfall Records & Books with John B. Ford. He lives in England in darkest Wiltshire just a few miles from the Avebury stone circle and Silbury Hill. He has been illustrating books and magazines since the mid 70s and has worked for Centipede Press, Lindisfarne Press, Mythos Books, and Rainfall Books, amongst others. With John B. Ford he wrote *The Night Eternal*, a dark Arabian fantasy. He is active in several bands including, The Chaos Brothers, Stormclouds, The Doctor's Pond, and The Ungrateful Dead. He is currently working on a new CD album titled *Dali's Brain: Dark Wings of Death*, a collection of short stories with John B. Ford, and a Bruce Pennington autobiography/retrospective titled *Cover Story*.

—End—